THE
OTHER
SIDE
OF
SILENCE

by
Joan M. Drury

spinsters ink
minneapolis

First edition
10-9-8-7-6-5-4-3-2-1

Spinsters Ink
P.O. Box 300170
Minneapolis, MN 55403

Cover art and design by Teri Talley
Production by: Melanie Cockrell   Lou Ann Matossian
                  Kay Hong   Mev Miller
                  Kelly Kager   Stefanie Shiffler
                  Carolyn Law   Liz Tufte
                  Lori Loughney

This is a work of fiction. Any similarity to persons living or dead
is a coincidence.

Printed in the U.S.A. on acid-free paper.

Library of Congress Cataloging-in-Publication Data

Drury, Joan M., 1945–
    The other side of silence / by Joan M. Drury—1st ed.
        p.   cm.
    ISBN 0-933216-92-0 (pbk.)
        1. Women journalists—California—San Francisco—Fiction.
    2. Lesbians—California—San Francisco—Fiction. 3. San Francisco
    (Calif.)—Fiction. I. Title.
PS3554.R827084   1993
813'.54—dc20   93-26211
                                                            CIP

Acknowledgments

I have never written alone. In my head, there have always been the voices of my friends and family and acquaintances—all clamoring for their point of view and their favorite character and this or that story that I "*must* include." It's been great fun—exhausting, stimulating, terrifying, and immensely satisfying. I have been wonderfully blessed with unruly, unconventional, insistent, opinionated collaborators. What a *fine* way to write a book!

I will try to list those most intimately involved and apologize now for any I forget (to all my beloved Daisy's). Marilyn Crawford, for loving and believing in my writing even when I didn't. Audre Lorde, for helping me to find my voice and conviction. My children—Kelly and Scooter and Kevin Kager, as well as new family additions Karie and Mirranda Kager—for ideas, suggestions, distractions, love. My parents, particularly for introducing me to mysteries. My first writing group in San Francisco, met through *Lesbian Uprising*. My first readers—Paula Barish, Pamela Mittlefehldt, and Ida Swearingen—such thorough and honest and helpful readers every writer should have. Kirsten Anderson, mostly for forcing me to buy and use a computer—which ended up making all the difference in the world—and, I think, for the ending. Judith Katz and our writing class for "unsticking" me when I was unable to make a crucial transition. All of the people who are involved in some part of J.D. Enterprises, making it possible for me to write, especially (but not necessarily limited to): Diane Cina, Melanie Cockrell, Roberta Cole, Marilyn Crawford, Marilyn Dahl, Lana Edmundson, Sheila Ehr, Karen Green, Nett Hart, Ellen Hawley, Ann Hazelton, Virginia Henrikson, Kay Hong, Kelly Kager, Kevin Kager, Therese Keogan, Lou Ann Matossian, Mev Miller, P.J. Mittlefehldt, Pat Olson, Deb Orris and Ron Peters, Teri Talley, Kay Thies, Jan Thornton, Liz Tufte, and Willie Williamson. Lou Ann Matossian, my excellent editor, and Kris Hoover, my unofficial but nonetheless helpful editor. Kay Hong, my conscientious and superb copy editor. All the women at Spinsters for their dedication and loyalty and care, but especially Liz Tufte for her tenacity and talent in producing this book. Teri Talley for perseverance and brilliance with the cover. Many women, not all of whom I'll remember, whose conversations or ideas found their way into this book or who just gave me love and support over the years: Lynn Anderson, Chris Cinque, Christa Donaldson, Skeet Huebert, Kathi Jaramillo, Roxanne Johanson, Julie Landsman, Laura McCamy, Melanie Vesser Moondagger Z, Barb Mersy, Lynn Rossom, Linnea Stenson, Kate Tyler, Corky Wick, Joan Wilder, Mary Wings. My characters, who never abandoned me, even when I abandoned them.

And finally, everyone who has touched me and this book in some way—all the women that I might have forgotten, wish I could forget, or will *never* forget. I extend my appreciation and gratitude toward all who had a part in this accomplishment: every conversation, every book I read, every piece of advice, all the work that was done for me so that I could do this, all of it counts, all of it matters, all of you matter!

To my parents
Barbara Houghtaling Drury and Edward Drury,
who gave me the gift of life and the love of words

...we should die of that roar which is the other side of silence.

—George Eliot

THE
OTHER
SIDE
OF
SILENCE

by
Joan M. Drury

WOMENSWORDS

by Tyler Jones

Most of the eyes at Jason Judd's funeral were dry. His widow was not crying, because his death had just freed her from twenty-some years of physical, verbal and psychological abuse. His daughter and son were not crying, because they'd both been witnesses to and victims of this abuse. Many of his colleagues, friends, relatives and acquaintances were not crying, because they'd just found out the extent of his abuse toward his family and were in a state of shock. After all, Jason Judd was a prominent physician, a learned and respected member of the American Medical Association and the American Surgeons Association as well as being a patron of the arts and an active member in many environmental organizations.

He and his family lived in prestigious St. Francis Woods in San Francisco as well as owning a beach house near Half Moon Bay. His children attended private schools from kindergarten through college. Fathers of such families don't give lectures at AMA conferences and then come home and push their wives and children around, do they?

Yes, some do. There are no profiles on the "usual" or "average" batterer. He might be rich or he might be poor or he might be in-between; he might be black or brown or red or white or yellow; he might be a doctor, a ditch digger, a lawyer, a factory worker, a school teacher, a mechanic, a minister, a police officer or he might be unemployed. He might even be a she. Sometimes he drinks or uses drugs and sometimes he never touches chemicals. He might be soft-spoken or he might be rowdy. He might have very little formal education or he might have a Ph.D. What they all have in common, these beaters of women, is that they beat the women they profess to love— women to whom they are married or with whom they live. And they do this in large numbers.

FBI figures tell us that 50 to 66% of all men in relationships with women beat those women (and these are FBI figures, admittedly conservative). Every 15 seconds, a man is beating a woman. Every 15 seconds. Count it out. One. Two. Three. At 15, say: one. At 30, say: two. In one minute, four men have beaten four women. In one hour, 240 men have beaten 240 women. In one 24–hour period, 5,760 men have beaten as many women. Day after day after day after day. This does not include rape or other sexual abuse. This is *just* physical abuse. Taking into account the enormous odds against accuracy, 4,000 women die each year at the hands of men who "love" them. That's 11 women a day, every day—dead, gone irrevocably and unnecessarily from the face of the earth.

This is war. War against women. If you are saying, "These

figures can't be accurate—why, I've never even known a man who beats his wife or girlfriend," believe me: you know such a man. There is no way you can't know such a man. But you are right, these figures aren't accurate. They only reflect the number of women who actually report such beatings—or projections that can be made from such reports. Most physical abuse goes unrecorded, unannounced, unbelieved.

The "beauty" of this war against women is that it is random: there are no patterns, there are no "hard" statistics, there is no predictability. The randomness of this violence makes it almost invisible. But don't be misled by this so-called randomness that would have you believe that wife-beating is an occasional loss of control. That is not true. If the beaters of women were uncontrollable beasts, they would also be beating their bosses, their co-workers, strangers on the streets. This isn't an occasional loss of temper. These men choose, carefully and deliberately, to store up all their anger and frustration and take it home to their wives, their girlfriends, where they know they can get away with this violence.

Justice? Very little. The legal system is geared toward protecting the defendant, not the victim. Judges, juries and the whole system are encouraged to be cautious and certain, beyond a shadow of a doubt. In court, it becomes his word against hers—whether it's battering or rape or incest or any other form of violence. How many violent men, do you suppose, inflict violence against the women and children in their lives in a public setting? And, even when there's irrefutable proof (videotapes or witnesses), juries frequently acquit men of heinous crimes. Our popular media—TV, movies, magazines, newspapers, novels—all conspire to convince the public, in subtle and not-so-subtle ways, that women ask for it, want it, enjoy it, deserve it.

Yes, there were mostly dry eyes at Jason Judd's funeral. But mine weren't dry. I was crying. I was crying for all the women who silently suffer men like Jason Judd. And not-so-silently, too, but the law does nothing to protect them. And all the children who are permanently damaged by physical and sexual abuse at the hands of men like Jason Judd. Damage, in some cases, that goes so deep that it can never be excised or healed. Maybe Judd didn't deserve to die, but the people who have been the victims—and survivors—of his abuse didn't deserve what they got either. We could talk about justice, I guess, but I can't even begin to make sense of that word. Women live in a different world than men do, one in which justice is rarely an issue.

I do the only thing I can: I keep putting one foot in front of the other. I keep moving forward—women's words propelling me on my way.

1

It was because of Aggie that I found the body. Later, Mary Sharon—who likes to think of herself as clever—said, "What did you expect? You name a dog after Agatha Christie and of course she's going to involve you in murder!" It happened during our usual 6:00 a.m. walk. No, I'm not one of those "morning people" who like to get up early and greet the day with joy and gladness. Actually, I wouldn't be too terribly upset if I'd never seen a sunrise in my entire life. I have nothing personal, mind you, against sunrises. They just occur too early in the day for my taste. So why am I out here every morning for the sunrise?

Simple. As a puppy, my golden retriever began "acting out" by chewing things. I would come home from work to discover a tennis shoe with a mangled mate, a shredded pillow, a faceless teddy bear. Aggie clearly needed more attention and more exercise on a regular basis. There was only one time of day that I could consistently guarantee availability. That was when I was normally still asleep in the morning. Five years have passed now, and Aggie's internal alarm clock is unerringly correct. Within a couple of minutes of 6:00 each morning, she can be found sitting next to my bed, leash in mouth, tail swish-swishing back and forth. The worst she might do, if I don't respond quickly enough, is to shake the leash a little insistently and let out a low moan, supposedly indicating the desperate state of her toilet needs.

Anyway, on that particular morning, we were strolling through the park, as usual. Well, to be more accurate, I was stumbling along barely awake, while Aggie was dashing about: snuffling here and there in the underbrush, giving chase to a squirrel or two, and keeping tabs on my reluctant progress. It was foggy, as it often is at that time of the day—especially in this part of San Francisco, west of Twin Peaks. Although it wasn't raining, the trees were dripping from the accumulated moisture, the excess pelting my head and arms. Being wrapped in a blanket of fog intensified my sleepwalking state: sounds and sights were muffled and dimmed. The distant lowing of the fog horn in the Gate barely penetrated this cocoon. The piquant odor of the eucalyptus trees was sharpened, as it always is when the leaves were wet. Cat piss. Mary Sharon says that eucalyptus leaves smell like cat piss, but what does she know? She is a recent emigrant and can't be expected to appreciate the subtleties of California mainstays.

Suddenly, I was jolted quite awake by the sound of Aggie's barking. In the years we'd been doing our morning routine, I don't think I'd ever heard her bark. I called, "Aggie! Come!"

She continued barking. This was highly unusual as Aggie almost always came when I called. I hurried toward the sound, feeling a bubble of anxiety balloon within me. As I rounded a curve in the path, I could see Aggie just ahead, barking into a clump of bushes. I hoped it wasn't a skunk.

"Aggie!" I hissed, mindful of the neighbors. "Hush up! What's the matter with you?"

When I reached her, both scolding and soothing, I snapped the leash to her collar and jerked her back sharply, with a quick glance toward the bushes. Then I stopped what I was doing and stood still, very still. Sticking out from under the bushes was a pair of shoes, shoes that were obviously on feet attached to legs attached to...Aggie continued to bark quite frantically, and I felt paralyzed. Was this a joke? If I pulled the bushes back, would this person jump out at me, laughing? Was it someone sleeping? But somehow I knew, with a spine-tingling certainty, I just knew this was not a person sleeping or even a person breathing. This was a body. A dead body.

Panic rose from the vicinity of my stomach and, at the same time, my throat began to clutch convulsively, as if to close off the panic before it reached my mouth and escaped in a scream. A fresh wave of panic seized me as I thought about someone else, someone who maybe caused this body to stop breathing. I looked inanely over my shoulder and decided it was time for Aggie and me to get away from there.

Aggie, thank god, quieted down the minute I dragged her away. The once-friendly fog now held menace. The early-morning stillness echoed with threatening sounds—the crack of a branch, the crunch of a leaf, the rustle of weeds. I ran. Aggie thought it was a lark, but I was gasping for breath and had a piercing stitch in my side by the time we reached my front door. I hesitated for a moment, then realized that I was more afraid to stay outside.

After calling the police, I gave Aggie her breakfast. Nothing ever interfered with her appetite. When the black-and-white pulled up outside my house, I glanced at the clock by my bed. It had taken them exactly two minutes and twenty-one seconds to arrive. Sometimes, when a man is beating his wife or girlfriend, it takes the cops as long as fifteen or twenty minutes to arrive. Of course, they take domestic calls seriously, know damn well that they might get hurt at them. I guess a dead body is less threatening. These are the kind of thoughts you have when you spend most of your adult life working against violence directed toward women.

I slipped out my door and noticed that the sun was now moving up over Twin Peaks, and the fog was already thinning and drifting away. The blue boys were just that—boys, looking hardly older than teen-agers.

"Miss Jones?" one of them inquired. He was white, sandy-haired and freckle-faced, reminding me of Richie in "Happy Days."

"Ms." I corrected him automatically and added, "Yes."

He wrote something down in a little notebook he pulled out of his shirt pocket as his partner, an Asian version of the same wide-eyed look, said, "You called about finding a ...body? That's right, isn't it?" His skin was tight and smooth as an apple, as it is on only the very young.

"Yes," I answered. "Come on. I'll show you." Emboldened by my escorts, I led the way across the street and into the park, stretching my legs assertively.

The white-boy-next-door asked, as we walked, "How d'ya know he's dead? Did you check the body?"

"No," I shook my head and stopped, peering at him but not seeing him—instead remembering that moment when I saw the feet. I shrugged. "I guess I don't know for sure. I didn't actually see him. Only his feet sticking out from under a bush. It was just...I don't know. Something about how still they were..." I suddenly felt sheepish and a little defensive. "I was alone in the park, and I was afraid. I thought I should just get out of there."

"Good thinkin'," he agreed, his youthful demeanor serious as he nodded solemnly, and I felt both mollified and a little silly.

As we recommenced walking, the Asian-boy-next-door asked me, "Do you run?"

I frowned, wondering how he could know I had run home. "What?"

"Run. Do you run?" When I continued to scowl at him, he gestured toward my clothes and said, "You've got sweats on. I just wanted to know what you were doing up here so early."

"Oh! I see. I didn't understand...no. No, I don't run. I was just walking my dog. We do it every morning."

He nodded as the other one again made a note.

By this time we were around the tennis courts and starting up the hill. "Come on, he's just up here."

"If ya didn't see him," the freckled one queried, "why d'ya always call him 'him'?"

"Mmmm." I squinted back to that moment of discovery again. "The shoes. They were men's shoes."

He nodded, once again making a note. Just as we were starting around the curve, I suddenly had the awful thought that the body would no longer be there. What if, after all, it had just been a vagrant who had since gotten up and wandered off? Or what if the murderer was hiding in those bushes and had since dragged the body to his car (her car?) and stuffed it in the trunk and drove off? I shook off that particular image, not wanting the panic to rise again.

But the feet with the men's shoes were still there, protruding from under the same bushes. One of the cops started to part the bushes, then hesitated, saying, "D'ya want to step back, ma'am?"

"Oh! Yeah. Sure." I moved out of view.

After a second, he said, "Call in. He's dead all right. Bullet hole between his eyes."

My legs instantly shook, the way they do after running uphill to catch a bus. I stepped back and leaned against a tree for support. At that moment, I was so glad that I hadn't had to see anything but his feet. I took several deep breaths, slowly expelling them to calm myself.

After a minute, the cop backed out of the bushes, took his notebook back out and wrote for a few seconds. Then he looked up and said, "Are you okay?"

"Yeah," I nodded. "I think so. It's just that..." I smiled weakly, "I'm not too used to finding bodies, you know? At least not before breakfast."

My attempt at humor was lost on him. Too young to be flippant, I thought. "It was real smart of you to get out of here right away. Suppose ya tell me exactly what happened."

I ignored his question. "A bullet between the eyes? Doesn't that mean...isn't that like an execution?"

He shrugged. "Hard to say. Anyone who watches TV might think that. Not something we can count on. And then, there's very little blood." It was as if he'd forgotten I was there, was talking to himself. "Of course, that's only true of the entrance area. Now the exit area," he said as he made an odd puffing noise with his mouth, "that's another thing altogether." My gag reflex kicked in as I got an all-too-vivid picture of what he was describing. He stopped abruptly.

"Are ya sure you're okay?" he asked again, peering at me. I nodded, swallowing obsessively, but I felt like saying—if I could've trusted my voice—no, I'm not okay, I'm going to puke all over you, you insensitive clod. But in deference to his tender youth and obvious earnestness, I said nothing. He prodded, "You were gonna to tell me exactly what happened this morning."

I took another deep breath and let it slowly out. I shifted from one foot to another. I described the little I had to tell.

"Now think carefully," he said when I was done. "Before your dog started barking, did ya hear anything else?"

I thought for a minute. "Just the foghorn. That's all I remember. Of course, I'm not too bright at that time of the morning, but...I think I would've heard a gun shot, if that's what you mean."

He nodded. "What about someone running? Or just moving around up here?" My throat constricted tightly as I imagined a murderer actually being up here with me. I shook my head, not trusting my voice to ordinary speech.

"How about at home? Before you came over here. Think carefully. Anything out of the ordinary. A car. What might've sounded like a backfire. Anything."

Again I tried to recreate that time. After a couple seconds, I shook my head slowly. "I can't remember anything different or unusual."

"Okay," he said. "What about the times? Can you give me a pretty close idea of what time you came over, found the body, and so forth?"

"Sure," I agreed and gave him a quick run-down. "Aggie wakes me up at 6:00 every morning. I always check the clock. This morning, it was 6:01. It's usually another five to six minutes before we actually leave for the park. We always go the same way"—I gestured, indicating our usual route—"and I'd guess it was maybe another five minutes before she started barking. That would make that"—quick calculations in my head—"about 6:11, I guess." I nodded. "Yeah, that fits because it was 6:14 when I called you."

He began by jotting down the information, but, by the time I'd finished, he was just staring at me with a look of amazement on his face. The other officer had rejoined us and he, too, looked surprised. I looked from one face to the other and finally blurted, "What?"

The first one shook his head and resumed writing while the other one said, "ma'am? You seem to have the times down quite precisely. Is there any special reason for that?"

Once I understood the source of their bewilderment, I grinned and decided a long explanation probably wasn't necessary. "Shall we just say, I'm a little obsessed with time?"

He raised his eyebrows and glanced at his partner, who continued to write things down. By now, others had begun arriving, and the area was being roped off with the usual yellow crime tape. The two spoke to one another in low tones for a minute, then the Asian cop said, "Come on, you can go home for now."

As we started back toward my house, we encountered a man and a woman in street clothes. He was white, tall with lots of reddish brown hair—on his head, chin, under his nose. He reminded me of a teddy bear. Well, actually, all of that was just a fleeting impression because it was the white woman with him who I was really noticing. She was about ten years

11

older than me, middle-to-late forties. Her neatly cropped hair, once dark, was now liberally salted. She had muddy brown eyes that I instantly adored. Her body was large and solid, and she moved with purposeful confidence. Our eyes locked for the briefest of moments, and I knew she was hearing the same "dyke alarm" that I was hearing.

The uniforms greeted the two of them deferentially. "Miss—Ms. Jones," at least he was educable, "Inspectors Dwyer and George." George was the woman. And she was. Georgeous, I mean. I know. That's "gorgeous," but you know what I mean.

I knew who she was. I'd heard of her—the first woman who cracked the elite all-boy club of the Homicide Division. We all knew she was a lesbian, but she had to be pretty closeted to make the grade in the police department. "Ms. Jones found the body. I was just taking her home, figured you could question her there." He indicated where I lived. It was almost but not quite a question. George and Dwyer nodded, dismissing us.

"Look, Ms. Jones," one of the uniforms was saying, as we walked on. "I think you ought to change your morning routine."

"Yeah?" I answered, rather inattentively. I've always been a sucker for brown eyes. I wondered if I had time to take a shower before they came knocking on my door.

"Your morning routine. I can't believe you do the same thing every morning at the same time. You even walk the same route every day!" I reluctantly let go of my musings and attempted to refocus my attention on this very serious young man. "You know, anyone casing your house would know exactly when it would be empty each day. Or when you'd be alone in the park. I don't want to scare you, but you just shouldn't make yourself such a sitting duck. It's really not a good idea to be so predictable." His baby face was creased in an effort to be stern.

I felt acutely embarrassed and wanted to snap at him—I know that—since, of course, I did know. These were simple, obvious rules exercising common sense that I would've pointed out to any other woman, but I just operate as if I'm invincible. "Of course, I see what you mean. It's just that, well, you know, if nothing has ever happened to you..."

"Yes," the other one agreed, "but now something *has* happened to you. Or at least in your neighborhood."

My throat tightened once more. Even though I saw and heard nothing, that didn't mean the murderer didn't see and hear me.

THE OTHER SIDE OF SILENCE

2

When we reached the street, Mary Sharon, her blond hair standing out in its usual spiky shoots all over her head, came running across to me, exclaiming, "Tyler! What's going on?"

The cops were staring at her odd hair-do and her flamboyant outfit. At least, I assumed that's what was riveting their attention. That day her slender frame was camouflaged by a billowing jumpsuit in an intense purple and sashed with a silky purple, yellow, and orange scarf. The yellow in the sash echoed her yellow LA Gear high-tops—her signature shoes.

The Asian cop recovered enough to say to her, "Excuse me, ma'am, but this is a crime scene."

I waved him off, "It's okay." I firmly took hold of her arm as we started across the street. "Come on, Mary Sharon."

Mary Sharon rented the studio apartment in my lower level behind my garage and was also my very dearest friend. Not for the first time, I was aware of the pale shadow I became next to her. Me with my ordinary brown hair, my watery not-quite-green, not-quite-blue eyes, my blend-in-with-the-crowd wardrobe. Even my nearly six feet of towering self was neutralized by the fact that it was a hefty six feet rather than a willowy six feet. Hefty. A polite word for fat. My mother, bless her motherly heart, used to tell me in my often tearful adolescence, "Honey, you're not fat. You're robust." Uh-huh. Robust, for chrissake.

Before we got far, one of the blue boys tapped my arm, saying, "You *will* stay at home now, yeah?" I nodded. "Good. Inspectors George and Dwyer will be over to ask their questions. Thanks for your cooperation. And ma'am? Please take our advice about your morning schedule."

"I will. Really. I promise," I assured him. I gripped Mary Sharon's arm as we finished crossing the street.

She stared at my grip, then transferred her curiosity to my face. "Tyler. What the hell is going on?"

I shook my head. "I found a body up there this morning, Mary Sharon. Or rather, Aggie did."

She stopped walking and her mouth dropped open. I thought to myself, that actually happens, mouths actually do drop open. "Tyler! Are you kidding?"

"Right. Yeah, I'm kidding. I made the whole thing up." I looked away from Mary Sharon at the two police cars, ambulance, and several other unfamiliar cars parked in the street. I glanced back at her face, then looked pointedly at the yellow tape already closing off the park. A cluster of neighbors was standing on the sidewalk, looking toward me eagerly. Others were peering out of their windows or standing outside their doors. Some looked as if they were about to move in our direction. I tugged on Mary Sharon's arm. "Come on. I don't want to talk to anyone right now."

I hustled us inside. Aggie greeted us with bounding enthusiasm, as if I'd been gone for hours instead of less than a half hour. She's been like this ever since I quit my job at the *Chronicle* and decided to work at home. Now she's so used to having me around that she's unhappy if I just go to the store.

"A body?" Mary Sharon breathed, almost reverently. "How exciting! Was it a man or a woman? What'd he look like? Or she? Was it a she? Come on, Ty, tell me everything!"

"Good god, Mary Sharon. This isn't a mystery book. Someone is dead."

She snapped out of it. "You're right. I'm acting like a jerk. It's just that nothing exciting ever happens to me."

"Oh yeah," I rolled my eyes, "lucky me. I get to stumble over bodies at dawn while you're still warmly tucked into bed like any sensible person."

"Come on, Ty! Tell me the details."

"I will but...I'll make you a deal. Have you got enough time to stay while I hop in the shower?"

"I guess so, but why?"

"You can let the detectives in if they should show up while I'm still showering. Okay? When I get out of the shower, I'll tell you everything." Not that "everything" was much of anything.

"Okay." She shrugged. "I'm going to make some coffee then, okay?"

"Great!" I agreed, moving toward the bathroom.

But I must've sounded a little too hearty because Mary Sharon suddenly peered at me, suspiciously. "Is something going on here, Tyler?"

I sighed. The problem with good friends is that they know you too well. I ran my hand through my short hair. "Nothing's going on here, Mary Sharon. I just want to shower before the detectives come to talk to me. Is that such a big deal?"

Mary Sharon just looked at me for a moment during which I felt like squirming but didn't. "Mmm," she finally said. "By any chance is one of these detectives a woman? Maybe even..."—she casually turned the corners of her mouth down— "...a hot woman?"

I stared at her with my best attempt at indignation. "Are you suggesting that I objectify other women?"

"I wouldn't call it *suggesting*," she drawled, "I think I would call it a simple statement of truth."

"Mary Sharon Andrews! I am deeply hurt! I thought you knew me better than that!"

"Mmm-hmm. Are you saying that one of these cops is *not* a hot woman?"

"Well, I guess it just depends upon how you define 'hot.' I think she's very attractive, myself, if that's what you mean by 'hot,' but it's because she has such deeply intelligent eyes."

"Mmm-hmm. What color are these deeply intelligent eyes?"

"Mary Sharon, I have just about had enough of your nasty implications. Are you staying or aren't you?"

"Oh sure," she answered. "I'd like to see these deeply intelligent eyes for myself." I narrowed my own eyes. She smiled sweetly and went into the kitchen.

It didn't take me long to shower, wash my hair, and pull on a pair of jeans and a t-shirt. The first t-shirt looked as if it had been crumpled in a corner of my closet, which was possible, so I changed to one that was less wrinkled. The smell of fresh coffee spurred me on. Why am I being so silly about this woman, I asked myself as I pulled a brush through my hair. There wasn't much, really, I could do with my hair. It did pretty much what it wanted to do. That's why I kept it short, not wanting to give it too much latitude.

Not that I wanted to get involved with anyone just then. It seemed to be taking all my energy just to stay involved with me. And anyway, I couldn't imagine being involved with a cop. Could I? It was all Mary Sharon's fault, goading me with her teasing. Then another little mental whisper said, Or is it just avoidance? Are you just trying to ignore any possible attraction to anyone? I shook my head impatiently. And my hair, of course, took that opportunity to go its own way.

I also realized something else at that moment: it probably wasn't about Georgeous George at all. It was about me. It was about me and this murder. About my all-too-familiar avoidance of conflict and scary feelings. Since I can't drink anymore, I have to find some other way to distract myself. Yes, it was a distraction. I felt pleased, relieved to make some sense out of this might-be "attraction."

This immediate reaction to George was typical of me. Even though I was doing a fine job of keeping my feelings at a distance, the whole murder thing *was* pretty scary. Too scary even to look at very much. But I could look at something—or someone—else, couldn't I?

"Where's my cup?" I asked Mary Sharon, who was sitting with her coffee at the kitchen table.

"I thought you gave up coffee," she said.

"You should talk, Ms. Perfect-Diet who wouldn't think of putting anything impure in her body-that's-a-temple." She made a face at me, and I shrugged, opening the refrigerator for cream. "I can't be perfect, Mary Sharon. It just isn't in me." She snorted, and I gazed forlornly at the spot where I used to keep my beer. I sighed, closing the door. "I sure would like a beer right now." I closed my eyes for an instant and could feel the damp, cold beer can in my hand, the sweet surprise of that first mouthful, the jump I felt as the electricity of it coursed down my arms and throughout my body.

Mary Sharon shook her head resolutely, saying, "Exactly why you gave it up, Tyler dear. Not even 8:00 in the morning, and you want a beer already."

"Okay, okay. So I'm not having one, all right? Anyway, Ms. High-and-Mighty, Ms. Righteous-Bones, are you telling me that if you had come across a body in the park, you wouldn't want a cigarette?" We sat at the kitchen table, the whole of the Sunset district spread below us, the edge of the ocean beyond just coming in to view as the morning fog receded. I wrapped my fingers around my coffee cup, sticking my nose deeply into the rising steam, sucking the odor in before taking my first gulp. The taste and temperature scalded my tongue and throat, burning away some of the intense need for booze.

"Actually, old girl, I didn't find any bodies, and I still want a cigarette. Tyler! Are you going to tell me what happened or not?"

I shared with her the scant details of the morning's events. Her eyes wide and still, she said, "Do you think the killer might have seen you?"

I shook my head and shrugged, trying for nonchalance. "I hope not."

"A body. It's hard to believe. In our quiet neighborhood..." After a moment, she continued, "Tyler, how're you feeling? Are you scared?"

I frowned, thinking (not feeling, you notice, but thinking). "I don't know. I don't...feel much of anything, I guess. I mean, it doesn't seem very real to me. After all, I only saw a pair of feet. And..." I let a rush of air out of my mouth. "I guess it doesn't really seem like it has much to do with me. You know? But, still. Yes, I'm scared. I'm not sure what that means. I just know that I am." And then I grinned at her as I added, "And I'm doing my best to stave off that feeling. By falling madly in love, for instance."

Mary Sharon nodded slowly, not picking up her end of our usual banter. "Now Tyler, these detectives are coming to talk to you?"

"Yeah. When they're done up there."

"Why are they coming to talk to you?"

"Why?" I frowned. "To hear about finding him, I guess."

"But didn't you tell that to the uniformed cops?"

"Yeah, but these are the homicide people."

"Maybe you ought to get a lawyer over here first."

"What?!" Mary Sharon was in her second year of law school and was sort of a nut about this kind of thing. At least, I thought she was.

"I'm serious, Ty. For all you know, they're thinking of you as a suspect. After all, it's only your word that the body was dead when you found it."

"For chrissake, Mary Sharon! Will you knock it off? I'm a

witness, that's all." She was scaring me worse than the body had. "Technically speaking, I'm not even that, since I didn't actually 'witness' anything, but that's the way they'll see it, I'm sure. You've either read too many mysteries or law school has fried your brain."

"I'm just telling you what I think, Ty. This is not any kind of official advice, mind you..." Her professorial tone and face were a little hard to take seriously, what with her punky hair and resplendent clothing.

"God forbid," I interrupted, "that you, a lowly law student, should pretend to be competent enough to give me advice." I knew, only too well, the whole schtick on professional responsibility in regard to law students "playing" at being lawyers.

Mary Sharon glared at me as she got up. "I've got to go. I've got a class at nine. If I were you, I wouldn't talk to them without a lawyer present."

"Thanks for the *advice*," I said rather meanly, and she shot a scowl at me as she headed for the door. I followed her, hands in the air. "Sorry, sorry! Suggestion. Thanks for the *suggestion*, Mary Sharon. I really don't think I need a lawyer yet."

Mary Sharon scowled. "Why don't you at least call Corinne?" Corinne Ngo was the staff lawyer at the domestic abuse agency where Mary Sharon and I worked. At the top of the stairs leading down to my front door, she hesitated. "Are you okay? I mean, we're being pretty flippant here, but, after all, you did find a body."

I gave her a hug. "Thanks for your concern, hon. I appreciate it, but I'm okay. I really didn't see anything, remember?" As I said this, the image of a blurry face with a bullet hole between the eyes arose in my mind. I resisted a shudder.

$$\boxed{3}$$

After Mary Sharon left, I walked back into my dining room and stared out at the ocean. Almost everyone I knew wanted to live on the bay side of this city, where it was sunnier. I occasionally did, too, especially in the summer when it sometimes seemed as if we went weeks without any sunshine—just a blizzard of fog instead. But I loved the ocean and had always known that when I moved back to San Francisco after college in Minnesota, I would live near the ocean or at least where I could see it. Ten years ago I came home, straight here to my Aunt Norah's place.

I'd liked living with Norah. My parents were in the midst of a long-overdue divorce, and I wanted to avoid being sucked into that maelstrom. Aunt Norah seemed steady and serene and ordinary in contrast. She lived in this typical San Francisco bungalow: the small living quarters—living room, kitchen with dining area, two bedrooms, and bath—on the second floor, a garage and rental space on the ground floor. She hadn't rented out the studio for years. It was only one large room with a kitchen alcove, but I didn't want or need anything more. I was coming home from a devastating breakup. The woman I'd expected to spend the rest of my life with had, instead, run off with a mutual "friend" of ours. I needed and welcomed the stability Aunt Norah was offering.

I leaned my head against the glass of my sliding doors, letting the sharp coolness calm me. The thought of Norah still probed like an ice pick inside my chest. She died a year and a half ago. The big C. At first, I wasn't sure I wanted to go on living. I drank more and more, without paying much attention. I wasn't surprised when I found out she'd left me the house, but I didn't think I could stand living here without her. Eventually, I not only came to appreciate and accept her loving generosity but to celebrate it. This incredible bonus—the mortgage was paid off—plus the income I get from the studio, enabled me to quit my job at the *Chronicle*, limit myself to a weekly column, and work on a book I'd been talking about for years.

Aggie nuzzled my hand. I dropped to the floor next to her, putting my arms around her neck. "Oh, sweetie, you loved her, too, didn't you?" Aggie had been like a gift Norah and I got for one another. We both loved dogs but had never felt we could have one because of work. Suddenly, it was ideal—Norah's retirement put her at home most of the time, and I was available for Aggie's more vigorous exercise needs.

I opened the doors. Aggie bounded out, and I followed. It was one of those days, frequent in the autumn here, that made you feel as if someone had washed your windows during the night—even when you weren't looking through windows. The colors were so vivid, the edges so hard and crisp. Maybe you have to live in San Francisco, where so much of the landscape is blurred by the ubiquitous fog, to really appreciate this kind of day. I gazed at the surf rolling in far below me. Aggie trotted around the deck, sniffing the plants and furniture, making certain nothing was awry before she scrambled down the stairs to the small fenced backyard. I fussed over the plants—picking out a dead leaf here, checking for bugs there, turning this one or that one to maximize the light received.

Norah and I had made a bargain. I loved doing the garden and just generally puttering around, and she loved cooking and cleaning. She had a domestic streak a mile wide. I kidded her about being a "closet homemaker." She willingly accepted the label but also insisted she'd never had any desire to get married.

I was watering the plants and Aggie was lying in the open patio doors when the front doorbell rang. Aggie tore down the stairs, barking viciously at the would-be intruders. I always find this amusing. It's comforting to know that most people, after witnessing this display of ferocity, would not attempt to force their way into my house. However, as I always point out to the attentive but noncomprehending Aggie, burglars don't usually ring the bell before entering a house.

After quieting Aggie, I let Inspectors Dwyer and George in, leading the way up to my dining room. I offered them coffee. Dwyer accepted while George demurred. I wondered if she was one of those pure ones who didn't put "junk" in her body. While I got the coffee for Dwyer and me, I observed her as discreetly as I could. She did not fidget; her hands lay loosely on the table. She looked around my living room, then at me. When I smiled, she looked away, out the sliding doors. There was, it seemed to me, a tightness in her shoulders, around her neck. I didn't think it was about coffee. Maybe she was just cautious about boundaries. She seemed so careful, so remote. Is that what intrigued me?

We sat at the table, Aggie by my side watching them closely for any suspicious moves or for any sign of encouragement toward her. George said, "I'm Inspector Carla George and this is Inspector Allan Dwyer." Dwyer nodded over his coffee. "We're with Homicide and will be in charge of this investigation." It was my turn to nod. "We would appreciate it if you would tell us everything that happened this morning."

Inspector Dwyer took notes while I, once again, related the morning's events. When I was finished, both Dwyer and George took me back and forth over some of the details. No, I hadn't heard anything like a shot or any unusual noises before

I left my house or when I was in the park. No, I hadn't seen any cars that seemed out of place. No, I hadn't seen or heard any activity at the park while waiting for the arrival of the police. No, I couldn't think of anything that I hadn't already told them. I described how I stood at my bedroom window to make the call. They asked to see this room, so I led the way (glad that I had made the bed—something I usually only did when I changed the sheets). They looked out the window down at the street and across at the park. I pointed out that there were lots of other ways out of the park.

"But you stayed here, overlooking the park," Dwyer asked, "until the squad car pulled up?"

I hesitated, thinking back through my movements. "No," I finally responded. "I called the police. Then I went to the kitchen and fed Aggie. Then I came back and stood at this window until the car pulled up. Almost right away."

Dwyer said, "Tell me what normally makes Aggie bark." Aggie had given up on their being either dangerous or affectionate and had long since lain down. At the sound of her name, she lifted her head and raised her ears. George smiled slightly and I thought, oh good, there's a human being in there.

"Mostly just people. Someone ringing the doorbell or slamming a car door—any noise outside, if she's inside. If she thinks someone's threatening me or if she's surprised, startled."

"How about at the park?" George prodded.

"She doesn't bark at the park. At least not usually." I thought for a moment. "I guess sometimes when she's being playful with other dogs."

"So you would say that usually what Aggie barks at is people—people ringing your bell or startling her or threatening you?"

I nodded, then thought perhaps I understood. I felt a little dismayed. "Oh. You're trying to figure out whether someone else was there, in the bushes, aren't you?" The base of my skull prickled. They nodded. "Oh, but...she could have been just barking at the...at the body. I mean, after all, that was a person and she wouldn't know that it...it wasn't anymore." They nodded again.

Then George said, "You go up there every morning at the same time?" I agreed. "You are aware, Ms. Jones, that we have a leashing law in this city?"

I sat very still. This was every dog owner's nightmare. "Yes," I said carefully, deciding to say no more though I was dying to blurt out that everyone in this neighborhood lets their dogs run loose at the park. It wasn't fair, however, to implicate my neighbors just to save my own skin. This issue, thankfully, was not pursued further.

Instead, George went on to ask, "How many people know that you do this every morning?"

I frowned. "Mary Sharon Andrews—she lives downstairs. She takes Aggie if I'm not here or if I'm not feeling well or something. I guess other friends know that I get up early and walk with Aggie but probably not the exact time. And neighbors. There are a lot of dog owners in this neighborhood. Although we usually go up earlier than others, some will be coming as we leave. We greet each other, know each other mostly by our dogs' names. Other than that...Why?"

George shrugged. "Just curious."

In a pig's eye, I thought, staring at her. "Are you wondering if someone deliberately killed that person there at that time, knowing I'd find him?"

"It's a possibility," she conceded.

"Not a very likely one," I said firmly.

"Why do you say that?"

"Because, I don't think it likely..." I stopped suddenly, feeling ridiculous. I shook my head and grinned. "I was going to say that no one I know would be likely to commit murder, but everyone must feel that way until it happens, I suppose."

Both of them smiled and agreed. Dwyer said, "Tell us about yourself. Your job, your co-workers, your friends, your family."

"My mother lives in Berkeley," I started. "I grew up in San Francisco. My parents are divorced now. My father and only sister live in the San Diego area." I thought of my family for a moment. My mother would be worried, would want to fuss over me. My father...he'll never know anyway. We don't have much to do with one another anymore. He never did like my being a lesbian; when he and Mom got divorced, it was an excuse to leave me, too. And Magdalene...Magdalene would be disdainful and self-righteous, somehow implying that it was my fault I got involved in tawdry situations like this. "I work right here, in my house. I'm a free-lance writer. And I work part-time for WINK—Women In Need of Kindness. That's a domestic abuse agency. What else do you want to know?"

"Tell us something about your friends, people you work with."

"My close friends are mostly women, women who are active in feminist politics. Then there are writers, especially journalists. I work part-time for the *Chronicle*, but that's just in the past year. Before that, I worked there full-time. Mary Sharon—my friend downstairs?—is my closest friend. We were roommates in college and have remained friends. A year ago she decided to return to school, got accepted out here, and moved into my studio." I stopped, thinking, How much do I have to tell them? Am I rambling?

Dwyer was looking at me intently, a slight squint to his eyes. He said, slowly, "Jones. Tyler Jones." I returned his gaze, wishing he wasn't going to make the connection I was sure he was working toward. He repeated, "Tyler Jones." He tapped his pencil against his teeth for a moment, George patiently watching him until the squint eased from his eyes, and I knew he'd figured it out. "Oh yeah," he said, his pleasant voice suddenly picking up a very slight but unmistakable edge. "You wrote that series on police officers who beat their wives and kids, didn't you?"

I nodded, deciding there was no point in saying more. I'd never been particularly popular with anyone on the police force since I'd done that piece.

"You won some kind of award, didn't you?" he pushed, obviously not impressed at all. I merely nodded again, my teeth clenching slightly. Not just "some" award. A Pulitzer! It was good work, factual and fair, but the cops would never forgive me for exposing the truth and placing any of their own in a less-than-heroic position.

George interrupted the silence growing between us. "You were an investigative reporter?"

"Not exactly," I responded. "I was called a special-assignment feature writer. It amounts to about the same thing. I quit a little less than a year ago. Quit full-time work, that is. I still write a Sunday column and do other free-lance work." I didn't volunteer the information that I was also working on a book about violence against women that included the info about cops.

Dwyer appeared to have swallowed his resentment and said, all business, "You specialized in crime, is that correct?"

"No, I didn't, actually. I investigated a variety of subjects. If there was any focus, and there was somewhat, it was on women and especially on violence against women." I added drily, "That, of course, is usually about crime."

"Quite possible that you made some enemies, writing the kind of articles you did?"

It was more of a statement than a question. I thought, The worst enemies I seem to have made are cops. Are you, Inspector Dwyer, suggesting that perhaps a cop killed this man, then planted his body in my park to frame me? Or scare me? With a kind of jolt I thought, Or are you suggesting that I killed this man myself? Some "enemy" I made working for the paper who came after me, perhaps? I scrutinized Dwyer's and George's faces. Both seemed to be waiting impassively for my answer.

I felt as if I'd been in something of a daze since first gazing at those shoes poking out of the shrubbery at the park. Suddenly, I shed this somnolent state and seemed to be returning to my body.

"Why are you asking these questions?" I redirected. "Do you think I'm implicated in this murder somehow? That maybe I'm being framed? Or terrorized? Or do you just think I did it?"

Dwyer responded, a slight edge back in his voice, "Just trying to cover all the bases, Miss Jones. Could you answer the question, please?"

"What was the question?" I snapped.

"Do you think you've made any enemies, writing about the stuff you do?"

"Sure," I barked. "Cops, for instance. Lots of other men who don't want to be fingered for their part in the awful violence that's done against women in this society." I changed direction before they could ask any more questions. "Who was the man up there? Any I.D. on him?"

A slight smile played around George's mouth. "We're here to ask the questions, Ms. Jones. Are your columns syndicated?"

"Yes," I responded, then continued, "I have a right to know who the body is. I found it. You're acting as if I'm a suspect. Do I have to call my paper to get the facts?"

"We don't have an I.D. yet, Ms. Jones. How many papers does your column appear in?"

"I don't know." That seemed absurd, even to me, but I honestly didn't know. "Maybe 20 or 25. I can check that for you if you really want to know. What difference can that possibly make?"

George said, "Do that, please. And also get us a list of the newspapers." When I opened my mouth, she interrupted, "It's possible you've made enemies over quite a wide area. I assume your column, like your reporting, covers the same kinds of controversial subjects."

"Yes," I agreed. "What kind of gun was used?"

Dwyer shook his head and George said, "We don't have that kind of information yet. How long have you worked for the *Chronicle*?"

"Almost ten years."

"Doing this—what did you call it?—feature work that entire time?"

"No. I started as a reporter, working my way up. The past four years were when I got to concentrate more on special assignments."

"Ms. Jones, if you could review the articles you did during that period—particularly the ones that might have been inflammatory to some individual or other or to some segment of the population—and come up with a list for us, we'd appreciate that very much."

I stared at her for a moment, then shifted my gaze to Dwyer. Again they returned my look impassively, patiently. Finally I said, "It seems to me that you're jumping awfully quickly to the conclusion that I might be involved in this murder somehow. After all, I'm just an ordinary citizen who happened to find a dead body in my neighborhood park. Don't you think it's rather a stretch to expect to find some connection between this body and me?"

Dwyer said in a soothing voice, "Just routine, Miss Jones. It doesn't mean a thing. We will want to know everything about everyone connected in whatever tenuous manner to this murder. We hope you're willing to cooperate."

I bristled at his tone of voice. "Don't patronize me, Dwyer," I snapped and then agreed to their request. While we talked, Allan Dwyer meticulously jotted everything down. I wondered idly if they took turns being the scrivener or did

Carla have seniority? Or maybe she just refused to do secretarial tasks, on the basis of historical expectations of women. Somehow I felt certain that thought was merely fantasy on my part. I didn't think the police would allow for "historical expectations of women" to play a part in decision-making. They probably took turns.

When they finally got up to leave, Carla handed me a card. "If you think of anything, remember anything, no matter how seemingly insignificant, please call us," she said. "We will need you to sign a statement. If you could come down to Homicide later today, we'd appreciate that." I nodded. "Do you need an address?"

"No. I know where it is."

"And Miss Jones—" Dwyer began.

"Ms." I corrected him, realizing he'd said that before.

"What? Oh yes, I see. Ms. Jones," he slightly exaggerated "Ms." the way people do when they are not altogether comfortable or familiar with the word or when they are annoyed at having to use it, "I think it absolutely essential that you alter your morning routine. Under any circumstances, such a regular schedule can be dangerous but under these circumstances..."

I felt a stab of tension between my shoulder blades, as if someone had just snapped a rubber band against my bare skin.

$$4$$

As soon as George and Dwyer left, I called Jeff Adams at the *Chronicle*. Jeff was on the crime beat at the paper, and we were old colleagues. I gave him the run-down on the story.

"You don't want to handle this yourself, babe?" Jeff had ways with words that I found intolerable, but I'd long ago given up on trying to educate him.

"Jeff, I can't. You know that. I'm too close to it. Anyway, you'll find things out that they'd never share with me. After all, you're not a suspect."

"They really think you mighta done it?"

"You know the schtick, Jeff. Everyone's a suspect during an investigation." We said that last sentence in unison. "Let me know what you find out."

The rest of that day was rather anticlimactic. Not that I wanted to start every day by finding a body in the park. It's just that I rarely talk to anyone in the morning, and then here was this morning filled with people, breathing and otherwise. Aggie was keyed up, too. I didn't know if she was catching it from me or just felt the same disruption of routine that I did. At any rate, I found it difficult to settle down to my usual morning of writing. I couldn't resist the temptation to call a couple of friends to share my grisly discovery. And then there was my mother. I hesitated about calling her, but I knew she'd find out sooner or later and just be hurt that I hadn't told her immediately.

"Tyler! How dreadful! Are you all right?"

"Mom," I said in my most soothing voice, "I'm fine. Nothing happened to *me*. Really. I just found this body, that's all."

"I'm coming over," she declared. "I'll just pack some things and stay with you for a few days."

For one split second, I was seduced by the thought of someone taking care of me. Then I quickly remembered what my mother was like. "No, Mom, that's not necessary. You're a dear, and I appreciate it, but truly it isn't necessary. I have lots of work to do, and I'm sure you do, too. We'll just end up getting in each other's way." And, I added, only in my head, I'd end up taking care of you more than vice versa.

There was very little hesitation in my mother's capitulation and, I'm certain, some relief. "If you're sure, honey? I am awfully busy now, but I could direct my activities from your house nearly as easily as from here." My phones would be tied up nonstop for hours, I knew, and I had no desire for the invasion of my mother's Central American relief organization.

"Everything's fine, Mom, really. Thanks a lot anyway." I rolled my eyes, just as if someone were there to appreciate my exasperation.

Thus easily persuaded, Mom happily moved on to her latest activities, filling me in on the details of her upcoming trip to El Salvador. Twice a year she drives her aging van with a caravan of other vehicles from all over the States to El Salvador or Honduras or Nicaragua or other points of need in Central America, bringing food, clothing, bedding, and other necessities. My mother fervently believes that the only life worth living is one of service and seems to be making up for the privileged years she'd spent as the wife of a robber baron. Our politics and values mesh very nicely, and many of my friends envy me my mom. Still, I sometimes tire a little of her fervor.

I turned to the book I was writing; work was always a

good escape. I was transcribing a series of first-person testimonies that would, eventually, be sprinkled throughout the more pedantic analysis and statistics of the rest of the book. The stories were horrific; hearing them filled me with a kind of fantastic, murderous fury. Oddly enough, however, it was soothing to put them into print—something about the breaking of silence, the piquant sting of women's words, calmed me.

MELODEE

My momma worked nights. She'd leave me with the lady next door until my poppa came to get me. I would cling to her skirts and cry and wail and beg her not to leave me but she did anyway. The neighbor ladies, they all just shook their heads and clucked their tongues about what a "momma's girl" I was. Sometimes my poppa came to get me real late because he had calls to make and then I'd be asleep and that neighbor lady would tell him to just let me sleep over and sometimes he'd do that and those nights would be the only nights that I got any peace. Excepting weekends when my momma was home. But mostly, even late, my poppa would hitch me up over his shoulder, calling me his "little sweet-potato-pie" and take me home anyway. I was the only one who wasn't fooled by that display of affection.

When we got home, my poppa'd tell me to get ready for bed. "Brush your teeth and get your pj's, on and I'll come say prayers with you." I hated prayers. I hated them so much that when my momma took me to church to hear my poppa preach and he'd say, "Let us pray!" I'd start to shake all over and cry. 'Course that was when I was still real little. Later on, I stopped caring.

It started so early, I can't remember exactly when, but I know I wasn't in school yet. My momma would go to work and when my poppa would come to say prayers with me, he'd say, "First I got to instruct you in the ways of the Lord. It is my duty to teach you how to be a good woman and a good wife. It is the duty of every father to instruct his daughters so." Then he would touch me all over but especially down there. And he would tell me to touch him places, too. And alls the time, he'd be telling me not to be a-scared and not to tell anyone about this because that was part of learning hows to be a good woman—that is, to keep quiet about the things that happen between man and wife in their own home. And that he knew I wanted to be a good woman and to grow up to be a good wife.

At first, when I was still real little, he'd have me lick that thing from between his legs. It would be all limp, kinda like a pickle that's been setting out in the sun too long, then it'd grow huge and hard and it scared me awful and he'd tell me, over and over, "Lick it all over jest like it's a ice cream cone, honey, oh yes, that's good," and then he'd tell me to "suck it like it was a peppermint stick" and if I started to cry 'cause I hated this part, he'd be so gentle and never yell at me or anything but tell me with such sorrow that he was so sorry that I wasn't gonna grow up to be a good wife and woman and then I'd cry some more but I would always, sooner or later, start sucking and he'd moan and groan and scare me so much and then that thing, that awful thing would throw up right in my mouth and all over my face. Then we'd say prayers together and he'd thank the Lord for giving him such a daughter that he knew was gonna grow up to be a fine woman and wife and I was supposed to thank the Lord for giving me such a fine father that was teaching me the ways of the Lord.

When I was still real little, he told me I wan't ready for him to do what he really wanted to do but he'd show me with his fingers. But sometime, I don't know when—'cause after a while I just stopped remembering anything—he musta decided I was ready and started putting it in me 'cause when I was 13, I alla sudden was pregnant. And, 'course, it was his baby 'cause there was no one else. My momma cried and moaned and wailed and he prayed and beat me— over and over and over again with a willow switch, saying, "The Lord has cursed me with a tramp for a daughter." I thought he was going to kill me and I didn't care 'cause I didn't want to go on living anyways.

Finally he quit and told me to get out of his house—that I was dead as far as he was concerned, that he had no daughter.

I went to stay with a school friend for a little while and then my momma came and gave me some money to "go away on the bus." I looked at the money and I looked at her and then I told her. I told her it was him, it was Poppa what done this to me and she slapped my face and said, "It's not bad enough you're a whore but a liar, too?" I never saw them again. I took a bus to Atlanta and got a job washing dishes and after the baby was born and took away from me—I never even got to see him or hold him—I went on the streets. I got out of the life and quit drugs ten years ago now. I still have nightmares about prayers.

$$5$$

I needed to move around after typing this story. Actually, I needed a drink. Since that wasn't an option, I made some fresh coffee. I threw some clothes in the washing machine. I vacuumed the living room rug, snapped the leash on Aggie, and we strolled downhill to a deli for some reinforcements. Coming back uphill was more of a struggle but just what I needed to purge myself of the feelings I had about this latest story, feelings I didn't really want to feel. A lunch on the deck helped even more. When the clouds began to move in, I was glad that I'd taken advantage of the sun while I could.

Later, I settled down to the process of going through my articles for the detectives. Luckily for me, everything I'd written was listed on my computer in order of publication. As I perused this fairly lengthy list, I jotted down notes of possible enemies. Some of it was pretty obvious.

The cops, for instance. I'd made myself unpopular with them more than once. Besides the Pulitzer-winning article about battering police officers, I'd also written an article about racism in San Francisco public offices, including, of course, the police department. I wasn't very popular with attorneys either—at least male attorneys—after I'd done that series on sexism in major law firms as well as sexism on the bench and how it operated. This investigation resulted in many interesting finds, including one about a major law firm that prides itself on being liberal and, of course, nonsexist—

even including two women as partners!—but nonetheless persists in holding its partners' meetings in a male-only club.

Which led me to an investigation of male-only clubs and organizations and their ties to influential politicos who shouldn't, ethically, be supporting organizations that were discriminating against women and, often, Jews, African-Americans, Asian-Pacific-Americans, Latino/a-Americans, and Native Americans. Oh, that series really made me popular. I wonder what Dwyer and George would think if I just said that my "enemies" were men? Would they even get it?

Journalism aside, what about all the men who resented my work with the women they'd abused? High on this list was Jason Judd, who once broke into my house while his wife was staying here. How many men had stormed WINK over the years, threatening me because I wouldn't tell them where their wives were?

I finally gave up and drove to the Hall of Justice. Dwyer and George were out, but they had turned the statement over to a desk jockey. I read it through, made a couple of changes, initialed them, and signed it.

Aggie and I then headed for Ocean Beach in my ancient but beloved 1974 VW Bug with the affectionate, if not particularly original, name of Lady Bug. While Aggie chased gulls up and down the shore, jumped in and out of the tide pools just before the surf came roaring in, tasted everything lying about and ran playfully with some other dogs, I walked along the water's edge, thinking. Thinking about what had happened that morning, going over all the pieces in my mind, trying to discover if there was anything, any tiny detail, that I wouldn't have recognized as important until after finding the body. I came up with nothing.

I shook my head impatiently, saying to myself, "This is absurd, Tyler. You've read too many mystery books. There is nothing you can do to solve this murder. Leave it alone."

I breathed deeply, pulling in the slightly salty, slightly

fishy sea air. I looked around. The beach wasn't crowded on this weekday afternoon with its partially overcast sky and sharp breeze. Other folks walked with dogs or alone with shoulders hunched against the wind and fists stuck deeply in pockets. Still others were obviously making their homes against the sea wall near the road. In this neutral territory, no one knew or cared who I was. I remembered the ball I'd brought for Aggie, took it out of my pocket, and spent the next half hour throwing it. By the time we left, both Aggie and ball fuzzy with sand, my body ached pleasantly from the fresh air and exercise. My car, of course, was the next object to get fuzzy with sand.

I was still in the garage, showering Aggie with the hose, when Mary Sharon came bustling out of her apartment. "Where have you been?" she demanded, standing with her hands on her hips.

I stared at her in amazement. "What?"

"Look, Tyler, don't play dumb with me. You were witness to a murder this morning. This is not an ordinary day. I was worried about you."

"Mary Sharon, I agree, this has certainly not been an ordinary day. But I did *not* witness a murder and am still going to operate in ordinary ways. That means, for one thing, that I don't have to ask your permission to go somewhere."

She had the grace to look a bit sheepish. "Okay, okay. I'm overreacting. I know I'm dramatic and silly, but how would I know if someone had kidnapped you or not?"

I couldn't help laughing. "Oh, honey," I hugged her. "You are a dear. Aggie and I just went to the beach."

We went upstairs and Mary Sharon collapsed on my pale yellow wrap-around couch while I got myself a coke. "Do you want anything?" I asked.

"Not from your house" was her answer, and I shook my head. She twisted the leaves of the large palm tree standing in the corner behind the center of the couch. "So. What do you know?"

"About the murder?" I shrugged. "Not a thing. I don't suppose they're going to tell me an awful lot."

"I'm sorry I wasn't here to meet your new interest with the 'deeply intelligent eyes.'" She opened her eyes wide in some kind of bovine look. I plopped down on the end of the couch and threw a dark brown pillow at her.

"Mary Sharon. She's not my new interest. I don't even know her."

"What's she like?"

"Ice water."

Mary Sharon pursed her lips. "Not much rapport, huh?"

I shrugged again. "Who knows? She has a job to do."

"Are you really interested in her?"

"Nah. She's cute, that's all."

"Mmm-hmm." Mary Sharon grinned. "You want to get something to eat? I'm going to bury myself in my books tonight and I need some sustenance."

I agreed readily. This was something we did fairly often. Perhaps too often, considering Mary Sharon's finances, or lack of them. Neither of us took much time to cook, but both of us liked to eat. We went to a nearby Japanese restaurant, not fancy but with solidly good food.

When we returned, Mary Sharon, as usual, retired to her apartment to study. Aggie, in her typical way, was as ecstatic to see me as if she truly believed I'd deserted her. Normally I liked living alone, liked having no one to answer to and only myself to set routines or deviate from them. Tonight, however, the house felt oddly still and quiet. I checked the phone machine; there was a call from Jeff. I dialed his home and listened to the phone ring over and over again. He hated phone machines.

I opened the door to the back and Aggie bounded out. I stood in the dark on the deck, admiring the lights spread out below but feeling uneasy. I knew it was silly because Aggie would be barking if there were anyone out there. Didn't matter. I still felt uneasy. These gardens actually were very safe, because they were all landlocked, hemmed in by other backyards that had no access to the fronts except through the houses. Of course, I thought, if the murderer lived in one of these other houses...And that would make sense, if the murderer was right in this neighborhood. Or knew someone in one of these houses. Maybe a lover who stayed overnight. Had a key. Wouldn't need a car to get to or from the park. Could easily scale my fence into my backyard.

"Aggie!" I called sharply. She came at once.

Damn, I thought, as we went back into the house. I hate this! I've never even thought of being afraid here. Nonetheless, I closed all my blinds—something I almost never did, except on the street side. I felt nervous, jumpy. I thought about going to a meeting. I glanced at the clock—too late. What to do? I put on some soothing Brahms and walked restlessly about my four rooms. I straightened wall hangings that didn't need straightening: the large fiber collage above my fireplace that a friend had made for me, the pair of O'Keeffe prints of her wild, sensual flowers in dazzling colors, and, in the dining area, the series of delicate watercolors that a friend of Norah's had done. I rummaged through, rearranged, pushed in, and merely touched the books heaped on the shelves lining one wall of my living room—all without really seeing the titles.

In the extra bedroom that I used as an office, I gazed at the photos hanging on the walls, like a pictorial archive. The black-and-white experimental studies that I'd done when I was younger. Very self-conscious artsy. I admired the outdoorsy photos that my friends had done. The journalistic photos also had special meaning. There was one of several sea birds being rescued from an oil spill; all but one of the six birds in that photo had died. And here I was with Pepsi, my first lover, hiking in Big Sur country. Julie, the true love of my life, lay with me in a hammock in a friend's backyard in Minneapolis. We were probably swatting mosquitoes, I thought ruefully. We'd been together for five years when she ran off with the friend who'd taken that photo. It took me nine years to recover enough from the pain of that betrayal to realize that I wanted to remember some of the good times, too. Only then was I was able to put this favorite snapshot up on the wall. There was a photo of Norah and me with Aggie when she was a puppy. We were at Mendocino, and Aggie was tearing through a field of wildflowers. My eyes misted. Next was a family portrait. Father looked relaxed and jovial, Mother appeared to be under some strain. Already, at eight, Magdalene had a saintly demeanor, and I—two years younger—wore a sly expression.

That picture moved me beyond sentimentality and away from nostalgia. Families. Was I seeing things when I looked at the photo of my family? Was I superimposing my adult views and experiences? After all, we *were* all smiling. Maybe we were just a typical, happy, American family. I snorted. Typical, oh, sure. Happy? I don't think so.

I spent a fitful night, waking from dreams with little memory beyond a feeling of tension. I lay in bed, listening to the little night noises of the house. Aggie was aware of my restlessness, her tail gently thudding whenever she knew I was awake.

Before Aggie came to the side of the bed in the morning, the phone rang, dismissing the image in my dream of a floating cave, a hole of some sort. I jerked awake and reached for the phone, mumbling, "Hello?"

There was a slight pause, then a voice whispered, "Aren't you going to the park this morning?"

6

I dropped the receiver as if it were burning my fingers. Then I quickly picked it up and gingerly put it back on its cradle. "Oh god," I said aloud. Aggie was dancing around, having no idea that something was wrong, just excited that I was showing signs of readiness before she'd had to prod me. I looked at the clock. 5:45.

I had no clothes on. I always slept with no clothes on. How could I get out of this bed naked? I didn't want to get up, but I desperately wanted, at the same time, to get up and check my doors, make certain they were all locked. I couldn't stay in bed.

"Knock it off!" I snapped at Aggie, who paused in her exuberance and cocked her head. I made myself get up, then went to my closet and pulled on a t-shirt that reached almost to my knees. With sweatpants on, I felt even less vulnerable. I padded into the dining room, checking the door to the deck. It was secure. Last night, I'd even put in the rod to hold the door closed, the one I only used when Aggie and I went away. I glanced down. It was still there, of course. I had to go downstairs to the front door but...

It was dark with just a bare indication of dawn around the edges of my closed blinds. I turned the hall light on, the one that illuminates the stairwell. The absence of shadows dispelled some of my tension, but I suddenly realized I wanted a weapon. I just couldn't go down those stairs without some extra protection. I looked around. Aggie was watching me, ears up, clearly puzzled. A baseball bat would be good. I had a bat somewhere, from high school when I was on the girls' softball team. Where was it? Probably downstairs in the garage. I went in the kitchen and considered the knives. Too scary. I got the little-used rolling pin out of a drawer and started down the stairs. Aggie thought, obviously, that this meant order was finally restored and went tumbling down ahead of me. The front door, of course, was still locked. The door to the garage was also locked. I breathed a sigh of relief and went back upstairs, trailed by a dejected Aggie.

5:57. "Oh baby," I said as I leaned over Aggie, hugging her head, "you need to go out, don't you?"

I went to the phone in the living room, hesitating before I picked it up again. I listened—just a dial tone. I dialed, then held my breath through several rings until a sleepy Mary Sharon answered, somewhat petulantly.

I exhaled. "Mary Sharon?"

"Yes." She sounded testy. "What is it?"

"Mary Sharon, I'm sorry. This is me. I just got a scary call. Can you come up here?"

She sounded alert now. "Tyler? What's going on?"

"Just come up. Through the garage. I'll open the door for you. Okay?"

"Okay."

I took the rolling pin again and started down the stairs. Aggie clambered down cheerfully, assuming we were *truly* going to the park this time. Mary Sharon's studio had a door that opened into my garage as well as one that opened into the backyard. Although the garage made me nervous, I was glad Mary Sharon didn't have to go outside just now.

I unlocked the garage door, opened it slowly, and said quietly, "Mary Sharon?"

"For chrissake, Tyler," she answered, her voice coming

from the direction of her own door, "turn the light on!" The only light switch was by my door.

I switched it on, and the spooky shadows in the garage disappeared. Everything took its familiar form again: the car, the lawn mower, two bikes, an array of garden tools. Mary Sharon, dear reliable Mary Sharon, shuffled across the garage in her ridiculous pink bunny slippers that matched her equally ridiculous fluffy pink robe. I shouldn't really malign it. Her mother made it to help fortify her against "those damp San Francisco nights." When Mary Sharon got near me, she stared at the rolling pin still gripped tightly in my hand and then casually let her gaze travel up to my face.

I guess I was the one who looked silly. "I felt like I needed a weapon."

She nodded but said nothing. She brushed by me into the house as I quickly scanned the garage. My Lady Bug appeared to be unharmed, and the rest of the room seemed in order. "Wait," I demanded as she started up the stairs. I dashed into the garage and grabbed my bat. Mary Sharon's eyebrows rose when she saw the bat, but she still said nothing. We went upstairs.

"Tyler, what the hell is going on?"

"I got this call this morning. Right before I usually get up. I'd had a bad night, nightmares and such, so I...Well, anyway, the phone rang. Words were running together in a rush, tumbling out of my mouth like coins out of a winning slot machine. "Someone just whispered, 'Aren't you going to the park this morning?' Then I hung up and checked my locks and called you."

"Did you call the cops?" She was staring at my windows on the ocean side.

I looked at her, then at the windows and back to her. "What's the matter?"

She turned toward me. "What do you mean?"

47

"Why are you staring at the windows? Did you hear something out there?"

"No, no," she said. "I don't think I've ever seen these blinds pulled before."

"Oh. Oh yeah. Well...I was kind of spooked last night."

"Tyler, you should've called me. If you want, I can sleep up here for awhile."

I pushed the offer aside with an impatient gesture of my arm. Then I caught myself. "I'm sorry, Mary Sharon. I don't mean to dismiss your generosity. I'm just trying to dismiss my chicken-ness. You know?"

She smiled, gave me a hug. "Of course I do." Aggie was dancing around us impatiently. "I think Aggie really has to go, Tyler. And I think you'd better call the police. I'll let her out back while you're calling. Okay?"

I nodded. "Yeah, that's fine." I bent over Aggie, ruffling her hair. "Poor little sweetie, you don't have any idea what's going on, do you?"

Mary Sharon moved toward the windows as I turned toward the phone. In that split second of motion on both our parts, I had a vision in my mind of an explosion centering on Mary Sharon silhouetted in my windows, and I yelled, "Mary Sharon!"

"What?" she yelled back, startled.

"I..." I shook my head slightly, then said in a more normal voice, "I'm sorry. Let me get the blinds."

"What are you doing?" she demanded of me as I strode by her and began pulling the blinds up, standing well back from the windows as I was doing it.

"Look. This is crazy, Mary Sharon, but you know? If someone was out there waiting to shoot me, like the guy in the park got shot, and then you opened the blinds, they'd assume it was me doing it and you..." I didn't finish.

Her eyes were as big as the proverbial saucers. "Maybe we shouldn't open the blinds?"

I shook my head again. "This is ridiculous. No one's out there. If there *was* anyone out there, they'd probably be at the park. Aggie's got to go out. Anyway, she'd be barking her head off if someone was out there." Wouldn't she? I removed the rod from the track of the sliding door, unlocked it, and slid it open. The sky over the ocean was pinkish-purplish gray, reflecting the first moments of sunrise behind us over Twin Peaks. Aggie looked quizzically at me and Mary Sharon, then she trotted out onto the deck. She stood still a minute, delicately sniffing the air, her golden-red hair moving slightly in the breeze. Then she looked back at us again as if to say, How come we're not going to the park?—and finally went down the stairs. We both let breath escape from our bodies, even laughed a little.

I went to the phone and dialed Inspector George's number.

$$\boxed{7}$$

By the time Inspectors George and Dwyer arrived, Mary Sharon had a coffee cake in the oven and was making a cheese-and-mushroom omelette. She wanted to make tofu patties, too (in lieu of sausage, I guess), but I didn't have any tofu (thank god!) and refused to go downstairs to get some out of her kitchen. Puh-lease! Wasn't a scary phone call a bad enough thing to start the day with? I'd suggested bacon but when she asked me if I wanted to cook my own breakfast, I dropped the idea.

"You can always tell my stress level by whether or not I start cooking," she told me.

"Why is that?" I couldn't imagine wanting to cook when I was upset.

"Association," she answered firmly. "Whenever I came home upset about something, Mom would make me something to eat. Stress and love and food. All mixed together. Clear association."

I smiled, thinking of Mary Sharon's mother as I always picture her, in an apron. True, she didn't wear one to Mary Sharon's graduation, but the only other times I'd seen her were in her home, and I'm pretty sure she never took it off there. Maybe to go to bed. I don't think my mother *owned* an apron. Not that she didn't cook, but cooking was a necessity to her, instead of a way of life. With my mother, eating was something you did to stay alive. With Mary Sharon's mother, eating was something you did to feel better. Or to celebrate. Or to express sorrow. "Your mother didn't only cook when you were upset," I reminded Mary Sharon, who looked up from her tasks and smiled.

"You're right. She cooked all the time. But the strongest memories I have of my childhood are of coming home totally devastated about one thing or another and her saying, 'Come on. Let's bake a cake.' Even when I came out to her, she baked a cake."

"Pretty stressful, huh?"

"Yeah, but you know, I've always thought she did it to celebrate, too."

"What do you think she was celebrating?" I thought of my own parents' reaction to my coming out and, believe me, "there was no joy in Mudville" would've been an understatement. Oh, my mother tried to be understanding and accepting, a good liberal mouthing platitudes like "some-of-my-best-friends-are" bullshit. She was obviously appalled, while my father—well, he didn't even try to be anything but disgusted.

"I think she understood that I'd just found myself," said Mary Sharon. "On the other hand, maybe I just made that up— it sounds good, doesn't it? At any rate, she put that cake together while we talked. Then we sat at the kitchen table and talked some more while it was baking. Then we ate it, without waiting for frosting, and by the time we were done talking, the cake was gone."

"The whole thing?"

"The whole thing. Those were the days, let me tell you. According to popular food mythology, I should be a blimp, shouldn't I? Instead of the whale that I am."

I shook my head and said, "Oh, surely not a whale. More like a walrus, I'd say. A slightly undersized walrus at that."

"Gee, thanks, Tyler. A walrus. That certainly brings to mind a fetching picture."

"What's the matter with a walrus? They have feelings, too, you know." I started to giggle. "A pink walrus!"

She narrowed her eyes, somehow resisting my inspired humor. "Mmm-hmm. Tyler dear, do you have any rat poison? Arsenic maybe? I could just slip it into this omelette instead of garlic and I'm sure you'd never notice the difference."

I shook my head. "You don't want to do that, Mary Sharon, the police are on their way. You know, you're not going to make a very good lawyer if you don't think of all the possibilities." This was a lot more fun than thinking about ominous whispers.

When the police officers showed up, it was hard to recreate that feeling of near-terror the phone call had caused. As I was introducing them to Mary Sharon, I observed George eyeing Mary Sharon's robe and slippers. I thought, Mmm, she's going to think we're lovers.

But Mary Sharon had caught the glance, too. She stuck a foot out and said, "Bizarre, huh? I grew up in Minnesota and, believe me, we Minnesotans are prepared for cold weather, come what may!" She added, "I live downstairs." George tilted her head in a noncommittal but acquiescent manner. Mary Sharon continued, "Want some breakfast?"

"Sure!" Dwyer answered as George said, "No, thank you." She frowned at Dwyer, and he exclaimed, "I haven't eaten yet!"

"Really," Mary Sharon insisted, as she set two more places at the table and began to bring the food out, "there's plenty. An old family tradition. You know the routine. You come home from school and say, 'Mom! I flunked an algebra test!' And she says, 'Come on, honey, let's make some cookies'."

Inspector Dwyer slathered butter on his coffee cake. "Did your mother really do that? My mother, excuse the language, kicked butt if we came home with news like that."

George held her hand up when Mary Sharon tried to

serve her some omelette. "I'll just have some coffee, thanks. Maybe a small piece of cake."

Oh sure, from Mary Sharon she takes coffee. And food. Mary Sharon, meanwhile, continued her babbling. "Oh, yeah, my mom thought food healed everything. Broken bones, broken bicycles, broken hearts. You name it, Mom had a food cure for it."

"I wish she'd been my mother," Dwyer said, his mouth full of egg.

George seemed to stifle another frown while glancing at Mary Sharon. "You don't appear to have been eating heartily all your life."

My teeth clicked against my fork as I bit down too hard. Great, now she's getting interested in Mary Sharon, who has, of course, turned on all that ingenuous Midwestern charm. Mary Sharon, in the meantime, was just staring at Inspector George. Suddenly, comprehension dawned and she glanced down at her thin self, only slightly camouflaged by her fuzzy robe.

"Oh. You mean..." she hesitated a minute, then said with great seriousness, "A person's size has little to do with food, you know." Mary Sharon used to have a fat lover, and she made it her business to understand the relationship between eating and size as well as people's attitudes about physical appearance.

George considered Mary Sharon silently while we all ate. Suddenly, she swung toward Dwyer and said, "Done, Allan? Can we get started?"

Dwyer grinned and said, "Sure," as he mopped himself up with his napkin. Mary Sharon and I were still eating, somewhat more leisurely. For me, this was heaven. I didn't get to eat this well in the morning unless I went to a restaurant, and I couldn't think of one restaurant that served homemade coffee cake. Dwyer turned toward Mary Sharon and said, "Thanks for breakfast. That was great. If I ever flunk an algebra test, I'll know where to come." She smiled broadly, catching my eye across the table.

"Now, Ms. Jones—" George had become all business again, "suppose you tell us exactly what happened this morning." She brought out a notebook and I thought, Ah, they do take turns. I told them about the phone call. When I was finished, George said, "That's all? Nothing else happened?"

"No." I looked toward Mary Sharon for support. "But you know, it was kind of scary, this voice whispering to me, just at the time I usually get up!"

She brushed this away. "I'm sure it was scary," she agreed. "It's just that your call came into the station at..." She looked at Dwyer, who flipped his own note pages back until he apparently found the notation, then read, "6:33."

"How come," George continued, "you waited at least a half hour to call us? Is that right? You did tell us the dog gets you up at 6:00 every morning, didn't you? And this call came in before you got up?"

"Mmm," I hesitated, remembering how I felt and what I did. "I just didn't think to call the police, I guess. I'd had a bad night, nightmares and stuff. My first thought was to get up and make sure my doors were locked. After I'd checked all the doors, I realized"—and here I reached down and patted Aggie, who was gazing hopefully at my plate—"that Aggie was still going to have to go out. I sure as hell wasn't going to go over to the park, but I was afraid to even unlock the door and let her out back." I grinned at Mary Sharon, feeling exceedingly silly. "I called Mary Sharon and asked her if she would come up."

George glanced at Mary Sharon, who had begun to clear the table, then back at me. "Mmm-hmm," she said, "I can certainly see that she'd be better at protecting you than we would."

I rolled my eyes and protested, "No, no. It's just that it all happened so fast!"

George genuinely smiled this time. "Really, Ms. Jones, I understand."

I smiled back, feeling the warmth of her rare smile, and said, "Tyler. Just call me Tyler."

Dwyer interrupted this touching exchange. "What can you tell us about the voice on the phone?"

I shrugged. "I don't think I can tell you anything. It's just, it was so ominous. He drew each word out..."

Dwyer waited a minute, looking at me, making me wonder what I was supposed to say next. Then he said, "He?" When I looked blankly at him, he continued, "You said 'he.'"

"Oh. I did, didn't I? I don't know. I mean, I don't know if it was a he or she. Whispers—whispers don't really sound male or female. Maybe I just thought it was a he because it was sort of like getting an obscene phone call."

"Let's try something," Dwyer said. "You close your eyes, Miss, uh, Ms. Jones. Okay?" I did so and could hear them moving around a bit and murmuring to one another.

Then someone whispered, "Aren't you going to the park today?" A chill slithered down my spine, and my eyes flew open. No one was sitting at the table. George said, "Don't turn around. Can you tell us who said that?"

It's okay, I told myself. It was just one of them. I tried to concentrate. "I don't know. I think...I'm not sure, but I think it was you, Inspector Dwyer."

Dwyer and George sat back down while Mary Sharon remained standing. Dwyer grinned. "It was her." He inclined his head toward Mary Sharon.

"Oh. I guess that didn't work so well, did it?"

"Actually, it was useful. We can pretty well establish that you really don't know whether it was a man or woman on the phone."

I nodded, and George asked, "Now, Ms. Jones—Tyler—no one else heard this phone call, is that right?"

For a second, I wondered what she was asking. Then I

smiled a little at Mary Sharon and answered, "That's right. I was alone."

"Is it okay if I leave?" Mary Sharon interrupted. "I need to get dressed and get downtown."

George nodded. "Sure. Do you have a work number we can have, Ms. Andrews? In case I need to get hold of you, talk to you later? We should have your home number, too." Oh sure, I thought, in-case-I-need-to-get-hold-of-you.

Mary Sharon, however, seemed oblivious to this ploy. "I work part-time, erratic hours, at Women In Need of Kindness. I don't think that number would be much help to you, but you can have it if you want. And I'm a student at Hastings."

"Law school?" Dwyer asked and pursed his lips in a silent whistle when Mary Sharon nodded. She wrote her home number and the WINK number on a scratch pad. "This woman place," Dwyer turned to me, "is that the same place you work, too?" Mary Sharon wiggled her fingers at me as she left.

I nodded. "Yes, but I'm a volunteer. Mary Sharon is on the paid staff. They usually have a law student or two part-time."

George was pulling a large photograph from a folder. "Do you know this person?" She handed it to me.

My breath caught in a ragged gasp. I did indeed know the man in this picture. He'd once broken my front door down and threatened to kill me. "Oh, my god" was all I could say.

They both nodded as George said, "Yes, this was the man in the park."

⑧

Aggie stirred, nudging me gently but insistently. I walked over to the deck door and slid it open. The morning was fresh and clear. I saw the Farallon Islands on the distant horizon, saw them without really seeing them, remembering, instead, petite Consuelo and her elegant, drunken husband, Jason. Dr. Jason Judd. Sighing, I turned back toward the table. George and Dwyer waited for me to speak.

"You must know I know him. Jason Judd. I had to call the police the only time he was here."

Dwyer nodded and George said, with a trace of warmth in her voice, "Why don't you tell us about it?"

I stood there by the door for a minute, then walked into the kitchen and stomped on the floor three times.

"What are you doing?" George's voice sounded startled.

"It's a message to Mary Sharon. If she hears this, she'll come up. I want her to know that it was Judd." I came back and sat at the kitchen table, where the two of them looked at me silently until I started again.

"My house is occasionally used as a 'safe house.' A place for women to stay for a day or two until the system finds a niche for them. These women may need to use a safe house for lots of different reasons. Maybe the shelters are all filled. Or maybe it isn't safe at the shelters because they've been there before, and their husbands know it. A few months ago— let's see, it was the beginning of April—Consuelo Judd came here. She couldn't go to the shelter because she'd gone there the time before, and her husband found out where she was and caused a lot of havoc. That's really bad for the shelters because, obviously, women need to feel safe at them. She was just going to stay here a couple of days—actually there's a rule that safe houses are used no more than four days in a row—and by then the system would have decided what to do with her to continue insuring her safety."

"What would they have done?" Dwyer asked. "I mean, if the shelters weren't secure and she had limited access to a safe house, what would the system do with her?"

"Well, we might've just moved her around from one safe house to another. Or—and I think this is what we were probably going to do—we would've found a shelter for her down the Peninsula or in the East Bay, some place her husband didn't know about. And we were putting together a temporary restraining order. She hadn't agreed to that before, but she was finally tired of being abused. At any rate, it didn't come to that."

I paused, putting both hands to my forehead and rubbing. It felt as if the skin was stretched too tightly across my forehead. After a minute, George pushed gently. "What happened?"

I got up and got myself more coffee. They both nodded when I offered it to them. I had to concentrate on not letting my hand shake as I poured.

It was evening. I was in my office, reading. I could hear the murmur of the TV in the other room. I was just thinking of getting a snack when the doorbell rang. Aggie let out a sharp bark, and I got up and opened the office door.

Consuelo was standing in the hallway at the top of the stairs, her body tense and leaning backward slightly.

Aggie brushed past her when the bell rang again, and

she jumped. "Consuelo?" I said. "What is it?" She turned to me as if in slow motion. Her eyes were large, puddles of terror. I grabbed her arm and said, "What? What is it?"

She whispered, "It's him."

Downstairs by the front door, Aggie's barks were nearly drowned out by a sudden pounding. "Open this door. Do you hear me? Open this door this instant! I know my wife is in there, so open up! I'm telling you, bitch, open this door or I'll kill you!"

Consuelo froze while I dialed 9-1-1. Aggie jumped frantically at the door as the yelling continued and a body began throwing itself against the door. "Aggie!" I called out sharply. "Come. Now!"

She came reluctantly but continued to bark. I got a grip on her collar and dragged her toward the bathroom, commanding Consuelo to follow us. She didn't move. "Consuelo! Come here!" My voice was sharp.

Her voice made me think of a sleepwalker. "He just wants me. I'll go down to him."

I grabbed her sleeve and pulled her toward the bathroom with us. "Consuelo, come on. The police will be here in a moment." I could hear the front door give way with an excruciating crunch as I closed and locked the bathroom door.

Consuelo said, "You must let me go to him. He just wants me. He won't hurt you if I go now."

I shook my head, trying vainly to calm Aggie down as we heard heavy footsteps running up the stairway. "Forget it, Consuelo. The police will be here in a moment." I hoped that was true. "I'm not letting that madman get his hands on you."

He was careening around my small house, pounding walls and knocking things over, all the time yelling about killing me, killing both of us. I tried to keep Aggie quiet, but of course she was wild. Consuelo seemed resigned, and I

*could feel the blood racing through my veins as my heart
thudded loudly in my chest.*

*Suddenly, he kicked the bathroom door in like a loose
pile of kindling. Aggie lunged as I grabbed for her collar.
"Get the hell out of here! Who the fuck do you think you
are? The police are on their way!" He raised his arm, I felt
what must have been a great adrenaline rush and let Aggie
loose at the same time that I threw my body between this
man and his wife. His hand slammed across my face, and
the pain exploded in my head like a lightbulb shattering. I
flew back and my head hit the shower door. A serene blue-
black darkness descended over me and the sounds around
me dwindled away.*

George and Dwyer were staring at me. Dwyer touched
my arm, saying, "Are you okay?"

Tears were running down my cheeks. I brushed them
away with the back of my hand and nodded. I got up and
poured myself a glass of water, though I was really wanting a
beer, whiskey, anything that would blot out the helpless fear
and anger.

I took a deep breath, slowly exhaling. "He found out
where she was and came here. He was drunk, pounded on
the door, yelled for me to let him in or he'd kill me. I called
the cops right away but...you know, it takes them a while
sometimes." I shot a look of anger at each of them, then shook
my head a little. I knew it wasn't their fault. Another deep
breath, slow exhalation. I didn't like remembering this.
Dwyer and George waited patiently. "Consuelo and I locked
ourselves in the bathroom with Aggie."

"What was Mrs. Judd like?" Dwyer asked.

I looked at him curiously. It seemed an odd question.
"What was she like?"

"At that moment. What was she acting like?"

"Oh. She was just kind of...patiently waiting. Obviously very used to this. Well, not used to it in a way. Her body was—it's hard to explain—all curled in on itself, protective. Here I was waiting for the cops, and she was just waiting for him to come hurt her again. Well, he did. He knocked me out. When I came to, the cops were standing in the doorway, and Aggie was licking my face and growling at them at the same time. Jason and Consuelo were gone."

I noticed Mary Sharon at the door to the deck, looking puzzled. "Did you stomp on the floor?" she asked. "I was in the shower, but I thought I heard you." Her hair was wet but still bristling, and she was dressed in her usual style—a bright fuschia-colored sweater that dipped down to the tops of her knees and equally bright yellow leggings. On her feet were black and white checked high-tops with laces that matched the fuschia of the sweater.

Only Mary Sharon, I thought, could somehow pull this together and look presentable. I knew that I would look ridiculous in such an outfit. I could just imagine the continual surprise she provided those staid, conservative law professors. She had certainly been a constant surprise to our professors back at the University of Minnesota. And it was obvious that she was a surprise to George and Dwyer—this transformation from demure pink rosebud to vivid primrose.

I handed her Judd's picture. "This is the man Aggie found in the park yesterday."

Mary Sharon gave a silent whistle. "Good old Dr. Jason," she said, looking at me as her mouth thinned and tightened. There was nothing more to say. Neither of us was particularly sorry about Judd's death. She came around the table, and we hugged. "I'm sorry, Ty, I gotta run. I've already missed my first class. This is your afternoon at WINK, isn't it?" I nodded. "Okay. I'll see you there then. Good-bye, Inspector Dryer—"

"Dwyer," he corrected her.

"Dwyer," she amended, "and Inspector George. Nice meeting you." She hurried off.

I poured some more coffee for Dwyer and me, but George put her hand over her cup this time. When I sat back down, she said, "So. You pressed charges against Dr. Judd. Correct?" I nodded and she added, "And now you have a civil suit pending against him, is that also correct, Ms. Jones?"

"Tyler," I said, and then agreed with her.

She looked at me curiously, then asked, "Why a civil suit? Most people would just press charges for assault and battery."

I smiled. "That was Mary Sharon's idea. It helps to have friends who know the law better than you do. Of course, WINK probably would have said the same. Civil suits make it tougher and tougher for men to get away with this sort of thing."

"And what about Mrs. Judd?" George continued. "Did she also press charges?"

"No."

"How about the temporary restraining order?"

"She dropped that, too."

"Do you have a gun, Ms. Jones?"

I was startled by the abrupt change of subject and hesitated. "A gun?" I repeated. "What's going on here? Why would you ask me that?"

"Just routine," Dwyer soothed. "Do you?"

"No. I don't have a gun. And," I added, somewhat defiantly, "no, I didn't shoot Jason."

They ignored my addendum. "Have you taken any self-defense classes or anything like that?"

"I've done some aikido. Nothing ongoing. In college I took a course in self-defense. Why?"

"You think self-defense is a good idea, but you don't own a gun?" Dwyer prodded me.

I looked from one to the other. "No. I don't like guns." After a moment's hesitation, I asked, "Do I need a lawyer?"

"You're certainly welcome to have a lawyer present, Ms. Jones," George said archly. "That's entirely up to you."

"But do I *need* one?" I persisted. "Am I a suspect?"

"I'm certain you understand that everyone is a suspect until we actually arrest someone. I can only reiterate that calling an attorney is at your discretion." I looked from one to the other again and decided not to worry about this just yet, although Mary Sharon would be appalled. Oh, well, let her worry about it, I thought, she worries enough for both of us. After all, I have nothing to hide.

Now it was Dwyer's turn to be formal. "Ms. Jones," his voice had a coolness that sounded ominous to my trained ear, "where were you on Tuesday night?"

This was Thursday, right? I found the body Wednesday morning, so Tuesday night...My stomach lurched as I looked at these no-longer-so-friendly police officers. I laced my fingers together, knotting them tightly. "I was at a meeting."

"What kind of meeting?" Dwyer pressed.

I thought: You bastard! You assholes! You know already! I know you do! Through clenched teeth I said, "An AA meeting."

"You're an alcoholic?" George asked.

"No!" I shot back. "I just go to AA meetings to meet people! You know? It's like a pick-up place for me."

Surprisingly, George seemed to be suppressing a grin. Dwyer asked, "How long have you been dry, Jones?"

Just "Jones"? Is this a compromise between "Ms. Jones" and "Tyler"? I missed Mary Sharon. "I've been going to meetings since July and quit drinking about a month before that, so...a little more than four months."

"Congratulations," George said, suddenly sincere again. I felt a little mollified that she was attempting to make this easier.

Dwyer broke the tentative rapport between us. "No

relapses?" I shook my head. "You didn't have anything to drink Tuesday night after your meeting?"

I was puzzled for a minute, then felt a stab of anger. So. They thought I'd fallen off the wagon, got my hands on a gun and gone and killed Dr. Jason Bastard Judd. The thought did have its appeal, I had to admit.

"What did you do after your meeting, Jones?" Dwyer again.

"I came home. Took Aggie out. Read a little. Went to bed."

"You didn't talk to anyone? See anyone?"

"No," I shook my head, thought a moment, then shook my head again.

"How about Mary Sharon?" George inserted at this point.

How come with her it was Mary Sharon and with me it was Jones? "No," I said again. "I don't think she was home when I came home. I heard her come in, or at least I thought she was coming in, later. She might've heard me moving around up here. I don't know."

"How did Dr. Judd find out his wife was here?"

"What?" These abrupt changes of subject kept me off-balance. Dwyer repeated the question. "Oh." I said, stalling a little. Surely it was all on record somewhere anyway. "She told him."

"'She'? You mean Consuelo Judd?"

"Yes," I agreed.

"When did she do this?"

"I don't know. She might've told him before she came, or she might've called him. That's more likely, but I just don't know."

"Wouldn't you notice if she called him?" George asked.

"Not if she did it when I was in the bathroom or out with Aggie or something. I wasn't here every minute and even if I am, I don't spend all my time monitoring someone else's actions. My purpose is to provide a safe place, not a prison."

Dwyer got up, walked to my bedroom door, and peered in. I told myself he'd probably seen unmade beds before. Then he poked his head into my office, right next to the bedroom. "This is all the room you have?" I nodded. "Where do these women stay when you have them here?"

"I only have one at a time. And I don't take kids. There just isn't room, plus they make Aggie nervous." I stopped, trying to remember his actual question. "The couch in my office is a futon. I sleep in there whenever someone stays over. If I need to work or just be alone, I can go in the office and close the door. It wouldn't be particularly hard for someone to use the phone."

"Why would she tell him where she was?" Dwyer asked.

I glanced at George for any sign that she understood better than Dwyer. She was waiting expectantly; if she knew more than Dwyer, she wasn't letting on. I sighed. WINK and other agencies constantly offered training courses to police officers about domestic abuse. So far, few police departments had made these courses mandatory. Even with those that did, some cops just didn't seem to pay much attention. "You have to understand a woman like Consuelo. She has been living with abuse for years. Consuelo and Jason had been married for twenty-five years." Annoyance grew in me. Why didn't these people take time to educate themselves? "He'd always been abusive, although it definitely escalated as he aged and, probably, his drinking escalated. Physical abuse becomes a way of life, becomes 'normal,' actually. It still hurts, it's still scary, it's horrid in every conceivable way. The one thing that keeps most women in these relationships, aside from fear and lack of resources, is that they believe, they really *believe* with all their heart and soul, that it will stop some day, that their men love them and will stop hurting them. So. Maybe Consuelo calls Jason and maybe he sweet-talks her—you know, 'Oh, honey, I love you, I won't hurt you ever again, I promise I won't, I'm so sorry I ever did that, I don't know what was the matter with me, I need help, I'll get it, really, just tell me where you are, I'm going to come get you and make it all up to you'—that sort of thing. She tells him where she is, because she wants so badly to believe him and also because she is in the habit of giving him whatever he wants. If she doesn't, she's likely to get very hurt. So..."

"Didn't it make you furious?" George asked. "That she told him she was at your house?"

I shook my head, gritting my teeth at their ignorance. "No. I've been involved with domestic abuse for too long to be surprised. You have to understand, women are under siege. Any of us might have done the same. I can't tell you how many women have told me, over the years, that they'd *never* put up with physical violence for a minute, and yet those same women are putting up with just as damaging verbal or pyschological violence." The corner of Dwyer's mouth twitched, and I forged on. "Look, it's not that she's stupid. Quite the contrary. Consuelo's very intelligent. She's just been beaten down, literally and metaphorically. When it comes to Jason, she's just trying to survive."

"Is this a cultural thing, do you think?" Dwyer asked, then stumbled on when I stared at him in amazement. "You know, because she's Mexican and used to this macho stuff."

My controlled impatience exploded. "Absolutely not! God, it's so infuriating to me they don't teach you people anything about domestic abuse!" I got up, carried our coffee cups to the sink and rinsed them out. I needed to be moving around some, so I wiped off the counters and washed out the coffee pot. "Consuelo Judd is Argentinian, not Mexican. Believe me, there is *nothing* about violence against women that is more common to any one group or race or nationality than any other. White women put up with it just as much as Hispanic women or any other women. Just like any color of man can do it. And any class, too—doctors do it, professors do it, *cops* do it, and laborers do it. As a matter of fact, even women do it to other women." There was a small silence in which I breathed deeply, remembering that as my anger rose, my breathing grew more shallow. "Consuelo just happened to be from Argentina. That had nothing to do with why she put up with Jason or why he beat her. And, by the way, this is about him. Not about her. *He* was the one who did the beating, don't forget."

George asked, "How about alcohol? That plays a big part in abuse, doesn't it?"

"Sometimes, sometimes not. I'm sure Jason had a drinking problem, but that doesn't explain everything." I returned to the kitchen table, sitting reluctantly, feeling drained from my outburst.

"How did you feel when you were in the bathroom with Mrs. Judd?" Dwyer asked.

I was getting used to these sudden changes. "I told you. I felt like I was waiting for the cops and she was waiting for him." I paused, thinking back. "But in some ways, I did feel like a victim. I felt..." I stopped again, feeling uncomfortable—no, embarrassed—at this admission. "I felt...a certain passiveness, helplessness maybe. It was *not* a good feeling."

"You don't think of your self as passive? As a victim?"

"I try not to. I live in a society in which women are raised to be pretty passive. And also victims. Obviously, I've been affected by that. But I try to be in control of my life as much as I am able."

"Do you think of yourself as aggressive, one who takes initiative?" Dwyer pressed me.

I nodded slowly. "Mostly."

"How about rage? Did you feel that when you were in the bathroom?"

I thought a moment. "I don't think so. I was distracted by Aggie and Consuelo and just...I don't know. No rage. Not then. Later I felt that."

"What did you do then?" George asked this time.

"I had a steel door installed downstairs. *No one* is ever going to break that door down again."

"But how did you feel toward Jason?" George prodded.

"What do you mean, how did I feel toward him? I despised him! Despised everything he stood for! The way he delivered a lecture at an AMA conference, then went home and beat up his wife! The way he came here, broke things up, then thought he could smooth it all over by apologizing and offering to pay for the damages. As if that's all he had to do! He treated me like *I* was the social misfit because I wouldn't let him in my house and talk 'reasonably' with him, because I wouldn't act like it was a temporary lapse in his usual manner. He was an asshole! Maybe he needed help. Maybe he, too, was a victim, but I don't really give a damn. No one deserves to be abused and no one has the right to do that!"

"Did you feel like killing him?" She wasn't going to leave me alone.

"Killing him? I don't know." How does one answer such a question? Of course I felt like killing him—but not *really*, not *literally*. Would cops, who have to be prepared to kill, understand the distinction? "I certainly can't, in all honesty, say I'm sorry he's dead. But if you're asking me if I *did* kill him, the answer is no. I didn't kill him."

"Do you think his wife might've?" Dwyer interjected.

I thought for a couple of minutes, catching my breath. "I don't know. It doesn't seem likely. Consuelo was—like I said— not stupid but had learned her lesson well: she was very passive." I wondered.

"Do you think it's possible she killed him?" George pushed me.

"Anything's possible, I guess. It doesn't seem likely," I repeated.

"What about their kids?" George asked this time. I shifted my attention from one to the other as they alternated questions.

"I don't know the kids. They're not at home anymore."

"Can you tell us anything about them?"

I shrugged, trying to remember things Consuelo had told me. "The older one, a daughter, apparently ran away in her teens, married her high school sweetheart. According to Consuelo, she mostly did it to get away from home and to bug her father—she married a Chicano from a low-income family. Anyway, I guess there was abuse there, too, but the daughter got out much sooner than her mother. She's divorced now and going to college. Mills, I think. The younger child is a boy. He goes to some school down in southern Cal. UCLA maybe. No. I think it's Cal Tech. A tough school. Consuelo was very proud of him."

"So she talked to you about her kids?" This time Dwyer. I was starting to think I could close my eyes and I wouldn't know who was Dwyer and who was George, even with the gender difference, because they sounded so much alike. I wondered if this was because they worked together or if cops just all sounded alike after awhile.

"Yes."

"How long was she here before Jason broke in?" Didn't he ask this question already?

"Two nights. It was the third night."

"So, long enough to see that you got up every morning at 6:00 with Aggie?"

I hesitated, then said, "Yes."

"What do you know about Consuelo Judd?" George changed directions again.

I was getting tired of this. "Surely you can get that information elsewhere?"

"Yes, of course, but we want to hear as much as we can from as many sources as we can."

"Not very much. I think she's from a wealthy family in Argentina. I don't know what Jason was doing there, but they met in Argentina and when he got back to the States, he sent

for her, and she came. He was in his thirties, I think, already
fairly established in his profession and she was in her early
twenties—very smitten with the worldly Dr. Judd, very enam-
ored of living the 'good life' in the States. Well, it's hardly
been good for her."

"Anything else?"

"Not really. She's been very involved in the 'proper'
charity kinds of things that wives of wealthy men seem to
do—Junior League or whatever, I really don't know. I don't
know the details about her family in Argentina, but with all
the political unrest there, apparently she's never felt she had a
home to go back to."

"Well," Inspector George said in a voice with finality
clinging to it, "we thank you very much for all your cooperation, Ms. Jones. If you haven't anything to add, Allan, I think
that's all for now."

Dwyer just added, "Ms. Jones, you should call us, any time
of day or night and *right away*, if you have any other phone
calls or any other incidents. No matter how insignificant they
seem."

I nodded, then stood up. "I've made a list of people that I
might not be particularly popular with. Because of some of
my articles."

"Good, that might be helpful." They followed me to my
office as I got the list. When I handed it to Dwyer, I asked,
"Was he killed in the park?"

George said, "The lab results are not yet conclusive." This
sounded like a rote answer. After a moment's silence, she
added, "Call us."

I nodded, walking them down to the street door. After
they left, I stood there at the bottom of the stairs for a few
minutes, resting my hand against the coolness of the steel
door.

9

After showering, dressing, and washing the dishes from Mary Sharon's enormous breakfast—oh yeah, I thought, she cooks when she's distressed but apparently doesn't do dishes—I found myself in my office. I needed the release of working without thinking. More transcribing, I thought, and pulled out another first-person testimony.

The phone delayed me. "Tyler girl, is that you?"

It was Jeff. "Hi."

"Didn't you get a message from me?"

"Yeah, I called last night, but you weren't around."

"Girl, you sound like you been run over by a truck one or two times. I guess you got the news, huh?"

"About Jason Judd, you mean?"

"Yeah. I found out late yesterday afternoon. Didn't think I should leave that kind of message on your machine."

"Yeah, well, I got a little visit from our 'finest' this morning. I think they think I killed him."

"Didn'cha?"

"Nice, Jeff. That's all I need—a vote of confidence from my co-workers. You got anything for me yet?"

"Nope. Just the I.D. I'll call you when I hear more. Sit tight, chickie."

I shook my head in disgust. "Bye, Jeff." I hung up the phone and turned to my transcription.

GERALDINE

My husband never laid a hand on me—except supposedly in loving ways. He never hit me or pushed me or kicked me. Still, his was a reign of terror. He threatened me, threatened me continuously.

He'd encircle my wrist with his thumb and forefinger and say, "I could snap this quite easily, you know." And there'd be an angry red stripe around my wrist when he removed his fingers. Or he'd put both his hands around my neck and slightly push his thumbs into my voice box and say, "It wouldn't take much pressure here before you'd be gone, you know." And there'd be two ugly red spots on the front of my neck when he removed his hands. Or he'd twist my arm up behind my back and say, "Just a little higher here and this would break, you know."

His voice was always soft and completely calm when he'd say these things. As if he were being totally rational. I hate that calm, rational voice that men use—as if passion negates your feelings or your reason or your instincts. And the lack of passion denotes sanity. Hah!

He had some other tricks he used. He had a bull whip that he kept in the bedroom closet. I kid you not. I hate to tell this part because it sounds like something I must've made up. It's almost too fantastic to be true. I remember that whip so vividly, the long plaited black tail attached to the stubby handle in his furious fist, the sound of it whizzing and snapping just inches from me. He only once actually hit me with that whip. Usually he'd take it out—either for me or for the kids—whenever we'd really pissed him off. Just the sight of it, as you can imagine, would strike terror in my heart.

He would slowly and sinuously wrap the whip around and around his clasp on the handle, talking all the while. "Someday, you know, someday you will just push me too far. I will have to really use the Marquis on you, you know." He called it the Marquis de Sade. Apt, yes?

Was this the day, I'd wonder? Then, without warning, he'd lash that whip out, snapping its end within inches of me (or the boys) and say, without raising his voice, "Are you going to do what I say?" The answer, of course, was always a given. Then, usually—for good measure, I suppose—he'd let the whip lash out once more.

And then he'd laugh. "You should've seen your face when the Marquis came at you. You should've seen it." I'll bet. I never said anything.

He did other things just to keep me off balance. They were mostly so subtle, I wouldn't recognize them as part of his siege against me and had trouble even remembering them. Until later—when I started to put it all together. Like he'd be out of town at a conference or on a lecture tour—always a great relief around our house— and the night he was expected home, he'd call and say he'd be a day late.

Then, that night after we'd all gone to bed, he'd break into the house. Either I'd hear him coming in and I'd lie there terrified—should I call the cops? or is it just Upton playing one of his games?—or I wouldn't hear him coming in and I'd wake up with this dark, menacing figure hovering over me. If I didn't wake up when he was coming in or when he was standing over me, he'd wake me by placing his hand over my mouth. Can you imagine waking up that way? Of course, after a while I never believed him when he said he'd be a day late, but then—sometimes he was. So, when I went to bed without him, I never knew if he would be sneaking in the house that night or not. It was impossible for me to get a good night's sleep under those conditions.

Another trick he liked to pull on me was obscene phone calls. Especially if he was out of town. He'd call in the middle of the night and whisper in a muffled voice the awful things he was going to do to me. It wasn't that they were so sexual, although they usually were, but it was the violence that was horrifying.

"I'm going to tear your arms off your body before I fuck you." I'd hang up, and he'd call back and say, before I could hang up again, "I'm going to get you, you know."

Sometimes he'd do that in the middle of the day. Any old time. At first I didn't realize it was him. I mean, who'd expect their own husband to do something like that? So I would call him at work, terrified, and he'd be so loving and soothing. Sometimes, when we were first married, he'd come right home and hold me and assure me it was going to be all right.

But it didn't take me long to figure out he was the one doing it. Even though I didn't exactly recognize his voice, there were certain things he'd say that were dead giveaways. Like repeating the words "you know" all the time—a habit of his. More than that, it was the intonation of his voice, a certain rhythm that was recognizably Upton's. I would scream at him to quit doing this and hang up and he'd just call back and I'd hang up again and then I'd finally take the phone off the hook.

When I confronted him, he would say I was completely insane, that everyone knew he'd never do anything like that. After all, he was a professor. I'd think he was right and feel contrite, but the next time it happened, I knew it was him. I finally gave up trying to get him to stop doing it.

Once, when he was out of town, I took the phone off the hook. He called the cops and told them he was out of town, his wife had a drinking problem and he was concerned about his sons because the phone seemed to be off the hook. Could they check his house? When the doorbell rang at three in the morning, I didn't answer it because I was so certain that Upton was in town, and it was one of his sick "jokes."

But the bell kept ringing and ringing and someone started pounding on the door, calling out, "This is the police, is there anyone home?"

While I cringed under my covers—refusing to answer the door because I was certain that Upton had just hired someone to pretend they were cops, one of my boys finally got up and opened the door. They thought, because I didn't respond to them and pretended to be asleep even when they came in my room, that I'd been drinking and I'd passed out. And, of course, to help them along with this conclusion, there was an empty bottle of wine on the counter in the kitchen. And it didn't matter how many times I told them I'd only had one drink before I went to bed, they'd already made up their minds.

They took my sons to juvie for the night and took me to a dry-up tank. You can well imagine Upton's reaction to all that. Although he played at outrage and dismay and refused to believe a word I told him—"the-cops-wouldn't-have-taken-you-to-a-dry-up-tank-unless-they-had-sufficient-proof"—he was, of course, secretly delighted that his latest prank had better results than even he'd imagined.

And me? I quit leaving the phone off the hook. I even quit hanging up when he called. I'd just sit there and listen while he talked of gouging out my eye and then fucking me in that eye socket or hacking off my boobs and carrying them with him always to fondle them whenever he wanted or how he knew I wasn't easily satisfied so he'd find things that were more satisfying to me, like sticking a baseball bat up my vagina or maybe a big firecracker or, probably best yet, a watermelon.

I thought about other things, maybe like a prostitute does, just surviving, getting through it. If I didn't…well, I didn't know, I guess, but I was starting to get scared that he was going to have me committed. He talked all the time about how T.S. Eliot had had his wife, Vivienne, committed—even though she wasn't really crazy, just a little difficult, a little eccentric. I knew this was supposed to be another warning but, like all his warnings, I never knew when he'd go further.

Of course, it seems to me now that I should have been committed. I mean, how could I put up with that stuff? But that's just too easy to say afterward. It wasn't like that then. It wasn't as if I sat down and figured out that he did all this stuff. I never put it down on paper all at once and realized, Jesus! this guy is nuts, not just cruel and abusive. Instead, everything that he did was isolated, seemingly at random. In between, he seemed like a dear, caring, intelligent man. It wasn't that I didn't know there was something wrong with him. It's just that I kept hoping that whatever he did, he'd not do it again. And he wouldn't—for awhile. Or he'd never do that exact thing again. It would be something a little different.

And I was scared. In the early days, before I had the boys, I said I was going to leave him after he'd threatened me about something or other. And that was the first time he brought out the Marquis. He fingered it so lovingly, told me how he'd taught himself to use it, coiled it so slowly, and then let it strike out toward me. I was dumbfounded—frozen with fear, waiting for him to actually hit me with it. Of course, he didn't. He just recoiled it and put it away, talking quietly about how he was sure I'd never really want to leave him.

I could hardly believe it had happened but I told a friend the next day, the wife of one of Upton's colleagues. Major mistake, as you can imagine. I was so naive, at that point. She, also, was dumbfounded and then told me, very pointedly, that she didn't believe me, that I had to be making up such a story, that everyone knew that Upton was the most soft-spoken, gentlest man in his department and that she didn't know why I'd do such a thing but that I'd better get help. I had thought we were good friends. It had never occurred to me that she wouldn't believe me. She went further—she told her husband who in turn told Upton.

This was the only time that Upton ever actually laid a hand on me—and even then, it wasn't direct—he let the tail of the whip strike me across my back. I was standing at the stove, cooking, had not heard him come in—which was usual, he was always sneaking up on me and scaring me when he came home. The first warning was the sound of that whip whizzing through the air. I just started to turn when it bit into my flesh with a blade-like ferocity, and I screamed, both in pain and fear. It had sliced right through my blouse and my flesh was cut open and bleeding where that whip had barely nicked me.

Upton serenely recoiled his whip, saying, "I trust I will never have to do that again."

And of course he never did. I stayed with him. I quit my job—as a researcher in the biology department, a job I adored—as soon as I got pregnant the first time, because Upton insisted there was no point in having babies if I wasn't going to stay home to raise them. I agreed with alacrity. I gave him two sons—exactly what he wanted—and I literally believed that I willed those babies to be boys. He was adamant about not wanting any dumb little girls—he'd say, "Girls are for beauty and fucking, boys get all the brains"—and I was terrifed what he might do, to me and to any little girls I produced. I obeyed, complied, groveled, whatever he wanted, whatever he needed.

Sometimes I felt like killing him. It seemed like the only answer. If I tried to divorce him, he'd look perfect and I'd look crazy—if my own friend didn't believe me about the Marquis, was a judge going to?—and I was convinced he'd get custody of the boys. And I knew I wouldn't get any alimony or help from him. I was sure of that and I felt incapable of taking care of myself, of being able to find and keep a job.

I spent years, literally years, planning how I would kill him and get away with it. I had my ideas so honed, so perfected that I probably could've pulled it off. Except I was so afraid of his power that I was convinced, in some perverse but real way, that if I killed him, he'd make certain I'd get caught. Sometimes, when I thought about that, I'd get scared that he might think of this on his own. I know this sounds crazy—it is crazy, all of it!—but I could really imagine him killing himself and setting me up for "murder one," the ultimate practical joke.

So it became obvious that I would have to kill myself, that that truly would be the only end to all this. I made careful plans. I couldn't stand the thought of him putting me down for being too incompetent to even manage killing myself. I would find the perfect method, then be convinced that I might screw up. Then I'd start all over, looking for a different perfect method. It's obvious to me now that all this careful planning was really a way of buying time, that I was hoping for another option, a better option.

Well, a better option did come along, finally, although I certainly didn't recognize it as such at the time. When the boys were both teenagers, Upton fell for a graduate student. He decided he had to have a divorce, so he could marry her. I was furious—all I'd put up with and now he was just discarding me? Here was my perfect out, and I didn't even see it. At least not at first. Anyway, the girlfriend didn't really like kids, so Upton was willing to let me have the boys and pay me both alimony and child support. Anything so long as I'd let him loose. We'd been married for twenty years at that point, and I never did a thing to free myself of his tyranny and then, when it was being offered to me on a silver platter, I wanted to fight to keep him!

Well, I didn't fight very hard or for very long. I'd never won any fight with him anyway. I did think about telling her what she was getting into, but I knew she wouldn't believe me—who would?—I would just look like I was the raving ex-wife. I also wanted her to pay the price for stealing my husband. This was, obviously, a bit prior to any feminist consciousness on my part. As far as that goes, it was a bit prior to any kind of consciousness on my part at all.

Once he left, it didn't take me long to realize that I was finally getting some peace. I went to graduate school—assuming that Mr. Nice Guy wouldn't remain nice forever, and I would need to be able to make a living. I fell in with what Upton would have called a "bunch of discontented, radical miscreants," but they were actually middle-aged women who had returned to college to finish educations that had been cut short by marriage and motherhood.

It didn't take us any time at all to discover that our major bond was our anger. These women changed my life. Six months after Upton left me, I found myself a feminist therapist and started piecing together the terrorism of our years together. And a year after he left, I sold the house, packed the boys' things up, and dropped them and their belongings off at Upton's condo. They were uncontrollable and attempted to terrorize me, just as they had seen their father do all those years. He had made it impossible for them to respect me, and I helped by being so passive. I wasn't going to keep trying to undo what had been done to them, mostly by Upton.

It was time for me to start living my own life. And I did. But I know, I know that there are so many other Uptons out there and so many other women totally paralyzed.

(10)

Usually I erected some kind of emotional barrier between these stories and myself, so I wouldn't get too close, too worn out, too touched by the intensity of them. Today, that barrier was too porous to shut anything out. Reliving Jason's attack had stretched my defenses paper-thin. I was crying by the time I finished transcribing Geraldine's story. I put my head down on my desk and sobbed—for her, for all the women who are brutalized, for Consuelo, for myself.

My own father never laid a hand on my mother or Magdalene or me. At least not that I remember. I think our family was pretty "ordinary." I was never raped or sexually molested or physically abused, but I still learned the same lessons that all women learn. Be careful. Be accommodating. Be nice.

My father was king in our house. At meals, he got served first and biggest and best. The largest chair in the living room was his. He never cleared a dish or picked up his newspaper off the floor where he'd discarded it or made a bed or washed any clothing. He decided what would be on the TV each night and what music would be played. He didn't even mow the lawn, like some dads I knew. My mom—and later Mag and I— took care of all the home needs. And all of his needs. Although it was never said out loud, my sister and I learned that men make money and go out in the world and do things, and women stay home and take care of them. I didn't learn well enough, apparently, and Magdalene learned too well.

It's always about power—whether someone's raping you or just sitting in the living room with his feet up while you wait on him or breaking down your door because you have the temerity to refuse him entry. I looked at the clock. 11:15 a.m. I checked my work schedule although I knew I didn't have to. I was ahead on columns, so I had no pressing deadlines.

"Come on, Aggie, let's do some sleuthing," I announced as we hastened down the stairs to the garage. I felt the excitement of impending involvement. "Hey! Where's your leash? Go on, girl. Go get your leash."

Aggie dashed back up the stairs to pluck her leash off the stair railing. Maybe I should call first, I thought. No. This is better. After all, Consuela owes me. Aggie was back immediately, leash in mouth, tail whirling. "Good girl," I patted her head. "Let's go."

Consuelo's house wasn't far away. One mistake, perhaps, of using my home as a safe space for her. Most of the city's wealthiest inhabitants chose to live in the mansions of prestigious, sunny Pacific Heights, rising quickly up from the bay and overlooking equally monied Marin County. Jason had decided to swap sun for staid, old-money St. Francis Woods. The houses were substantial though few reached "mansion" status. The ocean view could be spectacular when not obscured by fog. For some, the lack of sun, size, and impressive address was offset in other ways. Large yards, towering trees, and abundant open spaces were beautifully punctuated with numerous fountains, benches, terraces, and gates, all of stunning proportion and detail and bordered by brick-inlaid sidewalks.

Driving through St. Francis Woods always reminded me of the suburban communities farther south on the Peninsula—San Mateo or Palo Alto or Los Gatos, perhaps. While most of the city at this time of the year was thirsting for the winter rains after our usual summer of near-drought, not so here in well-watered, well-tended St. Francis Woods. Anything missed by the sprinkling systems was carefully tended by individuals with hoses and watering cans. I figured half the gardeners of San Francisco worked in this area. Here were lawns, shrubbery, and ground cover, all of lush green, spilling over terraced yards, sloping lawns, bricked patios. The streets were darkened by the presence of many trees—palms and eucalyptus, Monterey pines and manzanitas.

As I turned onto one of the curvy streets, no doubt intended to discourage drive-throughs, I hoped I remembered where Consuelo lived. I'd never actually been to her house. After the ordeal with the Judds, Mary Sharon and I had once driven by, curious to see where and how good old Dr. Jason lived. I turned again and swore, wishing I'd looked up the address. I always do this, think I can just drive to a place I don't really know. After a couple more turns, I breathed a sigh of relief as I recognized the house.

The Judds lived in a large Spanish colonial with white adobe bricks, arched windows, wrought iron trim, and a roof-top of curved red tiles. I parked my car in front, leaving the windows open.

"Stay," I commanded Aggie.

As I walked up the drive, I wondered if houses in Argentina looked like this or was this more typical of Spanish-Mediterranean areas? Or—probably the most likely—was this just a U.S. fantasy of a Spanish house?

I looped off the driveway onto a red brick walk leading to the front door. The doorbell echoed melodiously deep within the house. After a few seconds of silence, interrupted only by the chirping of a bird or two, the front door opened. I started to step back, feeling a cringe develop between my shoulder blades, but caught myself at once. Jason Judd, I reminded myself, was dead. This man who resembled him so disturbingly (minus thirty years, of course) must be his son.

"I'm Tyler Jones," I introduced myself. "I wonder if I could please see Consuelo Judd?" I held out my hand, but he left it dangling.

Jason's son frowned. "This is not a very good time. Perhaps you could leave a card"—his eyes took in my t-shirt and jeans—"or a message. Then she could get back to you at a more convenient time." Maybe he thinks I'm the Avon lady, I thought. No, probably not. My face was free of make-up.

I hesitated. How far does one go? I smiled sadly (I hoped) and said, "I know it's not a very good time. I found...your father's body yesterday morning." His eyes flickered, but otherwise he remained unmoved. "Your mother knows me. Would you please just ask her if she'll see me?"

He stared at me for a few seconds longer, then said, "All right. Wait here." He started to close the door, then opened it again and said, "What did you say your name was?" I repeated my name, and he closed the massive, carved oaken door in my face. I waited politely, just as if I had a choice.

The front yard was lush and green, with spots of color here and there. Around the corner, a movement in the bushes caught my eye. A brown creased face peered at me. The gardener, I supposed. I smiled tentatively, but he stared back without a trace of a smile. Mexican, perhaps. Or maybe Argentinian? Latinos were often the gardeners here because they were cheaper, especially if they weren't citizens. The front door opened.

The young man said curtly, "Follow me."

The interior of the house, beautifully appointed with very little color, left me with an impression of coolness. We passed white walls with a handful of paintings in only the palest colors, a white grand piano, white sheer drapes pulled closed on most of the windows and a smattering of dark oak pieces, not unlike the front door. A churchlike quiet remained undisturbed by our progress over plush white carpeting. I wondered how children could ever have lived in this house.

He led me to a lovely sunroom that bloomed with warm color, jutting out from the back of the house. Sparkling glass on three sides afforded fantastic views of the ocean far below as well as a lavish garden.

Consuelo was in the back corner, chatting on the phone. She smiled and waved me to a chair. Not wanting to appear to eavesdrop, I walked about the room, enjoying the garden. The young man was still standing by the door, but when I glanced over, he turned abruptly and left. I sat down at what I judged to be a neutral distance from Consuelo, who was, I suddenly realized, speaking in Spanish. My own Spanish, adequate for emergencies only, was not sufficient to understand her low murmurings.

The room was light and airy, filled with wicker furniture with bright splashes of yellow, green, and white. What I had taken to be a large orange cushion in a rocker suddenly stood up and stretched languidly, a cat. He sat and unself-consciously appraised me. Apparently he felt I wasn't worth much because he promptly turned around and leaped to the back of the chair, balancing precariously against the sway of the rocker. The birds outside chirped on, oblivious, as the cat's tail slowly swished back and forth.

Turning my attention to Consuelo, I found it hard to imagine a murder in this serene and cheerful setting. Even the beatings, which I knew had been a regular occurrence here, seemed a distant bad dream.

Consuelo was not looking at me, so I felt comfortable gazing at her. One night at my house, before Jason arrived, she recalled her first few months in this country. In those days, she told me, she looked the way women of upper-class Argentina in the 1960s looked—heavy make-up, hair elaborately teased to a towering beehive, ostentatious jewelry, clothes tight-fitting and revealing, and ridiculously high spiked heels.

"In short," she said, laughing a little, "I looked like a whore. In this country, anyway. Not so in my country." She went on to tell me how much disdain she felt for the women she met who wore such simple clothing, little make-up or jewelry. "I thought they were drab and flat-looking. At first, I thought my husband's friends just didn't have much money." Again she laughed. "I can just imagine what they thought of me!" Gradually, through observation and reading the fashion magazines, she began to realize there was a cultural difference, although for a long time she resisted changing. She was convinced that *Norteméricanas* would change if they could only see "how good they could look!"

Now, looking at her across the room, I thought how well she'd learned her lessons. Her blue-black hair, now streaked with silver strands, was pulled back simply, severely, into a thick chignon. Her off-white silk blouse, open at the neck, revealed a single strand of pearls, presumably real, the only jewelry she wore besides her wedding ring. Slacks the same color as her blouse had been expensively cut from fine linen. On her tiny feet were beige flats resembling ballet slippers. Whatever make-up she wore highlighted her already luminous beauty without appearing obvious.

As she turned her head slightly in the direction of the garden, the light played across her high cheekbones for a moment and brought to view a well-concealed or almost-faded bruise on her right cheek. I wondered if the cops had noticed that. I couldn't imagine the sharp eyes of Inspector George missing any such thing.

Consuelo turned again, smiling at me, and I remembered her curled under Aunt Norah's slightly frayed afghan, finishing her story. "Now, when I see women decked out the way I used to be, I think they look awful." She sounded sad, wistful. "It's all a matter of what you get used to, you know, and I've gotten used to U.S. ideas of fashion and class but..." She shrugged, not finishing the sentence.

At this moment in my reverie, Consuelo hung up the phone. "Tyler!" she said in a warm voice. She got up from her chair and walked toward me, her arms outstretched. "I am so sorry about the phone. My sister, you know, wanting to make certain I'm okay. It is so nice of you to come." She offered me her hands.

Maybe yes, maybe no, I thought. I took her hands and squeezed them. "I'm sorry, Consuelo."

She brushed this aside. "Come, Tyler, there are not reasons for you and me to lie to one another. There is little to be sorry about here."

I said nothing but nodded, my hand almost reflexively stroking my own right cheek. As she sat back down, she touched her cheek, saying, "Oh yes, it was still happening. This he did the night...that last night."

"Really?" I was staring, feeling some surprise at her honesty.

"Oh yes," she laughed a little, "it doesn't look good for me at all, Tyler. This is what happened. You want to know, yes?" I nodded, thinking this was going to be easier than I expected. "I was in my room, getting ready for bed. He'd been down here, not in this room, in his study"—she waved back at the rest of the house—"and suddenly came up shouting at me about some expenditure or other I'd made. I don't even know what—something for the house, maybe a piece of clothing for me. I remonstrated, it was so silly—it was not as if we were poor! And, of course, that was stupid. He just backhanded me and told me to shut up. Which I quite readily did, naturally. It wasn't bad. That was all. He yelled at me awhile longer, then left. Presumably to return to his study." Her voice was rich with the shadow of her Argentine accent.

"Did you call anyone? Did you think about getting out of the house?"

"No. I went to bed."

"Weren't you afraid? Did you lock your bedroom door?"

She smiled. "All these questions, dear. I don't get so afraid anymore. No locks. I used to do that, years ago, but he just—you know this—he just kicks doors down. And he gets madder if he has to do that. No, no locks."

She stopped, and I probed, "Then what happened?"

"Nothing," she shrugged. "I went to sleep. When Victoria brought me coffee in the morning, she told me that one of the courtyard doors was unlocked when she came in. She lives in quarters over the garage with her husband, Jorge."

"The gardener?" I guessed.

She nodded. "Yes, they are a good couple. Distant cousins of mine, actually. They're hardworking and devoted to me. I feel very lucky to have them. Anyway, she said that about the door, and I thought little of it. Assumed Jason had left early and just forgot to lock it. Or even left it unlocked all night. That happened sometimes, especially when he was drinking. Then the police came..." She gracefully raised her palms upward, shrugging at the same time. "I'm sure they think I did it."

"And did you?" I asked quickly, not giving myself time to ponder the appropriateness of this question.

Consuelo smiled. "Many times I have thought about killing Jason. Many times I have thought about how I might do it. Never have I considered a gun. I don't own a gun. I don't even like guns. No, Tyler, I did not do it. I am not sorry he is...gone, but I did not do it myself. I almost wish I had."

"Mother!"

I turned toward this outraged voice. In the doorway stood a young woman, obviously Consuelo's daughter. She wore scruffy blue jeans with a white peasant blouse decorated with intricate embroidery about the neck. Her feet were bare, her short dark hair was disheveled. Perhaps she'd just gotten up. None of this lack of attention to her appearance hid the fact that she echoed her mother's piercing beauty. I was most aware of her eyes, which appeared, from this distance, to be as black as wet obsidian and also seemed to be burning with anguish.

"Margarita," Consuelo said gently, soothingly, "it is all right. Tyler is a friend." Margarita said nothing, staring only at her mother with those tortured eyes. "Come here, dear." She indicated the chair next to her. When Margarita still said nothing and didn't move, Consuelo added, "This is Tyler Jones, dear. Tyler, my daughter, Margarita."

Margarita's eyes flickered toward me briefly, and I said, "How do you do, Margarita?" feeling like a total ass for being so awkward and formal. Margarita seemed to take no notice.

She shook her head, still looking only at Consuelo. "You should not talk like that, Mother."

Consuelo smiled sadly, waving her hand in dismissal. "I am not ashamed of the truth, Margarita. Especially not with Tyler. This is the woman who tried to help me. You remember, don't you?"

Again Margarita's eyes slid toward me and quickly away. "Lunch is ready."

Consuelo pressed her lips together and nodded. "Ask Victoria to set a place for Tyler." She looked at me. "You will stay, yes?"

I hesitated only a second. "Thank you."

Consuelo looked back at Margarita, who was now looking directly at me, not exactly with approval. "Margarita?" Consuelo said in a soft voice that was, nonetheless, an order. Margarita left the room.

Consuelo sighed. "You'll have to forgive my children, Tyler. This is a very hard time for them."

"I should think so," I murmured politely.

"Margarita feels enormous guilt about her less than loving feelings toward her father, and Peter—you met him at the door, yes?—is angry at me for not being devastated by his father's death. Part of that rage, of course, is anger at himself for probably feeling relieved as well as sad."

"Was Jason abusive to them, also?" I could not remember Consuelo and me ever talking about this.

She nodded briefly, glancing away. "Some. Not the same as with me. I was the buffer, I guess." There was a directness about her speech that seemed to have grown firmer since the last time I'd seen her. Or maybe just this week, since Jason's death? "So long as he had me to take his fury out on, my *niños* were somewhat safe. He was, on occasion, brutal with them. Children, you know, are rarely perfect. Although, I must say, mine tried hard to be. They were too terrified not to be. For them, it is different. Jason was their father. They hated him for doing what he did to me, for creating an atmosphere of terror, but—you know—they loved him, too. He was their father," she repeated. "For me, there was not love left. Only sadness."

"And anger?" I prodded gently.

She sat quietly, her hands perfectly composed in her lap, looking at me but, I sensed, looking inwardly more. After a few minutes of silence, she said, "Maybe. I can't seem to contact it. I don't know. What I feel...it just seems beyond anger." She stood up. "Let's go eat."

11

Consuelo led me to the kitchen where she and the cook exchanged words in Spanish. I could make out something about the dining room and Consuelo's reply that the breakfast room would be fine. When I asked if I might wash up, Consuelo guided me back the way we had come. There were three doors in the hallway, and she indicated that the middle one was the bathroom.

I hesitated, gazing out a two-story window to the garden, until I was certain that Consuelo had moved away. Then I deliberately moved to the first door, opened it and found myself staring at shelves of neatly folded linens. I bypassed the bathroom and tried the third door. Here was a dark-paneled room, the walls covered with bookcases except for the two windows and a dark brick fireplace. The only furniture was a massive desk placed in front of the windows and two high-backed, winged leather chairs by the fireplace. This room was obviously some decorator's idea of English baronial, a quintessential "masculine" room, probably Jason's study. I only glanced around—certain, anyway, that the police had gone over it with a fine-tooth-comb—then returned to the hall. Peter was standing by the kitchen door, staring coldly at me.

I smiled thinly. "This is not the bathroom, I guess."

"No," he agreed, icily. "It's the next door, this way."

"Thanks." I tried to exude charm but his expression remained frozen.

After a quick wash, I returned to the kitchen, where the cook pointed toward the rear, presumably the breakfast room. The woodwork was painted white, as were the table and chairs. The wall covering was a pale blue-and-white check, but the curtains and cushions on the chairs were a sparkling apple-green print. A bay window overlooked a sweet garden between this wing of the house and the garage behind.

Although the food was excellent—a shrimp salad served with a piquant but delicate dressing—lunch was a strained affair. While Consuelo seemed perfectly comfortable in my presence, Margarita's silence seemed almost ominous and Peter's seemed merely resentful and sullen. Their animosity made me so nervous that I began to chatter.

"What a cheerful room, Consuelo! I would never have thought of putting together these colors, and they are a truly delightful combination, aren't they?" I forked in some salad, hoping I didn't sound as inane to them as I did to myself. "And this salad is exquisite! I must tell your cook how delicious it is. Your gardens are so beautiful, Consuelo. It must be soothing to live surrounded by such beauty." Now that, I thought, is a truly stupid remark. All the beauty in the world couldn't soothe the ugliness of this household. But I guessed that Consuelo tried, inside and out, to counter that beastliness. I pointed toward the garage with my fork. "Is that your Mercedes, Consuelo?" When she nodded, I babbled on, "Red is my favorite color for cars. I've often thought a red Mercedes would be just what I'd like to have." Now when, exactly, have you ever given a moment to the thought of owning a Mercedes, Tyler? Red or otherwise? "Whose car is the yellow one?"

Peter stared suspiciously at me. Consuelo glanced at him, then said, "It's Peter's."

"Is that an MG?"

"No, it's a Triumph." Peter didn't look up to answer my question.

"I don't know cars very well, especially old sports cars. It is old, isn't it?" He nodded, offering no more information. "You're going to school in southern California, isn't that right?"

He just stared at me, not answering. Consuelo frowned, then said brightly, "Peter's at Cal Tech. It's his third year."

"Oh yes," I agreed. "I think you told me that before, Consuelo. I remember, Peter, years ago someone telling me that Cal Tech had the highest number of suicides in its freshman year of any college in the country. You know, because all the students going there were used to being number one in their high schools and, obviously, couldn't all be number one at college and that, coupled with the pressure of such a school..." Why in the world was I talking about suicide, for chrissake? "Is that still the same there?"

He answered stiffly, "I have no idea."

"Of course," Consuelo spoke smoothly, covering her son's obtuseness, "it is a school with very high academic demands, and the students by nature are very competitive."

"Yes, yes," I nodded, "exactly my point. What are you studying, Peter?"

"Physics" was the terse reply.

"Mmm-huh," I murmured, nodding politely. How in the hell did anyone have a conversation with someone studying physics? So. What do you think of Einstein? He was something, wasn't he? Actually, did Einstein have anything to do with physics? I turned toward Margarita. "And, Margarita, I think your mom told me you've recently returned to school, too. What are you studying?"

She stared at me, her eyes seeming a little wild. Peter suddenly burst out, "What are all these questions about? Do you work for the police or something?"

"Peter," his mother admonished him without raising her voice. "Tyler is my guest. She's merely trying to make conversation. Margarita?" This time it was a prod.

Margarita glanced at her mother, then at her brother and gave me a quick glare before lowering her eyes to her plate. Without looking up, she said, "I'm studying literature at Mills."

This time I said nothing, feeling silenced by the tension in this room. I attended to my food. Suddenly, the quiet was interrupted by the doorbell. Margarita bolted out of her chair, saying, "Sam."

Consuelo called, "Victoria? Put another plate on for Sam, will you?"

Sam, I thought, as Victoria brought dishes to the table, was apparently a fixture around here. Margarita's boyfriend, I guessed. A few minutes later, Margarita re-entered the room with a large blond man in his mid-thirties. Oh my god, I thought, more coincidences.

When Margarita made no attempt to introduce us, Consuelo started to do so, but Sam brushed it away, saying, "We know each other."

I half stood, reaching my hand toward him, and said, "Hi, Sam. How are you?"

He hesitated a second before grasping my hand. "I'm fine, Tyler. What are you doing here?" I blinked, and he went on before I could answer, "I thought you'd quit that job at the paper. What's this? A special assignment?" Now everyone was staring at Sam. "You are investigating this murder, aren't you?"

"You *are* a cop!" Peter sneered, which I thought was somewhat odd, seeing as how there was a bona fide cop in the room already—Sam was on the Berkeley force. "I knew it!"

I waved my fork in denial, saying, "No, I'm not a cop. I used to be a reporter for the *Chronicle*. That's what Sam's referring to, I guess. I'm not here in any official capacity, Sam."

"Tyler is a friend of mine, Sam," Consuelo said, then added, "And she found Jason's body yesterday morning."

Sam's errant left eyebrow lifted as he thanked Victoria for the food she brought him. "You found the body, Tyler?" I nodded but said nothing. "How did that occur?"

"Sam," I said, ignoring his question for the moment, "are you here in some kind of official capacity yourself?" Jesus, I thought, they do know he's a cop, don't they?

"No. Not official police business, anyway." He gazed solemnly at Margarita whose spectral look softened momentarily.

I looked from one to the other, then said, "I didn't think that the S.F. force would actually turn to Berkeley for help. Even though some individuals on the Berkeley force are obviously superior."

Sam laughed, visibly relaxing at my flattery. "Absolutely right. On both counts." I told him how I'd come to discover Jason's body. When I was finished, he said, "Quite a coincidence, the body showing up in the park by your house."

I shrugged. I told him nothing about Consuelo being at my house or the charges against Jason. Partly because I talked as little as possible about safe houses in front of others. And partly because I didn't know what Sam knew and what this family wanted him to know.

After a few minutes of silent eating, Peter suddenly blurted out, "What this bitch is not telling you, Sam, is that she's brought a lawsuit against my father!"

"Peter!" Consuelo finally raised her voice a little as Sam looked questioningly at me. "I've had about enough of your behavior, Peter. I know you are grieving and that is as it should be, but that does not give you the right to insult a guest of mine."

"She *pretends* to be a friend of yours, Mother!" Peter

shouted, jumping to his feet. "But she comes here asking all sorts of questions. She has every intention of soaking this family for all it's worth! Why don't you be honest with us?" He addressed this directly to me, and after a second added softly, "Bitch."

Consuelo also stood and said very quietly, "Peter. I will not stand for this behavior. I want you to apologize immediately to Tyler!"

I interceded. "Thank you, Consuelo, it's not necessary. Peter, I'm sorry about your pain. And I'm sorry your father was not the man you might've wanted him to be." His eyes flashed, but I continued before he could interrupt. "The suit I brought against Jason was just that—against him. It will be dropped now that he's...dead. It was never about money. Only about his behavior and the consequences of that behavior. I have no desire to extract any payment from your mother or you or your sister for what your father did."

Peter glared at me for a few seconds before stomping out of the room. His mother sighed but said nothing. Sam looked from me to Consuelo to Margarita. Finally he said, "Is anyone going to tell me what's going on here?"

I smiled a little but Consuelo said, "Oh, Sam. Family matters." She waved a hand, not in dismissal but in seeming frustration. "A few months ago I..." She hesitated. I thought, Good, she's aware of the compromising of a safe house. "I hid from Jason at Tyler's. When he found out where I was, he came and broke down her doors and knocked Tyler out and damaged some of her belongings..." Her voice trailed off. She said, almost in a whisper, "He was drunk, of course."

Sam's eyebrow lifted once more. "And then his body gets dumped..." He caught himself and said to Consuelo and Margarita, "I'm sorry. His body ends up in a park across the street from your house, Tyler? Pretty suspicious. Perhaps not such a coincidence after all, mmm?" He smiled crookedly. "I assume you're on the official list of suspects?"

I smiled in return. "I assume."

"And of course"—the crooked smile broadened—"you're not particularly a favorite of the police department, are you?"

I smiled in assent but said nothing. I liked Sam. I wondered if he would tell Margarita how we knew each other, wondered how much she knew already. Knowing Sam, I guessed she probably knew it all. He had worked hard to eradicate secrets from his life. Of course, it wasn't surprising that she'd fall in love with an alcoholic who beat his wife. Recovering alcoholic now. Ex-wife now. After I'd started the series on battering police officers, Sam had contacted me and told me he had a story I might want to hear. He was willing, astonishingly, to share his personal story and let me use his real name. It was, he told me, part of his recovery program. He needed to take responsibility for his actions in some public way.

From the beginning, it was clear that it was not easy for Sam to do this—like most cops, he wanted to protect "his own" from public scrutiny. I pointed out to him that I felt the same way about reporting on lesbian battering and violence. I think a respectful bond grew between us. One of the five articles in my series was entirely about Sam and his wife, his own background of family violence—his father, too, had been a cop—his eventual divorce and subsequent recovery. Sam's story had been a very important piece of the series, both educationally and emotionally.

Lunch was clearly over now, and the atmosphere had become subdued. I decided it was time for me to leave (poor Aggie came instantly to mind). I thanked Consuelo, and she took my hands again, touching her cheek to mine. "I'm glad you came, Tyler."

"I'm glad I did, too, Consuelo. If you need anything, anything at all, please call me. And I do mean that." I squeezed her hands and then reached one hand toward Margarita, saying, "I'm glad I met you, Margarita. I'm sorry it was under such difficult circumstances." She stared at my hand as if she didn't know what it was, then placed her own limply into mine, saying nothing. Finally I turned to Sam. "Nice to see you again, Sam."

"Yes," he agreed warmly.

Consuelo walked with me into the kitchen. I stopped to thank Victoria, in my halting Spanish, for the wonderful meal. Just as we began to move toward the front of the house, I heard Margarita say, "Were you lovers?" I looked at Consuelo, who pretended not to have heard but smiled slightly. The last thing I heard was Sam's laughter.

(12)

Aggie greeted me with abundant enthusiasm. I scratched her ears energetically, praised her for her reproachless behavior, and assured her we'd stop soon. I didn't think Consuelo's gardener would appreciate Aggie's calling cards. Getting out of St. Francis Woods was easy, and I pulled onto Portola, which took me up over the hill to Market Street, allowing me to catch a famous and much-loved glimpse of the city and the Bay Bridge before the descent into Noe Valley and beyond to the Mission. Aggie wagged her tail as I pulled into a spot next to Dolores Park.

I rolled my windows up and looked around. A couple of other dogs were running free, and it didn't appear there was anyone present who'd object to Aggie being off-leash. While she dashed about, I ambled aimlessly, thinking about the people in Consuelo's home. Did Peter's anger mask ambivalence about his father's death and his mother's apparent composure? Or did he have something to hide? And why did Margarita look so anguished? More mixed feelings? Had it been worse for her, worse maybe for both of the kids, than Consuelo wanted to admit—either to me or to herself? And could there have been sexual abuse?

"Aggie!" She was heading toward the playground where there were some children. Long experience warned me to keep her away from kids. She cheerfully altered her direction, paused to see if I was going to call her in, then dashed off in another direction.

Could it be, I wondered, that Jason's death had nothing to do with his family? Maybe someone else, some outsider, killed him. Maybe he was involved in something outside his home, something that got him in trouble. I smiled at myself rue-fully—you'd like that, wouldn't you, Tyler? You'd like this asshole to be a crook, wouldn't you? Being a beater of women is not enough for the rest of the world, why should it be for you either, huh? If he was a *real* crook, say a crack dealer or into child prostitution or something, then everyone would think he was awful, right? Okay, okay, you'll just have to do some more research into this guy. Maybe Jeff would have something for me.

"Aggie," I called again. She reluctantly gave up dancing around the base of a tree where a squirrel was scolding her. When she got to me, I snapped the leash on, and we left the park, Aggie walking smartly at my side. Just before we got to WINK, a couple of blocks from Dolores, we saw Lucie at her usual spot. Aggie began to wriggle and wag her tail.

"I hear my favorite girl coming!" she called out. "Come here, Aggie-girl, come here and give an old lady a kiss or two." Aggie obliged willingly, knowing full well the reward. "Huh!" Lucie snorted as Aggie covered her face with kisses. "You don't have to be quite so generous, you know. It's true you're the only one willing to kiss me these days, but I don't know that I'm this desperate." Aggie began to snuffle around Lucie's body, attempting to find the correct pocket. "So. Your true nature arises." Lucie reached into one of the pockets of her many layers of clothing. "You're not interested in this old lady at all, are you? Just want a little surprise, don't you? Just out for what you can get, aren't you?" Lucie pulled some unrecog-nizable scrap of food out and held it in her palm. Aggie eagerly picked it out of her hand and gratefully chewed it, act-ing as if she were starved.

I stopped worrying long ago what it was that Lucie was sharing with Aggie and whether she could really afford to share with a dog. This spot had been her "place" on sunny days for about two years now, and all of us regulars in the neighborhood knew she wouldn't hurt anyone, particularly not an animal. As to her ability to share, it just didn't matter what I thought—she was going to do it anyway. While she was having this exchange with Aggie, I got out a couple of dollars and dropped them in the hat sitting on the sidewalk next to her.

She squinted up at me, just as if she could actually see me, and said, "Thanks, Tyler." How she always knew who gave her money and who didn't, I have no idea. If there'd been the clink of coins, of course, it'd make sense. But she knew even when paper was silently slipped into her cap. "So. I hear you're the prime suspect in a murder case now."

I laughed. That was the other thing—she always knew what was going on. She may have been blind and "just" a street lady, but she had her "eye" on all of us. I lowered my voice and gruffly replied, "That's right, lady. I'm a dangerous character. You'd better watch out or I might blow you away."

She smiled with appreciation and continued scratching Aggie vigorously on her belly. "Uh-huh. Somehow I'm not too terrified. Are you, Aggie?" Aggie, who by now was lying on her back in complete abandon to the ecstasy of Lucie's hands, responded not at all.

"That dog," I said disgustedly, but in my normal voice, "is nothing but a common slut. She'd sell me for a mere promise of a rubdown."

"I doubt that," Lucie said, still scratching. "Would you, sweetie?" She switched her attention back to me. "But listen, Pickles, you be careful, you hear? This murder business is no joke, you know." She'd long ago dubbed me with this nickname, insisting I was too "sour" for my youth.

I shrugged before remembering that it was a useless

gesture in these circumstances. "I guess," I agreed. "Lucie, if you hear anything, let me know, okay?"

"Humphh," she snorted again. "What do you think a sightless old fool like me is gonna hear?"

"Plenty," I insisted. "Just let me know if it might pertain to this incident."

She squinted again. "You gonna play detective, Pickles?"

"Me?" I said, this time my voice taking on the sound of honeyed innocence. "No, no. I'm just curious."

She smiled, that kind of superior uh-huh-sure-you-are smile that can be so annoying on some people but just seemed conspiratorial on her. "Okay, Pickles, but tell me, is there anything you're more curious about than anything else?"

I pursed my lips a minute, thinking. "Just tell me if you hear anything about Dr. Jason Judd. Okay?"

She nodded. "Okay, but remember—curiosity killed the cat."

"I'll remember, Lucie. Thanks." I tried to put my smile into my words. "Come on, Aggie, we've got to get to work." Aggie gave Lucie one more kiss before we walked the couple of doors down to WINK.

13

Annie was saying to Louise, when I entered the WINK offices, "'Woman desperately seeking other woman in need of sex. Not picky about age, size, color, habits. Remember: desperate sex can be fantastic!' What do you think?"

Louise's thick, dark eyebrows, which matched her equally thick, dark hair, beetled together as she frowned. "Desperate sex?"

"Yes! Desperate sex can be wonderful! Why do we all steer clear of desperation?" Annie's pale blue eyes snapped with annoyance.

"Because," I interjected calmly, "we're all afraid that someone who is 'desperate' is never going to let go. You know, strangle us with their need."

Both women turned toward me. "Tyler!" Louise said first. "Are you okay?" She came around from behind the desk and enveloped me in the soft security of her ample body. When I looked puzzled, she said, "You know. The murder?"

"Oh, that," I shrugged. "Yeah, I'm okay. At least they haven't charged me yet."

"Are you seriously a suspect?" Annie nervously ran her long fingers through her silky, strawberry-blond hair.

"I don't think so, not really. The police department is going to suspect everyone until they have it solved, and—well, you know who was killed, don't you?" They nodded, and I continued, "So it does look kind of suspicious. After all, I hated this guy, and then he's found dead in the park right next to my house? I'm real glad I don't own a gun and never have."

Annie said, "Mary Sharon said you found the body." I nodded. "Was it dreadful?"

"I didn't actually see anything. Just his feet sticking out from under a bush. It was scary. The whole thing is scary."

"Our resident celebrity holding court?" Mary Sharon joined us from one of the inner offices.

I struck a pose. "Yes, dahling. Would you like my autograph?"

"I don't know," Mary Sharon responded. "Just how famous are you?"

I shook my head, returning to my own style. "Not famous enough or too famous for the wrong reasons. If this is Andy Warhol's idea of my fifteen minutes of fame, my immediate response is 'Spare me.'"

Annie made a clucking noise with her tongue. "Tyler. You already are famous, you know, for your writing."

I smiled, nodding my acceptance of her compliment. "Now, Annie, what is this 'desperate sex' stuff?"

"Desperate sex?" Mary Sharon asked. "Do tell!"

Annie seemed to flush a little but pointed at Mary Sharon, who wriggled her eyebrows in an imitation of a lecherous Groucho Marx. "See? Just say the words, and she's interested already. I'm just trying to write this ad for the personals column."

"Oh, that. I know about it. We've been talking about this for over a week, haven't we? Your latest version is about desperate sex?" Mary Sharon inquired, all of her previous lasciviousness dropped. Annie repeated the ad.

Louise said, "I don't think you should advertise desperation, Annie. I think it'll just scare people away."

"I don't know." Annie ran her fingers through her hair

again. "Honestly, I bet if I put that ad in the personals, I'd be swamped with replies!"

"Actually, I agree," I said. "I think you would. But what kind of replies? Imagine, Annie, what kind of weirdos you might get."

"Really!" Mary Sharon laughed. "I hope your bed works with handcuffs."

"Oh," Annie wailed, "you all can laugh. But you," she turned on Louise, "are happily married and have been forever, and you two"—she turned toward Mary Sharon and me—"are willing to be eunuchs or saints or something. You just don't understand what it's like to be single and lonely and horny!"

"I cannot speak for Tyler," Mary Sharon said solemnly, "but I assure you I am not willing to be either a saint or a eunuch. After all, Annie, it hasn't been that long since Clare and I broke up. At least not by my standards. Could I have just a little time to grieve before I go hunting?"

"I know," Annie relented. "I'm sorry." She slid a look at me out of the corner of her eye, clearly indicating that *I* was the one she meant anyway when she was talking about eunuchs and saints. I looked at Louise and Mary Sharon for support, but they seemed to be enjoying some private joke. Annie was stubborn. "I think that *all* of these ads in the personals are about being desperate. I'm just being honest. A lot of people might find that refreshing."

Mary Sharon nodded absently. "You're probably right. Print it."

"What?" Louise exclaimed as I said, "You've got to be kidding, Mary Sharon."

"You guys take this too seriously," she said. "Come on! If Annie sends this in, we can stop talking about it every day. Anyway, I think she's right. The personal ads *are* about desperation. Why not name it?"

"You're a big help," Annie said, grinning nonetheless at Mary Sharon.

I remonstrated, "I don't think it's fair to say that the personals are about desperation. You're saying, then, that everyone who puts an ad in or answers one is desperate. I don't think that's true. It's just a way for some people to meet new people."

"Have you ever put one in? Or answered one?" Annie asked me.

"No. But that doesn't mean I think everyone who does is wrong. Or desperate."

"Would you really send that in as is?" Louise asked Annie.

Annie's full mouth puffed out a little more fully as she said, "No. But what am I supposed to do? Practically all the women I know are ex-lovers or lovers of ex-lovers or lovers of friends or friends of lovers or lovers of my ex-therapist or therapists of my ex-lovers or are just simply not interested." She threw her hands up dramatically, and we all laughed. She scowled and went on, "I *want* to be with someone. I've had enough of this blissful singlehood right now. What am I supposed to say? 'My friends think I'm attractive, intelligent, sensitive, witty. I wash my hair daily, wear clean underwear, cook, and go to bed early. I don't fart, burp, or pick my nose (at least not on the first date).' How boring!"

"I kind of like that one, Annie. Some people *want* boring," I said earnestly.

She shot me a disgusted look. "God, Tyler! Some people don't want...anyone!" After which she flounced defiantly out of the room.

There was a brief silence. Then I looked at Louise and Mary Sharon in dismay. "Did I say something wrong? I thought it was all in fun."

They rolled their eyes at one another before Louise said, "Do you want to tell her or should I, Mary Sharon?"

Mary Sharon said, "You'd better. She never believes me when I tell her things like that."

"Things like what? What's going on here?" I demanded.

Both of them smiled at me. You know the kind of smile, that we-know-something-you-ought-to-know-but-are-just-too-dumb-to-figure-it-out smile. I narrowed my eyes in annoyance, and Louise, recognizing the signals of an impending storm, said, "Come on, Ty, don't get mad. We don't need *two* mad people in here today. It's just that..." She hesitated, glancing at Mary Sharon, who nodded. "It's just that it's pretty obvious that Annie has this big crush on you."

"What?" I almost shouted. "What are you talking about? Do you two get together at school, when you can't stand another minute of Admin. Law or Corp. Law or whatever you're taking this semester, and make these things up? I never heard of such a ridiculous idea!" I looked from Louise to Mary Sharon.

Mary Sharon was gazing off into space (or, into some inner space, I guess) and said somewhat dreamily, "It puts me in mind of Cordelia Wiggins."

I groaned. "Oh no." I started to edge toward the corridor, but Louise caught my shirt and said, "Come on, Tyler, don't you want to hear about Cordelia Wiggy..."

"Wiggins," Mary Sharon corrected.

"Wiggins," Louise confirmed Mary Sharon's correction and raised her eyebrows. "Wiggins? From Stony River, right?"

Mary Sharon and I said, simultaneously, "Louise!" and I clarified, "Stony River is the town in Minnesota where *my* mother grew up and I spent my summers."

Mary Sharon said, "I've told you a hundred times, Louise. I'm from Rocky Ridge. Rocky Ridge, Minnesota."

Louise shook her head. "Rocky Ridge, Stony River. Geez." She turned to me. "You do want to hear this story, don't you, Tyler?"

"Sure," I said, getting into the spirit of things rather languidly. "One of the Wiggins." When Mary Sharon nodded, I continued, "Aren't the Wiggins the ones who never got married?"

Mary Sharon nodded more vigorously. "That's right." She always loved it when I remembered any of her back-home stories.

"So?" Louise prompted. "What's the story? How could there be any Wiggies if they never got married?"

"Well," Mary Sharon said reasonably, "there weren't any after awhile, of course. But there were thirteen or fourteen Wiggins kids—their parents *did* get married—and they were all stretched out so they really covered two, almost three, generations. Cordelia was in the first-generation part of the kids, second from the oldest. When I was a little girl, she was already an old, old lady."

She seemed to slip into one of her memory stupors, and I prodded her, "Mary Sharon? Some of us have to work here. Could you get to the point?"

"The point?" She seemed genuinely puzzled.

Louise sighed. "How does this crush of Annie's put you in mind of Cordelia What's-her-name?"

"Alleged crush," I mumbled.

"Oh, that! Cordelia, you see, was the only one of the Wiggins who ever wanted to get married. She fell desperately head-over-heels in love with Morris Henderson. You know the Hendersons, they had the feed store?" she appealed to me, and I nodded as if I did know them. "She was forty-two and he was twenty-five. She mooned all over him and brought him presents and made herself available in every possible way. Well, he just didn't love her back, and finally he married one of the Murtha girls from Hanley Falls. Some think he just married her out of desperation, but who knows?"

"Yes," I agreed, "who knows?"

Louise looked disappointed. "This is it?"

"W-e-l-l," Mary Sharon drew the word out, "not quite. You see, Cordelia Wiggins, she just never really got over it. And forty years later, when she was in her eighties, don't you know"—Mary Sharon always started to sound more and more folksy when she told these stories—"she was still kind of haunting the house that Morris shared with Frannie. That was the Murtha girl's name."

"What do you mean? Haunting?"

"Once or twice a week—and mind you, she'd been doing this all those years although less frequently in the winter—Morris and Frannie would wake up in the middle of the night to the sound of something akin to howling, and there'd be Cordelia, circling their house and kind of wailing and moaning. Just think, all those years!"

"And they never called the cops or anything?" I asked.

"Oh, sure, in the beginning, all the time. Sheriff Kunkel would come and take Cordelia home and tell her to quit bothering them. But she'd do it again. And again. Finally, everyone just got used to it. Why, when Cordelia died back in the seventies—she was in her nineties by then—Morris and Frannie and their kids and their kids' spouses and their grandchildren all sat right up at the front of the church, just behind all the Wiggins, at the funeral, just like they were family, and Frannie just liked to have cried her heart out."

Louise and I just stared silently at Mary Sharon until she said, "What? Why are you doing that?"

Louise turned to me and said, "Do you think she makes these stories up?"

"Seriously? That's always been my guess."

Mary Sharon smiled benignly and then turned abruptly and walked away. I looked at her retreating back, then at Louise. "Speaking of serious, are you?"

"About Annie?" I nodded. "Yes, Tyler. We're serious."

I just stood there a moment, turning this thought over in my head. "Do you think that Mary Sharon was trying to tell me that Annie's going to start haunting my house?" Louise and I grinned at each other.

As I walked back to the volunteer room, I thought about Annie. It wasn't entirely unpleasant being aware that someone was interested in me. Annie was, well—I liked her. She *was* funny and smart and attractive. Not that I knew Annie all that well. She'd only been working at WINK for a couple of months. She was gathering her things when I entered the office we volunteers shared.

"Sorry I snapped at you," she said, not looking at me.

"Oh, that's okay," I responded, trying to convey that I hadn't noticed. "I'm sorry if I...er...well, offended you somehow."

She nodded curtly and left. I wondered if Louise and Mary Sharon were right. It didn't seem to make any sense that one minute we were bantering and the next minute Annie seemed so pissed unless...With an increasing sense of discomfort, I decided to dismiss the whole subject. The truth was, I felt flattered if Annie was attracted to me, but I also felt very wary of any relationships right now. Ten years since the breakup with Julie, I still had an overflowing attic of stored pain and resentment. Every relationship I'd had in the interim had been brief and mostly disastrous. My motto had become: Hurt them before they hurt you. Anyway, I was beginning to enjoy just being comfortable with myself.

I spent the afternoon writing the first drafts for a couple of grants. I'd done crisis-line volunteering for years and decided about a year ago that my own problems were more than enough for me to handle. Writing and doing office work allowed me to stay involved at a safe emotional distance.

Mary Sharon came in once during the afternoon and perched on the corner of my desk. "Are you okay?"

"You mean about Jason?" She nodded. It seemed like days instead of just hours since I'd found out who the victim was. "Yeah, I'm okay. It's a little spooky though, you know?" I paused. "I went over to his house today."

Mary Sharon's deep Nordic-blue eyes got round as only hers can. "You did?"

I laughed at her look. "Yeah. I'll tell you all about it later."

I called Jeff Adams over at the *Chronicle*. "Jeff? Tyler. What do you know?"

"A lot more'n most folk" was Jeff's clever response.

"Yeah, yeah," I agreed.

"That dude who got hisself iced was real respectable. You know what I mean?"

"We're talking about Jason Judd, right?"

"Right. By the way, babe, we figger your payment yet?"

"Dinner at the Washbag," I answered automatically. The Washington Bar and Grill was a time-honored hangout and reward for favors at the city's newspapers. "You got anything for me yet?"

"Nope. But I'll keep digging. This guy sort of important?"

"I don't think so. Why?"

"Just that the blues are playin' this awful close. Hard for me to get much info from my usual sources in the police department."

"Mmm." I thought a minute about what he'd said. "Could be they're being careful with you because they know I work for the *Chronicle*."

"I wondered. Anyway, I'll let you know soon as I know, Tyler."

"Check out any crime angles you can think of. You know, was he into drugs? Pornography? Prostitution? Anything at all. Any kind of connection with organized crime. Or unorganized crime. I'm not picky. Okay?"

"Will do, Tyler. You think someone was tryin' to frame you?"

"Maybe. My guess is...just trying to involve me." This was a new thought, which I tucked away for later. "Thanks a lot, Jeff. Anything you find, just call me at home. Okay?"

At five, I went looking for Aggie. She had a habit of wandering away from me to any co-worker willing to pet her. When I poked my head into Rachel's office, she waved toward a chair. Rachel Wallerstein, phone cradled against her shoulder, was the executive director of WINK and hence one of the few paid staff members.

At last she said, "Hi, Tyler. What's this I hear about your being involved in a murder?"

I shook my head. "Rachel. I hardly call accidentally finding a body 'involved.'"

"But you knew this person?" I nodded. "Come on, Tyler, don't make me drag this out of you. Tell me what's going on."

So I filled her in on the details and the connections between Jason and myself but left out my visit to Consuelo that very morning.

She nodded, thoughtfully tapping a pen against the edge of her desk. "Okay. Keep me posted, will you? I don't see how it can be any trouble, but, well, the fact that you work here and his wife stayed with you when she left him...I just want to make sure it doesn't cause us any problems. Does this whole incident strike you as being curious?"

"You mean his body being in the park by my house?"

"Yes."

"Yes, I find it to be very curious."

She tapped her pen for a couple of seconds. "You don't think it's just a coincidence, do you?"

I shrugged. "I'm not sure what I think. I guess it seems pretty far-fetched to be a coincidence. But I'll tell you one thing, the police don't think it's a coincidence."

She started a little at this. "They don't seriously think you did it or had anything to do with it, do they?"

"Let's just say they're not ruling that possibility out."

Tap, tap, tap. "It would probably be a good idea if you talked with Corinne, don't you think?" Corinne Ngo was our staff attorney.

I nodded, saying, "Yes. I intended to do that."

Rachel put her pen down decisively and dismissively. "Good. As I said, keep me posted." I agreed and started to leave the room when she added, "And Tyler?" I turned back.

"I'm sure you didn't do it, and I'm sure I speak for everyone here when I say that."

I thought that statement was a little condescending, but I tried to appreciate her intent and said, "Thanks. I didn't do it, Rachel, but I can honestly tell you I'm not particularly sorry he's dead."

Naturally I found Aggie in the cubicle where the law clerks, Mary Sharon and Louise, worked with Corinne. Aggie greeted me with her usual tail-wagging enthusiasm, acting as if I had abandoned her instead of vice versa. Mary Sharon was the only one in the room.

"Corinne's gone?" I asked her.

"Yeah."

"Are you almost done? We could go get something to eat before going home, if you're interested."

Mary Sharon nodded, looking up from some papers spread out on her desk. "Absolutely. I want to hear *everything* that happened today. I have to make two phone calls and straighten up here. Okay?"

I nodded. "Fine. Aggie and I are going to the park, so just meet us there."

Aggie leaped excitedly at the familiar sound of the word, "park." It wasn't quite 5:30 when we got outside. Lucie was no longer at her usual post. The streets were busy with cars and people on their way home. At Dolores Park, I let Aggie off leash but kept her close.

Momentarily I thought of the column I might write about Jason but then was distracted by the thought of Jason's shoes jutting out from under that bush in my neighborhood park. Why was he put there? Or had he been there already? Could it have been a coincidence? But then why did someone call me this morning? Was that someone watching the house? What was it, exactly, that had been said? "Aren't you going to the park today?" Something like that. At the time, I felt someone was watching the house, had seen that I hadn't left. But now I wondered. I had answered the phone, so whoever it was *knew* I hadn't left the house. Would something have happened if I hadn't answered the phone?

Like what? Like going to the park and putting a bullet between my eyes? Oh, cut it out, Jones. It was growing dusky now, fog creeping across Twin Peaks and sliding down this side of the city, and a little shiver ran down my back. I guess someone had succeeded, one way or another, in scaring me.

Aggie. Where was Aggie? I looked around and didn't see her. "Aggie!" I called, forcing myself to stay put but swiveling slowly around to peruse the park. "Aggie!" I called again. Why didn't she come? She always comes. "Aggie?" My voice faltered a little. Not Aggie, I thought. Tears sprang to my eyes as I thought of Norah and said aloud, "Not Aggie, please. Don't hurt Aggie." I swiveled around once more, scanning the territory. "Aggie?" At that moment she came bounding out of a group of bushes in one corner of the park, another dog leaping with her.

"Aggie!" I shouted joyously. Wiping the tears back, I leaned over to snap on the leash. As we headed toward the car, I saw Mary Sharon walking toward us. We ran across the grass to her.

(14)

All through dinner, Mary Sharon listened to the details of my visit to the "grieving" family. Finally, she said, "But why, Tyler? Why would anyone dump that body in the park by your house?"

I shook my head, chewing a mouthful of enchilada before answering. "I don't know. I keep trying to figure that out. If someone was trying to frame me, why didn't they leave a gun in my house? Maybe they were just trying to implicate me, you know, throw the cops off somehow?"

She nodded, biting into her burrito and wiping a dribble of salsa off her chin. "Of course, maybe he was killed in the park. Have you heard anything about that?"

"No, nothing yet. Jeff is having a little trouble getting info from the cops. I asked George this morning, but she said they didn't know yet. I think she was putting me off. After all, I am sort of a suspect, so they're not likely to give me any information."

Her eyebrows shot up. "A suspect? You seriously think so?"

"Absolutely. You should've heard them this morning, Mary Sharon. It got very...formal there for a while."

Mary Sharon pursed her lips. "Tyler, have you talked to Corinne yet?"

I laughed at her seriousness. "Tomorrow."

"You'd better not talk to those cops again without her being present."

"Mary Sharon! You're advising me to not cooperate with our illustrious police force?"

She held her hand up in quick protest. "I'm not advising anything. I'm merely making a good suggestion."

"Well, anyway, dear heart, I should have some more information by tomorrow. Jeff will find a way to get what we need."

"That's good." She took a swallow of her mineral water and said, "Who do you think did it, Tyler? Who had motive, opportunity?"

I shrugged. "We don't have enough information."

"Come on, Ty." She was getting out paper and pen. Mary Sharon was a compulsive list maker. I'm sure this was why she was such an excellent student and would make a fine lawyer. "What about Consuelo?"

"I guess the most obvious motive was that she was fed up with his beatings. Interesting that he hit her the very night he was killed."

Mary Sharon was writing everything down. "Maybe more than interesting. Alibi?"

I shook my head. "Home asleep. No one to corroborate her story, apparently."

"Do you think Consuelo killed him?"

I frowned, thought for a minute. "I guess I think it's possible, but I don't think she did it. I think I would've gotten a sense of her lying—if she was—when I asked her if she'd killed him. I could be wrong, but I don't think I am. And don't ask me why," I said, putting up a hand to forestall the obvious question forming on Mary Sharon's lips. "I just don't think she did. Intuition or something. And even if we ignored my feeling about this, it's hard for me to imagine how she got the body to the park—presuming the killing was done elsewhere. Or if she had a gun and forced old Jason to drive to the park and forced him to walk by those bushes and then shot him, why? Why would she want to involve or implicate me? That doesn't make any sense at all."

"I agree," Mary Sharon said. "How about the daughter? What's her name?"

"Margarita."

She wrote that down and said, "What do you think? Maybe to protect her mom? Or maybe he abused her more than her mom thought or will admit, and she finally did him in?"

I grimaced and shrugged simultaneously. "Yeah."

"Yeah what?"

"Yeah maybe."

She looked at me intently. "What's the resistance here, Tyler?"

I pursed my lips for a couple of seconds of silence. "Maybe I just don't want it to be anyone in his family. Or maybe I just don't know what I'd do if it were."

"And Margarita specifically?"

I made a clucking noise with my tongue and ran my finger through the hot sauce on my plate. "There's something there. It could be a lot of things, but she seems tortured." Mary Sharon said nothing, waiting for me to go on. I shrugged, noticing that I was shrugging a lot. "There was something about her eyes." I remembered the anguish burning in her. "I don't know, Mary Sharon. Something seemed wrong with Margarita, not just grief but...Either she did it or she's terrified her mother or someone she loves did it. That's what I think." Actually, Margarita's tortured intensity could convince me, more than anything, that her mother did do it. "If she did do it, I have the same problems with her transporting the body. Unless..."

"Unless what?" Mary Sharon pounced.

"Wild speculation."

"Tyler, at this point, it's all speculation."

I conceded the truth of that. "Well, what if her brother was in on it? Or Sam? Then the transporting of the body wouldn't be such a problem."

"Give me a 'for instance,' Tyler," Mary Sharon insisted.

"Well, let's just say Margarita and Sam were there when Jason started hitting Consuelo. Maybe he hurt her more than she told me; maybe he was really beating the hell out of her. And Margarita shot him. Then they moved him to the park—"

"But why the park by your house, Tyler? The only person, it seems, who would truly want to implicate you would be Jason himself."

"I know. It doesn't make any sense. This whole thing about the body being moved—where was he killed? No blood in their house or garden? In the car that moved him?"

"Do you know there was no blood at the Judd house or in any of the Judd vehicles?"

"No, but I think there would've been an arrest by now if they had found any blood traces anywhere."

"You might be right, but we can't deal with those things, Ty. We'll just have to hope the police find that kind of stuff, and we get access to it. Does she have an alibi?"

"Margarita? I was really going to ask questions like that, Mary Sharon. 'So, Margarita, where were you the night your father was killed?' Hopefully Jeff will come up with some of this."

"The boy's name is Peter?" I nodded as she wrote it in. "Probably same motive as the daughter's. Protecting his mom or maybe reacting to his own abuse. Alibi?"

"Presumably he was down in L.A. Isn't that where Cal Tech is?"

"Pasadena, I think," she said, as she continued writing. "What about him?"

"Possible. He's a real hothead." Something about Peter... what? Something just out of reach of my consciousness. Peter. I couldn't bring it into focus. "But, I don't know. It'd be easiest to think it was him. He seems to have inherited—or learned, I suppose—his father's temperament." I looked at her list. "Pretty slim pickings. No wonder they're considering me. I suppose you'd better put Sam down, too."

"The boyfriend. You think a cop might have done this?"

"Well, that's true," I said, my voice heavy with sarcasm. "It's not likely. Cops are so opposed to violent solutions." She grinned as she wrote "protecting girlfriend" with a question mark. "Truthfully, Mary Sharon, I don't think Sam would've done this."

"Love is a pretty strong motive, Tyler," Mary Sharon pressed.

"Do you have a scenario in mind?"

This time she shrugged. "Suppose Sam found Jason beating Margarita. The shock of it, Jason's action and Sam's reaction—maybe then."

"You could be right," I agreed. "The odd thing is that something about this whole scene doesn't add up to a crime of passion. It feels—I don't know why exactly—planned."

We were both silent for a minute until Mary Sharon said, "Alibi?"

"For Sam? Don't know," I said. "This seems really far-fetched, but if we were cops, we'd consider every possibility. I think you should add the cook and the gardener."

"Names?" Mary Sharon asked and wrote down Victoria and a question mark as I couldn't remember her husband's name offhand.

"I think Consuelo told me his name, but I just can't remember it now. They seem devoted to Consuelo. She told me they were related to her, cousins or something."

We both looked at the list for a minute. "Anyone else?" Mary Sharon asked.

I shook my head. "I don't think so. Not without more info than we have at this point. Maybe you could make a separate list and just call it POSSIBILITIES." She wrote this down and looked at me for clarification. "I was just thinking of things we don't know yet. Problems with Jason's co-workers? A mistress? He's a doctor, maybe he was involved with drugs somehow. I don't know. Some business problem we couldn't possibly know about? Debt. Gambling bills."

"And maybe Consuelo had a lover?" Mary Sharon interjected.

"Very good, Ms. Marple," I agreed. "Or—I don't think this likely, mind you, but the cops seem to think it's possible—maybe the murder had nothing to do with Jason at all. Maybe it's about me. Someone who really hated me for the stuff I wrote about. Or my irresistible personality." I smiled my most winsome smile. "The likeliest here seem to be men in power: cops, politicians, attorneys. Anyone with a stake in maintaining the status quo. And I've done a lot on prostitution and pornography, so...?" I shrugged. "That brings in the mob, I guess, or at least a bona fide criminal element. Although it's hard for me to believe that anyone thought I was so threatening that...And of course there's always the "New" Right, the white supremacists, the anti-choice crowd. I certainly rattled a few cages when I did that series on all the groups that convene against choice."

"And you've written about that group in Oregon or Idaho or wherever they were—the neo-Nazis who preach hate and violence against anyone who isn't white."

"And the skinheads. Some of those folks are just crazy enough to do something like this. On the other hand, why would they? The fact is, Mary Sharon, it's hard for me to take this idea seriously—that someone killed Jason Judd to somehow get at me or implicate me. It just seems like too weak a link."

"I agree," she said, "but who knows?" She was writing furiously.

We both said nothing for a few moments, staring at her list. Then I laughed and said, "Well, maybe it's like *Murder on the Orient Express.* Remember? They all did it together? In collusion?"

"Could be. Yeah, I kind of like it," Mary Sharon agreed.

15

When we got back to the car, Mary Sharon agreed to hang out at the park with Aggie while I attended a nearby AA meeting. I blew kisses to both of them as I walked briskly away, calling, "It'll only be an hour." Aggie watched me attentively for a moment before she refocused on Mary Sharon, who was clearly, to Aggie's mind, choosing the better option.

Mary Sharon was deeply engrossed in a law book when I returned. She looked up, startled at my greeting, and said, "Surely it hasn't been an hour."

"No," I agreed and added, "Let's go." I moved immediately toward my car as Mary Sharon scrambled to collect her things.

"Hey!" she said. "What happened?"

I shook my head in a motion of disgust as we got into the car. "Just one of those meetings where they begin with the Lord's Prayer."

"Oh," Mary Sharon responded, clicking her tongue sympathetically against her teeth and knowing enough to say no more.

I felt thoroughly conflicted when it came to the so-called spiritual aspect of AA. My spirituality, namely my feminism, would not tolerate this father-in-heaven bullshit, and I was not willing, as many women I knew were, to substitute "mother" for "father." I felt the entire 12-step program should undergo a massive overhaul and purge itself of all of its sexist trappings.

However, I had yet to find very many participants who shared my concern. Consequently, I "took what I could and left the rest" by literally walking out when I felt the sexism was too flagrant. On the other hand, I wasn't ready to abandon its aid in my struggle for sobriety.

That night the house didn't seem as alien, as scary as it had the night before. Partly, I think, because I was angry about the meeting I hadn't gotten to attend, and so my energies were directed elsewhere. Aggie happily settled herself down in her favorite spot—the corner of the couch—while I paced around.

Eventually, of course, my thoughts turned back to the murder. I knew I should just let this go. I also knew I wasn't going to do that. So I made a mental list of what I needed to do to find out more about the bad doctor and his son. Besides hearing from Jeff, I should check the archives at the paper. And Peter? Windy, I suddenly realized, was my ideal source. She was already down in L.A. and research was her game. I dialed her number immediately.

As the phone rang, I figured she probably wasn't home anyway. She and Lexie were probably out at a film premiere or a big studio party. Some kind of Hollywood gala. Maybe Sharon Gless was there. Lily Tomlin. Who knows? Maybe even Katharine Hepburn. Well, not likely, I guess—she didn't live on the West Coast. My fantasy of Windy's life was interrupted by Windy herself answering the phone.

"Windy? Tyler Jones."

"Tyler, honey! Good to hear your voice! You coming down here to visit me?"

"Not that I know of, but it's a tempting thought. Have you seen Sharon Gless lately? Or Lily Tomlin?"

"What?"

"Just a little joke, my dear friend."

"Honey! When's the last time you had biscuits and gravy for breakfast?"

"Cut that out, Windy! You're appealing to my baser instincts."

"Are there any other kind?"

"Enough of this seduction stuff, Windy. Where's Lexie anyway?"

"She's on location somewhere in the jungle. South America. Africa. I forget." Hah, I thought, she knows exactly where she is. "Who knows when she'll get back? A woman's got needs, you know. Urges."

"Uh-huh, sure, Windy. This is big talk and that's all. You know it and I know it."

"Huh! Someday that girl's gonna be sorry she leaves me all alone like this!"

"Actually, Windy," I tactfully changed the subject. "I've got a favor to ask you."

"Big surprise. People are always just wanting me for my fine mind when I want to be wanted for my great bod!"

"Life is tough," I commiserated. Windy was one of the best trackers in the newspaper business (as well as having, indeed, a great super-sized body), and I was glad I could call her a personal friend and be able to use that friendship for the help I might need. "I want you to get me whatever info you can on a student at Cal Tech—name of Peter Judd. He's in his third year. I want to know anything, everything. What kind of student he is, what teachers think of him, what students think of him, his grades, his friendships, his extracurricular activities—both official and not so official. And I particularly want to know what he was doing Tuesday night this week. Okay?"

"That's all? No identifying marks? His sign, maybe? What he ate for breakfast, perhaps, a week ago Sunday?"

"Windy? Is this a bad time? Or just too much to ask? Tell me the truth."

She laughed abruptly, not really humorously. "Sorry, Tyler. I'm cranky. I get this way when Lexie is gone. Like—

what the hell am I doing with someone who is always gone? Know what I mean?" I knew I didn't have to answer, and she continued, "Shouldn't take it out on you, honey. Anyway. I can do this shit for you. Might take a day or two. *The Times* does pay me to work for them, you know."

"Just tell them it's reciprocity with the *Chronicle*. Yes?"

"Mm-hmm. They do love that shit." We both laughed.

"Anyway. Whatever you can get would be great. And whenever, too. The most important item—if you don't have time for the rest—is the one about Tuesday night. Okay?"

"Okay. What's going on, honey?"

I filled her in on the events of the past two days. "At this point, I don't know. I'm just gathering details, seeing if there are any threads that lead to one another. I guess I should just leave it to the police but..."

"Oh yeah! Fat chance of you doing that! Okay, honey, I'll get what I can for you and get back to you soonest."

"Great! Thanks a lot, Windy. And listen, why don't you come up here for a weekend? You can make biscuits and gravy anywhere, can't you? And I'm sure you could stand a break from La-La land anyway! We'll sit on the deck, drinking something exciting like iced tea and you can bitch about wayward lovers and I can bitch about no lovers."

"You seriously in the market for a lover these days?"

"Nah." I always started talking like Windy after a few minutes of listening to her. "I'm about all I can handle right now. Some days, you know, I have these fantasies. But, no, I'm not seriously in the market."

"I might just come visit you. Yes, ma'am, I might. In the meantime, I'll find out what I can about your boy here. Get back to you soon, honey."

I turned the lights off when I got off the phone, so I could stand on the deck without being backlit. Even though I felt less spooked than I did last night, I was still wary. Aggie scrambled down the stairs to the backyard, and I leaned on the railing. There was nothing to see; the fog was thick and soupy. I couldn't even see Aggie down below. After a few minutes, I whistled. Aggie didn't respond. I felt a chill start at the base of my spine. I shook myself mentally. Don't do this again, I admonished.

"Aggie?" I called softly, then more firmly. "Aggie, come!" She trotted up the stairs and jumped up, placing her front paws on the railing next to me. She liked to be on the same level as my face. "Oh, baby," I whispered into her ears as I nuzzled her. "I'm really getting paranoid, aren't I? Let's go to bed."

I put Art Tatum on the CD player and slid gratefully into bed, suddenly exhausted. Almost at once I drifted into that delicious floating state somewhere between consciousness and unconsciousness, where everything is clear and sharp and yet, at the same time, as fuzzy as a Monet painting. My limbs lost all their substance, as if they were drifting in water or levitating, while my mind seemed to focus with increasing clarity. I always felt as if I wanted to write when in this state. Of course, I never did because the effort to pull back to full consciousness would have shattered the state itself.

There was suddenly an unattached, half-formed thought whirling around with me in this never-never land. I couldn't quite "think" it, like not quite being able to see someone's features in the dark, but was perfectly aware of its presence, nonetheless. Something to do with the murder, with...who? With Peter. What about Peter? The thought skimmed over the edge of my mind, refusing to settle. The effort to pursue it was clearly going to jar this timeless, weightless, breathless state I was in, so I let the thought go. The next thing I knew was Aggie shaking the leash in my face.

16

It must be 6:00, I thought, opening one eye and squinting at my clock. Yes, indeed. My other eye opened and both of them gazed at the phone next to my clock. It wasn't ringing. I moved over a little and patted the spot next to me, saying, "Come here, Aggie. Come on. Let's just snuggle a little."

She eyed me curiously as I continued to pat the bed, encouraging her to lie down next to me. This was clearly unexpected behavior. With a final shake of the leash, she let it drop and crawled up next to me. I put my arm around her, whispering some endearments in her ear before falling back asleep. In this manner, I bought myself a little more time. It was close to 7:30 before Aggie's wriggling was insistent enough to wake me up again.

"Okay, okay, sweetie," I crooned as I extricated myself from her presence as well as the tangled covers. "This murder business has sure played havoc with our schedule, hasn't it?" I pulled on some sweats and a warm sweater and picked up Aggie's leash from the floor. "Come on, girl," I said to her.

Instead of going to the park, I drove over to the beach by Crissy Field on the bay. Aggie was beside herself with ecstasy by the time I parked, this being her favorite beach in the entire world. She adored swimming, and the waves were generally benign enough here so she could swim far more easily than at Ocean Beach, where the crashing surf discouraged her. After she'd jumped in and out of the water several times, thoroughly drenching me by shaking next to me each time she got out, I found a stick and we spent the next half hour playing fetch, in and out of the water.

Then we walked for a while. That is, I walked while Aggie rocketed back and forth, chasing sea gulls and jumping into the bay to swim after a duck or two before giving up in the face of their superior aquatics. The sun rose above the Berkeley and Oakland hills, making the bay sparkle and the white sharpness of the cityscape seem almost luminous. In the other direction, the Golden Gate Bridge beckoned in all its solid splendor, competing with the undulation of the Marin headlands behind it. I blinked tears away, thinking of Norah. We often came here together, allowing Aggie the joy of running and swimming while we walked arm in arm. Norah was a particularly satisfying confidant: she listened carefully and nonjudgmentally, and just as carefully expressed opinions or suggestions. I missed her.

"I don't know why I bring you to the beach," I muttered, when we returned to my car. "You're perfectly uncivilized. You don't care at all about me or Lady Bug." Aggie cocked her head to one side, ears forward, her tail thumping on the back seat as I drove home. "Will you quit that?" I demanded. "You're getting sand all over the back seat!" Her tail just thumped more.

When I got home, I had to give her a shower with the hose and rub her down. I hated to do that because San Francisco was too often in a state of drought or semidrought. Most of us living here, or at least most of the people I knew, tried to conserve water. However, her long curly hair had to be cleaned or I'd end up feeling like I lived in a sandbox. As Aggie happily gobbled her food down, I used my minivac to remove some of the sand from the back seat of the car, grumbling all the while. I always came home from the beach feeling decidedly cross about all this work, yet I loved going there with Aggie, too.

After showering off the salt and sand that Aggie insisted on sharing with me, I made toast to eat with my coffee and once again tried to make sense of the past days. I doodled on a sheet of paper as I sipped my coffee appreciatively and wandered through the labyrinth of events. I wrote words and names in a random fashion. Dr. Jason. Consuelo. Murder. Park. Aggie. Foghorn. Margarita. Gardener. Safe house. Bitch. Shoes. George and Dwyer. Bullet. Peter. Cook.

Wait a minute. Bitch? Where'd that come from? I sat still, thinking. Bitch. Bitch. I turned the word over and over in my mind. I looked at the other words and names I'd written down. Peter. Oh yeah, he'd called me a bitch. Why was that sticking in my mind? I sat motionless, not wanting to disturb the mental process, feeling that a buried thought wasworking its way to the surface much as buried tires do. Suddenly it broke free, and I knew immediately that this was the thought that had been teasing me last night at dinner and also just as I drifted off to sleep.

Peter clearly knew who I was, by name if not sight. He'd called me a bitch when he was railing about my suing his father. And yet—before that—he'd pretended not to know me. At the front door and when he asked if I was a cop. If he knew who I was, knew I'd filed a lawsuit against his father, why was he playing dumb? I felt a sharp tingle of expectation.

Was he the murderer? He seemed perfectly capable of it to me. I am, for good reason, suspicious about men—especially when it comes to violence. An occupational hazard. Also, the threat of men's violence was as much a threat to me as to any woman. I knew, of course, that sons of violent fathers often learned to be violent themselves. Peter's outburst suggested a certain tendency toward violence, although, I had to admit, that was a long way from physically beating someone, let alone actually murdering them.

Why would Peter kill his father? Could he have done it accidentally? Or was it planned? Did he come up here from southern Cal to commit murder? Or did he come up for some other reason? Did he hear his mom and dad arguing, see his dad hit his mom, and vow to stop it somehow? Was he even up here?

I took my coffee to my office. The little red light on my phone machine was blinking, so I pushed the button and immediately heard Jeff Adams. "Hey babe! Don't stay home, don't get the info!"

I shook my head, grinning. Jeff liked to talk to people, not machines, something that's getting harder and harder to do in this society. I dialed his office and, luck being with me, he was in.

"Jeff. Tyler here. What have you got for me?"

"'Bout time you be calling me back. You out overnight somewhere, doll? You holdin' out on me, not updatin' me on your wild sex life?"

"Jeff," I assured him, "I just got back from taking Aggie to the beach."

"Hmphh. You still just sleepin' with that dog?" When I didn't answer, he continued. "Okay. Here's what I got. Good old Dr. Judd was hit on the head before he died."

"The ubiquitous blunt object, by any chance?"

"What?"

Me and my dumb mysteries. "Any ideas what he was hit with?"

"Oh yeah, I see. Yeah, 'blunt object' works. In fact, it works very well because"—he paused dramatically—"they found it. Lying right next to him, practically. A flat rock."

"They're sure?"

"Oh yeah, a little blood and a couple of hairs plus it matches the dent in his head."

"The dent in his head?"

"You gonna get squeamish on me?"

"No, but...wasn't the back of his head kind of, well, messed up from a bullet going through there?"

"Good question, Jones. Very good. Yeah, a shot like that would definitely result in one mighty big hole in the back of your head. Apparently the rock came down near the top of his head, leaving an identifiable indentation."

I wrinkled up my nose. "But the rock didn't kill him?"

"Nope. Just knocked him out."

"Any rocks like this in the doctor's garden?"

"Nope."

"Any in any of the suspects' yards?"

"Yours is the closest."

"What does that mean?"

"The rock matches other rocks in your park."

"Oh." I turned this over in silence for a few seconds, then said, "He was conked on the head by a rock, and it happened in the park?"

"Yep."

"And they know this because of the rock?"

"Yeah, the rock, and the fact that he wasn't moved after he got knocked out or after his death."

"They know that for sure?"

"Pretty sure."

"How can they tell things like that?"

"It's pretty technical, babe."

"Yeah, yeah."

"Primarily it just has to do with blood loss. There was a break in the skin where he was hit with the rock. Doesn't appear to be much loss of blood before his blood source was cut off more permanently."

Again, I silently thought for a few seconds. If someone took him to the park, say at gunpoint, why would they knock him out first, then shoot him? Wouldn't they just shoot him? Someone sneaked up on him and hit him on the head with a rock and when he fell back, shot him? Why not just shoot him in the first place? And if someone sneaked up on him, had he gone to the park on his own? What was he doing there in the first place?

"Yoo-hoo!" Jeff made a tapping noise on the phone. "Anyone there?"

I nodded before realizing that wasn't going to help him. "Jeff. I'm still having problems with this 'dent' on the head versus the hole in the back of his head."

"You're good at this detail stuff, Tyler. How come you never worked crime?"

"Too many violent men, Jeff. What about this rock and hole? Can you explain this so it makes sense?"

"I can try. The hole caused by the bullet came through the base of his skull. The rock dent was higher up, near the top of the head."

I mulled this over. "So apparently he was shot by someone taller than him, holding the gun at a downward angle."

"Not likely, babe. I mean, what, a giant? Either the doc was kneeling and someone was holding a gun, pointed downward, between his eyes or just shot him while he was lying on the ground, knocked out from the rock. Which, actually, seems to be the case."

"Oh yeah. That makes sense. Was there anything taken off of him? I mean, could it have been simply robbery?"

"The police thought of that, too. However, his wallet and other pocket stuff, including I.D., were all sitting on his desk at home."

"Like he'd intended to go to bed, emptying his pockets in preparation?"

"Maybe. But the wallet was empty. According to his wife..." I could hear him rustling papers.

"Consuelo?"

"Yeah, according to his wife, Consuelo, that was unusual. She insists that he always carried large amounts of cash."

"This is so weird."

Jeff ignored me and continued with his report. "They haven't entirely ruled out the possibility that someone intended to rob him, knocked him out, found he had no money on him—"

"Then shot him? Out of anger?"

"It's not exactly a hot theory over at the station, Tyler. Just one theory."

"Then they have to assume he was already at the park. Yes?"

"I guess so."

"This really doesn't make much sense," I thought out loud. "Someone came in with a gun, made him get up, get in a car, took him up to my park, hit him on the head—how? Walked around behind him, leaned over, picked up a rock and hit him? Then shot him? Or he just got a yen to walk around the park across the street from my house, and someone saw him, thought, 'Oh goody, I'll get some dough,' knocked him out, discovered he had no money on him and then shot him?"

"Tyler, I write about crimes. I don't try to solve 'em."

"Aren't you curious, Jeff?" We'd had this conversation before.

"Babe, you know I read the ending of a mystery first. I leave puzzling to you brainy types."

"You're a disgrace to your profession. Why don't you write for the society pages?"

"The thought's occurred to me, actually, but I don't own a tux."

I snorted. "They found the rock, how about the gun?"

"Nope."

"Identify it?"

"Not exactly."

"What does that mean?"

He sighed his I-always-gotta-teach-'em-everything sigh. "The easiest way to identify a murder weapon is to find the weapon itself. No such luck. The next thing they look for is empty casings. No casings. Sometimes the bullet helps. If it's recovered—which it was in this case. Unfortunately, it's not much help."

"Why? I thought it was routine to identify a gun from the bullet."

"Only in movies, Tyler. In real life, too many variables. They think the gun used in this case was probably a .38 Special."

"What's that?

"A pistol, a handgun."

"Jeff, what I want to know is...I don't know exactly. I guess I want to know if there's anything unusual about this gun. Very large? Extremely small, what's usually called a 'woman's' gun? Anything particularly distinguishing about the use of this gun?"

"Nope. Routine. Ordinary. Maybe the Macintosh of guns. The kind of gun every nighttime security guard is usually issued. Most cops carry them. Not very expensive, medium-sized, easy to use and buy."

"Any of the suspects have one?"

"Not registered. No one has a gun registered to them except Dr. Judd himself. And he kept his in his house. It was still in the wall safe when the officers asked Mrs. Judd to open it up. And it wasn't a thirty-eight. And it hadn't been fired anytime recent. Oh yeah—another thing about that safe. Apparently the old man kept large sums of cash in there, too. All of that was gone as well."

"Now what could that possibly mean?"

"Don't know." His tone implied "don't care."

"Jeff. This is too strange. Did he take all this cash out of his safe before he went to the park? Was he meeting someone there? For some sort of payoff? And then something went wrong and they killed him?"

He just mumbled again, "Don't know."

"Mmmm. When was he killed?"

"That's a little hard to figure exactly. It was cool that night, which throws off the body temperature, but the coroner guesses between 2 and 5 a.m."

I turned all this over in my head, and this time Jeff waited patiently. "Was his car around the park somewhere?"

"Nope. His car was at home in the garage. No prints on the steering wheel. None. Not even his."

"Wiped clean?"

"Would seem so. Or maybe he always wore gloves when he was driving. You know, some of these ritzy types like to wear driving gloves, affect a racing style."

I thought about this a moment. The cops must've thought of this, too. "What did Consuelo say to that?"

"Nope."

"Nope, she didn't say anything or nope, he didn't wear gloves?"

"Didn't wear gloves. At least not that she was aware of."

"This just gets weirder and weirder. What do we have here? Someone drives him or makes him drive to the park or he drives himself there to meet someone, this someone knocks him out, discovers he has no money on him, shoots him, drives back to his house, wipes the prints off the steering wheel, and gets the money out of his wallet on his desk? And out of his safe? Or maybe that was already out. But if he were meeting someone for a payoff in the park, wouldn't he have taken his wallet? And why would they take the car back to the house? Or did he go to the park in someone else's car? But then why was his steering wheel wiped clean?"

"Your guess is as good as mine. No, probably better."

"Or he goes up to the park on his own, a mugger hits him, finds he has nothing but keys on him, drives his car...but how would a mugger know where he lived?"

"Beats me."

I jotted down the info Jeff had been giving me, and some

of my thoughts, even though they seemed nearly incoherent to me. "Alibis?" I finally asked.

"The usual. Not very good. Wife was home in bed. Alone. Son was in L.A. area, goes to school down there and lives in a dorm. His roommate said he was there all night. Daughter has the best alibi, she was shacked up with some Berkeley cop— Sam Ogwicz, you know him, don't you?—which also gives him, the cop, an alibi. Gardener and cook, Jorge and Victoria Alvarado, are married to one another, have an apartment over the garage. Both were asleep, together. They're related to Mrs. Judd. And you"—he chuckled slyly—"were home alone. Asleep. Doesn't seem to be any other suspects."

"Anything else? Anything on the 'good' doctor himself?"

"Clean as a whistle, at least that I can find. No whispers even of crime connections. I'll keep digging, of course. And"—pause—"there's a girlfriend."

"Big surprise. This kind of guy shouldn't even have a wife, let alone a girlfriend."

"Everybody loves somebody..." Jeff began to sing.

I ignored his musical attempts and interrupted. "Give me the stuff on her."

"About thirty—"

"About?" I interrupted again.

"Okay, okay." More rustling of papers. "You gung-ho types always want every minute detail, I swear. Here it is. Thirty-three. Lives on Telegraph Hill. You want the address, Tyler?" When I agreed, he gave it to me and finished, "An artist. Name is Laurel Scott."

"How long had they been seeing one another?"

"Don't know. Sounds like quite a while. Apparently he paid the rent. A regular sugar daddy, you know."

"Do the cops know about her?"

"Don't know. Used my best persuasive powers to get this info from a sweet lil' thing working as a nurse in his office. I might be a step or two ahead of them, but if I could get this info, so can they."

"Mmm. Any other info you've given me that the cops might not have?"

"Not that I know of. If I know it, I assume they also know it. Sooner or later, if not already."

"Okay. Give me your instincts, Jeff. What're the cops thinking?"

"They're certain it's an inside job—someone in the family. Or close to the family like the boyfriend or you or the at-home help. And they're checking out the people who worked with him—his receptionist-nurse at his office, the aforementioned sweet lil' thing, other doctors, all that stuff. But they don't take that very seriously. They think it's someone closer."

"So I really am a serious contender?"

"Right now, as serious as anyone else. Here's one sup-po-si-tion they all is kicking around: suppose the doc decided to buy you off, you know, give you 'boo-coo' bucks to drop your case. He arranged to meet you in the park by your house, you take the money and he tries to beat you up and you, let's just suppose, push him down. He hits his head and blacks out and you decide to finish the job. Bang-bang. Then you drive his car back to his house to muddy the waters, wipe the prints off and walk back up to your place and—ta-da! find the body."

I whistled. "Wow. That's a little scary. It certainly makes more sense than any of the theories I've come up with."

"I thought you'd like it," Jeff agreed.

"Only problem is, it didn't happen."

"Says you," he shot back.

17

I looked at all the notes I'd made while talking with Jeff. Then I looked out the window at the park. The same questions kept spinning around and around in my head. I leaned back in my chair and closed my eyes, pressing my fingers against my forehead. I was tired of thinking about this murder. None of it made sense. The scenario the cops designed for me—would that work with someone else? He met them (but why in that park?) for some kind of payoff, a fight ensued, he got knocked out, they shot him? But who's "they"? It seemed, more and more, that he had to have been in the park already—either with someone or alone. But why? Why, why, why? *Why can't I just have one drink a week?* My eyes snapped open. Cute, Jones, real cute. Sneaky, too.

Time to do some work, think about other things. I pulled out some research I was doing on date rape among high school kids and wrote a rough draft of a column about the subject. I still wanted a drink. Maybe several drinks. Maybe several bottles.

I pulled out another testimonial to type.

MINA

I was ten the first time my brother, Jerry—who was fourteen—made me have sex with him. I guess I really mean to say the first time he raped me. I still have trouble saying that. Rape. I never thought of it as rape. Not back then, when it was happening. I don't know why. I guess 'cause rape was something that some strange man did to you. Not to you, actually, but to other girls. It wasn't something your brother did to you. And anyways, when I finally did tell people, they all acted like it was my fault, like I coulda stopped it or like maybe I really wanted it to happen. And I didn't know if maybe they weren't right. Maybe it was my fault. Probably it was.

It's still hard for me to say it, say rape, like someone is going to say I'm lying or making it up. He'd do this every now and again—rape me, I mean—whenever he felt like it or whenever he got his hands on a porn magazine. Sometimes he'd bring a buddy or two and they'd take turns. Watching and laughing and egging each other on.

Years later, in court, they asked me—didn't I fight? Didn't I scream or cry for help? I didn't. I didn't do anything. Well, at first, I'd said no! and tried to push him off, but it never made any difference. And after he did it the first time, I went to my mom. I remember it so well. I was crying—those big hiccupping sobs that hurt deep down in your chest and stomach. I tried to tell her, I told her Jerry was doing something not nice to me and she just dismissed it and said he was "just teasing me" and I shouldn't be "so sensitive." So, I wasn't sensitive anymore. And I never cried again. I was passive. I didn't seem to have any choice, so I didn't do anything about it.

My mom had a brother much younger than her. He was always broke, so he'd stay with us until he found someone else to sponge off. Whenever he came, Jerry and him raped me together. Mom would go shopping or out to play cards or to work or somewhere, and they'd come to my room and do it. This went on for a couple, three years.

When I was fourteen, I tried to kill my brother. I stabbed him three times with a kitchen knife. He didn't die. I wish he had. I still wish that. Mom called the police. I was put in a place for crazy people. I was there for four years. They gave me shock treatments and a lot of other things, too. Things that I guess they aren't allowed to do anymore. It didn't really matter to me. Nothing was worse than being at home.

We were like guinea pigs. The attitude was "let's-try-this-and-see-what-happens." Sometimes, at night, when it was just us patients and the orderlies and maybe one nurse who was asleep in the building somewhere, the orderlies would come to our rooms and rape us—one by one. I learned more about being a good, passive girl.

When I got out, I didn't remember much. I moved away from my family and got a job. If a boy wanted sex with me, I'd let him. What did it matter? I was "easy." I took some night courses at a community college. I was taking a Women's Studies class and something snapped. I freaked out, stood up in class and just started screaming. I was terrified, thought they'd lock me up again. But this teacher, this Women's Studies professor, never reported me to anyone. Instead, she took me to a shrink—a woman—who was totally different than all the male psychiatrists I'd been to.

It all came out, everything that had happened. Eventually I contacted a lawyer and started a civil suit against my brother and uncle. I got a lot of support from the other students, my therapy group, my feminist lawyer, my professors—we were all so sure we were doing the right thing.

My mother got on the stand and said I was crazy, that I had always caused trouble and made up stories to get attention. She said I was jealous of my brother who'd never been in any kind of trouble, and told them about my trying to kill him. We lost the case. It was longer and more involved than that, but the bottom line is still the same—we lost the case.

After that, I didn't bother trying to kill someone else. I tried to kill myself instead. I didn't succeed, but back I went to the loony bin. I wasn't crazy. I had never been crazy. I wonder what crazy is? Women who struggle against their abusers? Women who expect reparation for irrevocable damage? Or a society that turns its back on those women? I wasn't crazy, but it sure has made me feel crazy, all these years, to have no one believe me or even act like it mattered. It did. It did matter. I matter.

Oh, great. Terrific. Now I *really* wanted a drink. Mina's voice was flat and emotionless, somehow more chilling than if she'd been hysterical.

I walked around restlessly, letting Aggie outside. I paused, staring at the rolling surf down below—another bright, sunny day. Fall is almost the only time of the year that San Francisco can count on frequent sunshine. I walked out and leaned against the railing of the deck, drinking in the glory of the ocean. I tried to empty my mind. Why couldn't this beauty be enough?

After a minute or two, I went back in—leaving the door open for Aggie. I stripped my bed and shoved the sheets in my washing machine in the garage, picked up my bedroom, plumped some pillows in the living room. I wanted a drink. I watered my plants, cleaned the bathroom, washed the handful of dishes sitting in my kitchen sink. I still wanted a drink. I glanced at the clock. Not yet noon, and I wanted a drink. I can think better, I protested, if I drink. *Bullshit!*

I finally gave in and checked my AA schedule book. This is ridiculous, I told myself, you just went last night. Well, you tried to go. *So? You're not limited to a certain number a week, you know.* But I'm an adult. I shouldn't be so helpless. *Oh? You're in control, right?* I guess I'm not, but I feel like I *should* be. *I know, but you're not. You can't do this alone. You can't do this at all. Alcohol is in control here. You can only triumph over it with the help of a power greater than your own.* Yech! This is the part I always resist. *Come on, Jones, a power greater than your own doesn't have to be a white man with a beard sitting on a throne. It can be the collective energy and love of all recovering alcoholics. Or the collective energy and love of all the women in the world. Or the mist that emanates from the Marin hills. Or the whispery shade of the giant redwoods. Or the gnarled beauty of the bent-over Monterey cypresses. Whatever works for you.*

Whatever feels more powerful than you alone. It can be just you and one other person on the phone.

At this thought, I looked at the phone. Then I went back into my office and got out my phone list from my home ΛΛ meeting. I called the first name. I got a machine. I called the second name. She couldn't talk right then, could she call me back in about a half hour? I wanted to respond, "I don't think so. I expect to be dead drunk in a half hour," but I didn't. I called the third name. No answer. I called the fourth name. She could talk. She could listen. She did both. I felt stupid, and I told her that. She understood. I wanted a drink. She understood that, too, and asked what I was doing about it. I said I was calling her.

"That's good, what else?"

"I'm going to a noon meeting."

"That's good, what else?"

"I wasn't taking a drink."

"That's good, what else?"

"I think that's all."

"That's good, what do you need?"

I felt better when I got off the phone. I still wanted a drink, but I felt better.

I drove down to the Mission to a meeting, feeling resentful, not of them, but of my alcoholism. Why couldn't I just drink and be done with it? Why did it have to become a problem for me? I did a little whining, internally and externally, and felt even better when I left the meeting.

At a deli by my house, I picked up a turkey sandwich and some potato salad, then walked down the street and got a chocolate malt. The phone was ringing when I let myself in the door. I rushed to beat the machine, just barely made it, and was breathing hard from running up the stairs.

"Now that's a delightful sound," Jeff Adams said cheerfully. "Catch you in the middle of something, Tyler dear?"

"What's up?" I ignored his innuendo.

"Have you ever heard of F-U-C-K?" He spelled it.

"Fuck? It does have a familiar ring to it."

"No, babe, get your mind out of the gutter. Capital F period, capital U period, capital C period, capital K period."

"There's some sort of organization called F.U.C.K.?"

"I don't know. I'm asking you."

"No. The answer's no. I've never heard of them. Why?"

"I'm not sure. The truth is, I'm not sure that I didn't just make it up."

"Jeff, what are you talking about?"

"I'm trying to tell you, Tyler. I don't know what I'm talking about. All I can tell you is that I was doing some nosing around about Dr. Judd and one of my informants said—after I'd told her some details—she said, 'Fuck!' And I agreed, 'Yeah, ain't it so,' and she looked at me kinda funnylike and then she laughed, and I suddenly got the idea that it wasn't 'fuck' she'd said but F.U.C.K.—or something like that. I pushed her a little, but she just clammed up and said I was imagining things but—really, Tyler, my guts are telling me I'm on to something here."

"F.U.C.K.? I don't suppose you'd tell me the name of your informant?"

"You know better than that, Jones."

"I know, but...I just wonder if she might tell me something she wouldn't tell you. You know, because I'm a woman..."

"And I'm obviously not? No way, Tyler. I get your point, but you know I can't do that."

"Yeah. I wonder...Tell me this, Jeff, is she a street person?"

"Yup."

"A prostitute?"

"Might be."

"You really think there's something to this?"

"Honestly, Tyler, I don't know. But...yeah, I think there's something to it."

When Jeff hung up, I remembered Corinne Ngo, the attorney at WINK, so I called her and sipped my malt while telling her the events of the past couple of days. She cautioned me to cooperate fully with the police but also to contact her if they tried to question me again.

18

I was just dialing the *Chronicle* number when the doorbell rang. Aggie, of course, beat me down the stairs, barking. After shushing her, I looked through the peephole and saw my mother.

"Mom," I said, giving her a big hug when I opened the door.

"Hi, dear." She hugged me back. "Are you all right?"

"Yeah, yeah, I'm fine, Mom. Really," I added, meeting her skeptical look. She bent to nuzzle the now-quiescent Aggie before starting up the stairs. "What are you doing here?"

"I had some errands to run over here, picking up donations at drop-off points and such, and just decided to stop by and see you." She stopped suddenly, halfway up the stairs. "Is that all right? Are you busy? I can leave if you're in the middle of something." I'd once given my mother hell for not respecting me enough to understand that I worked during the day, even though I was at home, and she'd always been very careful of not overstepping those boundaries since.

I reassured her. "It's fine, Mom. I'm not totally engrossed in anything right now anyway. I want to finish one little thing, then I'll join you in the kitchen. Okay?"

"Sure," she agreed. "Want me to make some fresh coffee?"

"That sounds terrific," I said as I headed for my office.

I called the archives at the paper and hooked up my modem to their modem so I could peruse the data storage without having to go down there. I indicated on the finder that I wanted a copy of every reference to Dr. Jason Judd and also specified every member of his family. Then I left the computers to do their magic and joined my mom.

She'd carried the coffee pot and cups and saucers out to the deck. She'd included napkins and some biscuits she must have brought as well as cream cheese and jam. No amount of radical politics had ever blunted my mother's natural inclination toward a certain graciousness. For a moment, I felt cherished and taken care of, and I put my cheek against my mother's before I sat down.

She smiled faintly but said, "What was that for?"

"Mmm," I murmured around a biscuit, "I love you."

"Well, I love you, too, dear. We really should take time to see one another oftener."

I nodded, stretching out more languidly as I let the afternoon sun soak in. To answer would have been pointless. We always said the same words to one another, and nothing ever changed. We were both busy, we both loved the way we lived, and we were both likely to continue in this manner. We were comfortable with the fact that our lives only intersected occasionally and peripherally.

We chatted idly and inconsequentially for a while. She told me the latest news of my sister's kids, Jonathan and Mary Ellen. I wasn't very interested—Magdalene had decided that a lesbian aunt was not a good influence for her children, so I hadn't seen Jonathan since he was a baby and had never seen Mary Ellen—but I listened dutifully. They were, after all, my mother's grandchildren. Then she talked of her upcoming activities with SALSA (Strong Alliances with Latinas and Sud Américanas)—the relief organization she had co-founded. I told her what columns I had coming up and how the book was progressing. I started to feel there was something else waiting to be said.

She gestured toward the ocean, saying, "A perfectly

gorgeous day. Norah had an ideal spot for sunny days, didn't she?" I smiled my agreement. "You're very lucky she left you all of this, dear."

Inwardly I bristled at my mother's matronizing tone, but I sidestepped confrontation and said, "I know."

"Well," she said, returning her gaze to me, "you deserved it. It wasn't just luck." The bristling subsided, and I smiled at her. She hoisted her omnipresent oversized purse to her lap and commenced rummaging in it. "I want you to see something, Tyler." I felt a slight tension in my neck. She pulled a letter out of her bag, handed it to me, and said, "I know this probably has nothing to do with anything but..."

The envelope was addressed to my mother, Louise d'Alma, in letters cut out of newspapers. No one called my mother Louise; she'd been Weezie all her life. The missive itself was composed on a typewriter, one that clearly needed a new ribbon because the print was faint and smudged. It read:

> Mrs. Louise d'Alma,
> You must stop meddling in areas you don't know about. Drop all your connections with AMIGAS or you'll be sorry. This is none of your bisiness. If you are not cooprative, we will get you through your famly.
> A Freind

"Mother! This is dreadful!" She nodded her agreement. I read it again, turning the paper and the envelope over to see if anything could help identify it. The postmark was San Francisco, dated a week and a half ago.

I looked at Mother, who was watching me intently. "What's AMIGAS?"

She answered in Spanish, which I didn't much follow—
apparently the meaning of the acronym—then she elucidated.
"It's a new organization, started by Chicanas in the U.S. and
women in war-ravaged Central and South American countries. It's quite radical, advocating women's rights in the
workplace and politics as well as better conditions for
mothers and wives at home. It's aligned itself, naturally
enough, with the more left-wing elements but is pushing
them, too, on their sexism and their general weaknesses in
regard to women's issues."

"Good for them," I responded.

"Yes, well, some old-time liberal, male-dominated organizations—both in this country and in Latin countries—hate it, of
course. They say these mixed-blood *Norteaméricanas* don't
understand their cultures, that we're rabble-rousing reaction-
aries bleeding energy away from the 'real' issues, meaning, of
course, the men's issues. Nothing new. Same old stuff."

"Really," I agreed, feeling angry. The liberal boys always
sounded just like the conservatives when they went on about
"rabble-rousing" and "bleeding energy" away.

"And of course the more conservative elements oppose
AMIGAS because of their basic socialistic stance, so they're
not popular with anyone. We could, obviously, go on and on
about this." She obviously saw my coming explosion. "Our
usual habit of the converted railing at the converted. But the
point is, does this particular threat have something to do with
the murder in your park?"

I frowned. "Go on."

She shrugged. "At SALSA, we've just made some overtures
to AMIGAS about a possible collaboration between our two
organizations. It seems like a natural to us. And they're
interested, too. Of course, any support that a new organization like AMIGAS gets from an older organization like ours
helps to strengthen it. And some people don't want AMIGAS
to succeed. Or even exist."

I read the letter again. "Do you get things like this often, Mom?"

She dismissed the notion with a sweep of her arm. "Occasionally. No big deal. The thing that made me scrutinize this a little more closely is that I don't think I've ever gotten a threat before that actually mentioned my family in any way. And then—you find this body..."

I nodded. "I guess we'd better tell the cops."

19

George and Dwyer weren't available, but I left a message for them. Mother was washing up the dishes in the kitchen when I rejoined her. Fog had started to roll in and had obliterated the warmth of the sun, so we settled down in the living room on opposite ends of the couch. Aggie looked from one to the other of us, trying to determine the best opportunity for attention, then settled next to me with her head comfortably in my lap. My mother pulled a mass of brightly colored yarn from her bag and began to knit.

I smiled at the familiar sight. Throughout my entire life, I've watched my mother's flashing knitting needles. Knitting was her only apparent domestic talent, one that enabled her to make use of every minute. Time was very important to my mother.

"What are you making?" I asked her.

"Oh," she scrutinized the shapeless tangle as if she'd forgotten what it was. "Right now, socks. But it could be anything—slippers, scarves, sweaters. Whatever the youngsters might need." There was a time that everything she knitted was for her own children or nieces and nephews or grandchildren. Now almost everything was for the recipients of SALSA. Without looking up, she said, "Tyler, give me an update on this murder business."

I was telling her about the Judd family when the phone rang. According to the dispatcher at police headquarters,

George and Dwyer were nearby and would swing by my house. I wondered if they were down at the Judd house again. When I finished my story for Mother, she continued knitting for some minutes, silent and intent. The dance of her knitting needles was exquisitely elegant, not unlike someone doing tai chi—slow, graceful, purposeful. At last she said, "I wonder if anyone in Consuelo's household might be involved in AMIGAS?" Then the doorbell rang.

We reassembled at the kitchen table. I got coffee for Allan Dwyer while he and Carla George studied the letter. They held it carefully, just touching the edges. Mother's and my fingerprints, I thought, have probably wiped out anyone else's. While George slipped the letter and envelope into a plastic bag, Dwyer said, "We'll have to keep this, Mrs. d'Alma."

My mother nodded, saying, "It's not 'Mrs.' Ms. will do or you can call me Weezie, actually."

"D'Alma is your maiden name then?" Dwyer asked.

"No," my mother answered. She looked at Dwyer and he looked back, obviously expecting an explanation but receiving none.

George finally broke the stalemate by saying, "Excuse me, Ms. d'Alma, but we need all the information we can get. Even the little things might be important in ways that aren't apparent. Your daughter and you have different last names. We're only trying to place the context."

"My last name is my father's name," I volunteered.

"And my last name," my mother smiled at me, "is from my mother's first name. Alma." She added no more.

This time George took notes while Dwyer led with the questions. "Mrs....Ms. d'Alma, tell us about this letter."

My mother related to them, in some detail, the tenets of SALSA, followed by what she knew about AMIGAS and the tenuous connection between the two. When she was done,

George asked, "Is there anything else? You haven't told us anything that would seem to warrant such a threat."

Mother shrugged and looked evasive, I thought. "There are whispers but...who knows about rumors?"

Dwyer pounced. "What whispers?"

Mother shrugged again, looking at the fog hanging just outside my windows.

"Ms. d'Alma?" George prodded.

Mother's attention came back to the table. "In the first place," she started quite firmly, "I've been dealing with Central and South American politics and personalities for some years now. There is a certain...drama, you might say, that seems present in most Latin dealings. Warning or threatening letters are not unusual in this business. In the second place, I'm not interested in passing on vague rumors. I can only tell you that I and colleagues of mine have *heard* that AMIGAS *might* be funding certain underground and/or illegal activities that will help their cause. Not things like drugs or things that would have an impact on this country. More like contraband medicine and supplies for the needy, maybe arms for self-defense, that sort of thing. Maybe some help in smuggling individuals at risk out of their countries and providing refuge here. I emphasize: these are only rumors, not things that I *know* about."

I felt pride bubbling up inside. My mother's integrity was so clear and clean. Dwyer swung to me. "Are you involved in your mother's political activities?"

I shook my head. "Not really. Well, indirectly, I guess. I've given some money. I have, on occasion, offered services—such as picking up supplies for Mom or distributing flyers to other organizations. And I have written about the Latinas' plight, both here as refugees and in their home countries. I totally support what my mother's doing, but I don't work directly with her or her organization."

They asked us a few more questions, nothing new, before

they left. At the door, George said, "Thanks for calling, Jones. Every little piece of information might make a difference."

Back upstairs, my mom had bagged her knitting and was preparing to leave. "Mom." I suddenly felt awkward.

"What, dear?" she smiled inquiringly.

"I don't know. I just wanted to tell you that I'm really proud of all you do. Your commitment and dedication. You're pretty terrific, you know?"

Her smile spread. "Well, Tyler, I'm proud of you, too." We hugged again before she left.

I spent the next couple of hours going through the information my computer had extracted from the paper's archives. Aside from his arrest last spring for assault and battery—which I made certain got in the paper—Jason Judd's life seemed above reproach. He was a member of the American Medical Association and the American Surgeons Association, the National Wildlife Federation, the Opera Guild, the Sierra Club, and a host of lesser-known but no less respectable organizations. He gave speeches: technical ones for doctors, general ones on health for women's and poor people's clinics, passionate ones on animal rights and wildlife conservancy. He went to opera openings, film premieres, and art shows. He was on the board of directors of an Asian immigrant organization, two art galleries, a Hispanic health clinic, and a small medical supply company.

The rest of the Judd family surfaced only in relationship to Jason, as "wife of" or "children of." I wondered how Consuelo covered the bruises when she went to the opera or an art opening. I suppose he was careful about bruises. But it did make me wonder more about the final mark he left on her cheek.

Late in the afternoon, when I began to think about supper, the phone rang. It was Windy. "Just a quick flash for you, Tyler. This Judd kid? He gave his roommate $500 to say he was in the dorm all night on Tuesday."

"What?!"

"That's right, you heard it here. He left his room about 7:00 p.m. Tuesday night. On Wednesday morning he called and offered his roomie the money to lie."

"So this roommate lied to the cops?"

"Apparently. He's pretty nervous now. I haven't got all the details yet, but I think this kid is probably hooked on something and my guess is that Peter-boy was his supplier."

I whistled. "You're amazing, Windy! How'd you get all this so fast?"

"Never mind, honey, I got my ways. I just—you know—leaned on him a little." I laughed, knowing full well how intimidating Windy's 250 or so pounds of black beauty could be. "This is just a start, but I thought you'd want to know right away."

"I sure do. Thanks a lot. Oh. Windy, I'm going to have to tell the cops about this—I'll be in big trouble if I don't. Any problems with that?"

"You don't have to tell them how you know, do you?"

"Of course not."

"No problem then. They should know anyway. This kid'll spill on his own, if we wait, but if you want to push it, fine. I'll let you know if and when I have any more on your boy."

I glanced at my watch as I hung up. 5:30. Peter. So Peter *could've* been here on Tuesday night. Why would he come up?

20

I called the inspectors once more and left a message. Then I sat tapping my finger against the phone while staring out my window. Abruptly I said, "Let's go for a walk, Aggie," and she nearly jumped into my arms at the sound of those familiar words.

I took her leash. Although she wouldn't need it, one never knew when the SPCA people might do a surprise raid. Just as we left the house, Mary Sharon came trudging up the hill from the nearest MUNI station. After dumping her books, she joined us.

As we crossed the street to the park, I realized I hadn't been there since Wednesday morning. Aggie dashed ahead of us, clearly unconcerned about finding anything untoward—like a body. I was feeling much less enthusiasm than she was and particularly glad that it was afternoon, and that I wasn't alone.

At first, Mary Sharon and I talked of law school and WINK, anything other than the murder. When we got to the place where Jason's body had been, I stopped and stared at the ground. There was a faint smudge of chalk in the grass where the police must have marked the body's exact presence. Aggie rambled by, pausing long enough to sniff casually in the vicinity.

Mary Sharon said, "This is where it was, huh?" I nodded,

and when I said no more, Mary Sharon nudged me. "Think out loud."

"It doesn't make any sense, Mary Sharon. He came to the park, either with someone or alone. If he drove his car, someone else had to get that car back to his house. Maybe he came in someone else's car. From his house to here is about a mile and a half uphill. He doesn't strike me as the kind who would take a stroll like that in the middle of the night."

"Or any other time, either," added Mary Sharon. We began walking again.

"Then someone hit the not-so-good doctor, apparently from behind, with a rock."

"What? What's this about a rock?"

"Oh yeah," I said. "I forgot. You don't know the latest developments." I told her about the coroner's report and other info from Jeff, my mother's visit with the poison pen letter, and Windy's call about Peter.

When I finished, she snorted. "Well. A very interesting day, yes? I hope Peter has a good lawyer."

"Yeah, it doesn't look too good for him, does it?"

"No, it doesn't," Mary Sharon agreed. "But then, it's still not very clear, is it?"

"That's just what I was saying. Someone hit Jason with a rock, then shot him between the eyes. Why would someone knock him out and then shoot him?"

Mary Sharon shook her head and shrugged. "Gives a whole new meaning to the word 'overkill,' doesn't it?" We had to look away from each other so as not to giggle. "Could there have been two different someones?"

I grabbed her arm. "Wait a minute! Couldn't he have hit his head on that rock when he fell, after he was shot? That would make more sense than anything I can conjure."

"I don't know," Mary Sharon demurred. "Wouldn't the medical examiner determine that? I thought you said he was knocked out before he was shot."

"Yeah, I guess," I agreed glumly. "Maybe someone was pointing a gun at him and he was backing away, stumbled, fell and hit his head on the rock."

"That makes some sense. You'll have to ask Jeff what the cops think."

By now we had walked around the park more than once. "Still, once he's dead, what next? Did someone drive his car back to the house, go in, and get his money out of the wallet? How did they get in the safe? Or did someone take the wallet and other pocket items off his body and leave them on his desk to make it look as if he'd left them there? Did he bring the money from his wallet and from his safe when he came here to meet someone?"

Mary Sharon shifted our attention slightly. "What do you make of that letter your mother got?"

I frowned. "Who knows? I mean, as long as we're just speculating here—what if, for instance, Victoria..."

"Who?"

"Victoria. The cook. What if she is an AMIGAS member and...what? I don't know how to make it connect."

"Well..." Mary Sharon drew the word out deliberately. "Okay. Suppose the husband—what's his name?"

"Jorge," I supplied.

"Fine. Suppose Jorge is in some radical South American organization, one that's opposed to AMIGAS, and he is lifting money from his employer and is caught by Jason. He's already been told to threaten you to get at your mother and her organization, so he decides to do both by bringing Jason to the park by your house. Jorge kills Jason and leaves the body for you to find." She took a deep breath. I looked at her skeptically, and she laughed.

"I don't know. Maybe. The thing is—anything's possible, isn't it? Peter makes more sense, don't you think? Can we make some kind of case, if we just go ahead and cast him in the role of villain?"

"Okay," Mary Sharon agreed. "He drove up here Tuesday night. Why?"

"If Windy is right about him supplying his roomie's habit, where does he get the stuff? His dad? Or maybe just money from his dad?" Giving up on our circling, we headed for a park bench at the top of the hill. On a clear day, you could see both the ocean and the bay from this vantage point. Today was not one of those days.

She shrugged. "Whatever. Let's just say Peter was here that night. What happened?"

"If they came to the park together in Jason's car, Peter might've driven it back to his folks' house afterward."

"After what?"

"After he killed his dad, I guess."

"Why?"

"Why did he kill his dad?"

"No. Why would he drive the car back to the house."

I frowned, turning over possibilities in my head. "He had to get back to the house where his own car was?" She bobbed her head from side to side in a "maybe" signal. "So. They were walking around in the park—"

"Why would they be walking about this park in the middle of the night?"

"Oh, leave me alone. You know I can't answer that. They just were! Okay?" She scowled but didn't say more. "So. They were walking around, they got into a fight, maybe Peter pushed Jason, Jason fell and hit his head on a rock. I like that! Then Peter shot him, took his wallet and stuff, drove back to the house and left everything on Jason's desk. He took the money out of the wallet and out of the wall safe and took off. I'll have to find out how he supposedly found out about his father's death."

Mary Sharon nodded, "Maybe. Maybe it was something like that."

We sat in silence for a little while. Aggie breezed by every few minutes, just to make sure we hadn't left her. Suddenly I got up. "Mary Sharon. I have to look at where the body was again."

We walked back to the spot. I poked at a thick-branched bush and walked around behind it. Mary Sharon looked puzzled.

"Jeff said the body hadn't been moved after being hit by the rock, yes? But look at this bush," I said. "Someone couldn't fall *through* here. I've been assuming the body got dragged out of sight here after the murder. But Jeff said the body hadn't been moved." I pointed to the front of the bush. "His legs were sticking out here, but most of his body was behind this bush. I can't see how he got in that position unless..." I looked at Mary Sharon for a couple of seconds before saying it aloud. "Was Jason sitting behind that bush, waiting for someone, when he got hit by the rock?" Mary Sharon's eyes opened wider. A squiggle—of excitement or fear, I wasn't sure—scampered down my spine.

Mary Sharon said, "And who would he be waiting for behind that bush?"

I grimaced. "Exactly! Who else but me? What time did Jeff say the coroner had estimated time of death?"

"Didn't you say between two and five?"

"I wonder. Could it have been later? Like closer to my usual six o'clock walk with Aggie? Jason is squatting behind this dense bush, and suddenly he gets hit with a rock from behind. He falls backward, and his legs end up protruding through the front here." I pointed to where I'd seen those shoes. Was it only a couple of days ago?

"If he wasn't moved after being knocked out and shot, then he *must've* already been behind that bush!" Mary Sharon said excitedly. "Maybe, just maybe, he was here on purpose. Maybe he already knew your schedule and was waiting for you to pass that bush."

I clasped my hands, trying to contain the excitement I

was feeling. "But what was he going to do when I came by?" Neither of us answered my question.

We turned our steps toward home; I whistled for Aggie. I still felt some elation, although it began leaking out of me like air out of a balloon at the creepy thought of Jason lurking in my park. Still, this was the first theory that at least made *some* kind of sense about why he'd been in this park.

As we crossed the street, Mary Sharon asked, "So. Are we going to eat at this shindig or are we going out to eat first?"

I looked at her blankly. "Shindig?"

"Tyler. Has this murder fried your brains or what? Tonight is Jude Becker's party."

"Oh yeah," I smacked my hand on my head, "I forgot all about that."

"Well?"

"What?"

"Food!"

"Oh. Let's eat there. The food is always fantastic."

"Okay, but I don't want to leave any later than seven or seven-thirty then. I'm starving."

"Fine," I agreed. "I just have to shower and change. Maybe talk to George or Dwyer, if they're available. I'll come down at seven. Okay?"

"Terrific." We parted at my front door.

There was a message on my machine from Inspector George. I tried her number again, and this time she answered the phone.

"Inspector George, this is Tyler Jones. Thank you for returning my call."

"Sure," she responded easily. "What's up?"

"I've got some info you should have. I found out that Peter Judd left his dorm around 7:00 p.m. on Tuesday night and didn't return until the next morning. He promised his room-mate $500 if he'd lie about his being in the room all night."

There was a little pause before she inquired, "Where'd you get this information?"

"I can't tell you. I'm sorry. Just some newspaper sources I have. But it was made clear to me that this kid, the roommate, is ready to spill everything now."

"Okay. We'll check it out. Anything else?"

"Just a theory, a thought I'm playing with."

"Shoot."

I winced but didn't respond to her choice of words. "I got to thinking about that bush the body was under and realized that I'd always thought Jason had been dragged under there for cover. If he wasn't moved at all after the assault, then what was he doing under that bush? And I started wondering if, perhaps, he was sitting under that bush—or behind it, I guess—waiting for *me*. Like maybe he had an idea of inflicting some kind of revenge on me." When she didn't respond immediately, I added, "After all, you've all made it clear to me that my schedule is so predictable that anyone could've easily figured it out."

Still no response. I felt a little uncomfortable. What had seemed like a brilliant idea moments ago now seemed pretty ordinary. Finally George said, very carefully and precisely enunciating each word, "How do you know whether the body was moved or not?"

Oops! In my excitement, I'd forgotten that I really wasn't supposed to be privy to that information. "I'm sorry, Inspector George..." I let the sentence dangle there.

"Well?" she snapped sharply.

I shook my head, even though she couldn't see it. "I can't tell you. Confidential sources, you know."

"More of this newspaper mumbo-jumbo?" She was angry, very angry.

"Yes." Damn! I could've shared all my guesswork without letting her know how much I knew. How could I have been so stupid?

"Ms. Jones," her voice was icy, "are you attempting to investigate this murder on your own?"

"I'm just looking into it. It does concern me, you know."

"This is police work, Ms. Jones. I am ordering you to stay out of it. No more inquiries. No more investigation. Is that clear?"

"Yes, ma'am," I agreed affably. "What about my idea?"

"We'll look into it. In the meantime, Jones, call off your sources, your helpers, whatever it is you're doing. I repeat, this is police work and is best done by professionals." I didn't respond this time. "Do you understand me?"

"Yes," I said. "I understand you perfectly."

And, of course, I did understand her perfectly. Not that it made the slightest difference to me.

21

Jude Becker's party merited careful preparation. I found a pair of seldom-worn black gabardine pants and ironed my favorite shirt—a white cotton pullover with a Russian-peasant feeling to it: slit neck, smocking, and puffy sleeves. Mary Sharon called it my poet's shirt. I hated ironing, but this shirt was worth it. With some idea of dressing up, I pulled a black-and-white tweed vest over the shirt and attempted to tame my hair.

A legend in her own time, Jude Becker was a wealthy, older dyke who'd been out and active in lesbian circles and feminist philanthropy most of her adult life. The story was that she'd inherited tons of money from her father, a famous criminal lawyer who got Hollywood mega-stars out of jams all through the 1930s and 1940s. And, the story further went, she'd inherited her preference for women from her mother, who stayed married to her father while loving Hollywood's leading ladies behind closed doors.

Jude had this party once a year, at her fabulous Pacific Heights mansion, to make the presentations of the Becker Awards for Achievement. Perhaps this annual event recalled her childhood in the glitzy world of Hollywood stardom. Fantastic food, strolling musicians, and opulent surroundings supplemented by women decked out in an array of brilliant outfits—ranging from my determinedly casual attire to haute couture. The Becker Awards were bestowed on women in the

Bay Area who were recognized for feminist contributions. I'd
won one for journalism a couple of years ago. It was the feminist lesbian social event of the year.

I called Mary Sharon and said, "I'm ready if you're ready.
What do you say?"

"Ready." she responded. "Or almost. What are you
wearing?"

"You're not dressed?"

"Yes, but I just want to know if it's totally stupid."

"Mary Sharon. Why don't you just tell me what *you're*
wearing?"

"Tyler!"

"What is the big deal? I'm wearing those gabardine pants,
my poet's shirt and a vest. Okay?"

"Oh," she hesitated. "That's a nice outfit."

"What's the matter? Are you embarrassed to be seen with
me?"

"Of course not. It's just that...I'm wearing a vest, too. I
don't want us to look like twins or anything."

"We will *hardly* look like twins," I said drily, thinking of
her blond, blue-eyed Nordic look next to my middle-Euro-
pean, nondescript look: darkish hair, high cheekbones,
greenish-bluish eyes—nothing dramatic enough to be "exotic."
Not to speak of the fact that her vest probably reached her
knees and was made of peacock feathers or some such thing.
"What's going on here, Mary Sharon?"

"Nothing. I...I just want to look good tonight."

This was so unlike Mary Sharon, who dressed with such
elan and seemingly total disregard for anyone else's opinion
that I had to pause. Finally I said, "So. Is there someone there
tonight that you're hoping to impress?" Mary Sharon's lack of
response confirmed my suspicions. "Ahhh. Let me see. Who
would this be? Maybe that woman at the health clinic? The
one you always seem to be talking about these days? What's
her name again? Marsha? Marilyn?"

"Maura" was Mary Sharon's succinct response. "Knock it off."

"O-kay. Are we ready to go or what?"

"Come on down, I'll be ready."

I assured Mary Sharon that she looked stunning as she climbed into Lady Bug. Actually, for her, this outfit was rather subdued. Black silk pajamas partially covered by a vest of ribbons of dazzling color that actually dipped below her knees. The rhinestone-studded hightops would've seemed tacky on anyone else. I often wondered where she found these shoes. In sheer numbers, I bet she could give old Imelda a run for her money—though I doubted Ms. Marcos would be caught dead in any of Mary Sharon's shoes.

We barely got in the door when Joanna Barnes accosted us. Perhaps I shouldn't say accosted. Joanna's okay; she just comes on a little strong. And I definitely shouldn't say Joanna Barnes because she changed her name, quite awhile ago now, to Red Annachild. "Red," she always said when someone would ask, "because it's a woman's color. You know, the color of menstrual blood." Anna, of course, is her mother's name. But I've known Joanna/Red since high school, and it's still hard to think of her as anything but Joanna.

"Tyler!" she screeched as she enveloped me in her arms. "Oh, hi," she added vaguely in the direction of Mary Sharon.

"Hi, Joanna, how goes it?" I asked, knowing I shouldn't have been so mean, but her cavalier attitude toward Mary Sharon always brought out the worst in me. Joanna was wearing a slinky satin evening gown that looked suspiciously like a nightgown. It made me think of Carole Lombard. "Fabulous dress," I added, assuming it was a dress.

Her slight frown turned to dimples as she rushed on. "Listen, sweetie, you have to meet my new lover. Geri!" She called out, then turned around to find this Geri-person right behind her. "Oh, honey, I want you to meet one of my oldest and dearest friends." I winced. I would hardly call Joanna a friend, let alone oldest-and-dearest, but Joanna, who thinks of me as a "star" in the lesbian community, likes to exaggerate our relationship. "Geri, this is Tyler Jones. Tyler, Geri."

I tried not to buckle as Geri squeezed my hand in a bone-breaker. She was dressed entirely in black leather—tight pants and a vest with nothing underneath (and it was *not* buttoned). She had a spiked collar around her neck and her bare arms were festooned with chains. Parts of her hair were blond, other parts were bright purple, and still other parts were chartreuse. All of it looked like a badly mowed yard.

I was attempting, not very successfully, not to make facile judgments. The last time I'd talked to Joanna, she was vehemently against S/M. Had she changed her mind? Joanna had been especially mad about the way it made us look to the straight world. I was less optimistic about mainstream approval and more concerned about sadomasochistic practice itself.

"Oh, yes," Joanna was adding, "and this is Mary...Mary Beth, is it?"

"Mary Sharon," I sourly corrected her. For some reason, Joanna had taken an instant dislike to Mary Sharon and always made a point of slighting her. I rolled my eyes at Mary Sharon, but she shook hands with Geri and grinned back at me, being more tolerant of Joanna than I was.

"Guess what?" Joanna leaned toward us and spoke in a conspiratorial whisper. "I went to an S and M potluck!"

"Really?" I said, my eyebrows escalating while I wondered how Miss Manners would have responded.

After a slight pause, Mary Sharon, with what I recognized as a rather gleefully malevolent grin, asked innocently, "I wonder what one brings to an S/M potluck? What do you think, Tyler?" I looked blank. "Battered shrimp, do you suppose?" She drew the words out torturously and I giggled, for the moment forgetting all about Joanna and her new lover.

"I think ladyfingers, don't you?" I answered, wiggling my fingers sensuously.

She nodded vigorously, "Oh, yes! And what else? Minced ham perhaps. Or smothered chicken?"

I grimaced. "How about mashed—or is it smashed?—potatoes?"

"Definitely," she agreed, "and I think, perhaps, chopped liver and surely some ground beef?"

We were really getting into it. "And a light dessert, something adorned with slivered almonds, yes?"

"How about black-and-blue berries with w-h-i-p-p-e-d cream?"

At this point, Geri interrupted. "At our next potluck, we're serving smeared queers or maybe butchered bitches. Hope to see you there." And she stomped off, her chains rattling a little.

We watched her for a minute and then Mary Sharon shrugged. "And they say *feminists* don't have a sense of humor."

"You guys are really rude, you know that?" Joanna snapped. "There's sure no point in ever expecting any support from you, is there?"

"Support?" I said, feeling truly amazed. "Is that what you wanted, Joanna? Support?" She just glared at me some more, saying nothing. "Listen, maybe we were having a little fun at your expense, but I think you were expecting a bit too much to want support from us."

"What do you know about it? Have you ever gone to any S and M events? Do you know any S and M-ers?"

"Apparently we do now," Mary Sharon said brightly.

"Joanna," I said testily, "you seem to forget I did a whole series on S/M last year for *off our backs*. I am a journalist. And a feminist. It's true, I do have my biases, but I think I did a lot of research and attempted to present both sides of the story."

Joanna sort of snorted but before she could say any more, Mary Sharon said, "Look, Red, I'm sorry if I just dismissed you. You're right, that was rude. The truth is, 2,000 women are raped *every day* in this country. Every 14 seconds, some man is beating a woman. One in three girls has been sexually molested by the age of eighteen. I just don't have much time—and truly can't support—women who want to 'play' at raping or beating. You don't have to be into S/M to get raped or beaten, you just have to be female and alive. And sometimes 'alive' doesn't even matter. You think I don't understand what S/M's all about? You're right. I don't understand anyone who wants to link violence with eroticism. I don't understand it any better than I understand war games. War is not a game; it is not fun. Neither is any other kind of violence. Do you need to hear more?"

"No," Red said stiffly, "I don't. You do, though. But it's not going to be from me." And she stalked away.

"Well," Mary Sharon said, her voice faking a lilt, "welcome to the party. Hope you're gonna have a swell time." Suddenly I started to laugh. Mary Sharon nudged me. "Be nice now, you commie pinko feminist."

"I think someone might call me a feminist fascist more than commie pinko." I laughed some more. "Oh, Mary Sharon, I can't help it. Battered shrimp! You were too much, you know that?"

"Mmmm." She was looking around as if she wasn't listening to me. "Do you think there are battered shrimp shelters?" We both broke into giggles, and she added, "You weren't too bad yourself. What's next for Red, do you think?"

I got my mirth under control. "I don't know. She'll probably organize butch/femme support groups. Really, she does seem to try everything, doesn't she?"

Before Mary Sharon could answer, Jude came swooping down upon us. She was a large, handsome woman with a cloudlike explosion of white hair surrounding her face that barely contained her generous mouth and intense blue eyes. The crinkles that crisscrossed this animated face reflected passion and joy.

"Tyler! Mary Sharon! What are you doing skulking about the front door? Get some food! Get something to drink! Enjoy! Enjoy!" Her voice boomed out as if she were on stage, trying to project to those in the back row, every word a pronouncement. After hugs around, she whirled on me. "Tyler! What are you up to these days?"

"Ah..." I hesitated, feeling as if I'd been thrown off-balance by her verbal style. "I'm writing a book, Jude. And my columns, of course. And the usual, working at WINK."

"A book?" she shouted. "Marvelous! About women?" I nodded. "Of course! I want an autographed copy, yes?"

"Yes, Jude, of course," I agreed.

"And Mary Sharon," she wheeled abruptly, "you still in law school?" She had a fabulous memory.

"Second year," Mary Sharon agreed.

"That's fine, just fine! We need some committed women lawyers. Show these scoundrels how to do it right! Teach them the meaning of integrity, yes?" Mary Sharon smiled and nodded again. "Off you go, now," Jude insisted, steering us toward the dining room. "Enjoy!"

Mary Sharon shook her head as we strolled through the house. "She is something, isn't she?"

"Oh, yeah," I agreed as we poked our heads into the room that was obviously for the lesbians-with-babies lesbians—the babies mostly present. The mothers were breast-feeding, changing diapers, and talking to one another while the children, mostly boys, it seemed, were hitting one another on the head or whining or sleeping. "Jude Becker is bigger than life." Mary Sharon and I smiled as tolerantly as we could and backed out of that room, looking at one another out of the corners of our eyes.

"You say a word," I muttered, "and I'll 'whip cream' you."

"Don't worry! I think I'm more afraid of the mothers than I am of some bone-crushing S/M-er. Are we real lesbians anymore?" she asked, when out of earshot of the mothers. "We don't do S/M. We don't have or even *want* babies. We're not butch or femme."

At this point, I interjected, "Some people think that you're pretty femme-y and that I'm pretty butch-y, Mary Sharon."

She snorted but otherwise ignored my remark. "We're not witches," this as we passed the roomful of goddess-worshipping lesbians who seemed to be initiating some kind of ritual. They were all in a circle, something was burning in a pot in the center—incense or sage—and their eyes were closed as one person was solemnly calling on the west wind or maybe it was the wet wand. I don't know. "How do we fit in? Of course, you're doing your part by being in a 12-step program. That's just about as trendy as babies these days."

I narrowed my eyes at her. "You *could* do your part, too, you know. Somewhere there's an Al-Anon meeting just waiting for you."

"Really, Tyler, such an edge to your voice. I thought you pure program types didn't get pushy with apostates."

"I'm new at this," I said disdainfully, "I can still make mistakes. Like punching you in the nose."

Her eyes got all round at this. "Wait," she said, "I think we just passed the leather den. Maybe you'd like to join them?"

22

The dining room was crowded, with three tables set up in a U for maximum access. Although the food was plentiful and varied, what really hit the eye was the luscious presentation. A handful of red and purple primroses were scattered on the edge of one platter; a branch of vivid scarlet bougainvillea spilled onto the crisp white tablecloth between two platters of neutral-colored rice dishes; and a crisp pink hibiscus adorned yet another platter.

We loaded our plates and made our usual disparaging remarks about one another's choices. "I swear, Mary Sharon, you and I must have gotten switched at birth. You are, at heart, a true-blue Californian and I must be a Midwesterner, don't you think?"

"Your observation"—she narrowed her eyes—"is based on the assumption that all Californians are health-food nuts and all midwesterners are junk-food junkies. You and I should be proof to the contrary."

She was right, of course. My plate was stacked with meatballs, cocktail weiners, chicken wings, mushrooms stuffed with caviar, pâté, potato chips and dip, nachos and various gooey, sweet things while hers was a pile of artichokes and guacamole, tomatoes stuffed with more rabbit food and delectable fruits, pasta and unfamiliar salads called unimaginable things like tabouleh. Mary Sharon was a vegetarian, and I was a confirmed omnivore.

"Do you want to stargaze?" she asked me, when it was clear our plates could hold no more.

"Sure," I agreed. "Where? The staircase?"

She nodded, and we headed for the front of the house where the winding staircase overlooked the ample vestibule, allowing us to see everyone who arrived and left. We were sidetracked two or three times, separately or together, by various people. Jude's parties brought together friends, acquaintances, present lovers of ex-lovers, and ex-lovers of present lovers. I smiled, nodded, and chatted my way through this throng of women, assuming Mary Sharon was doing the same. At one point, Jude herself peered at my plate and gave me a nod of approval.

Once we had settled halfway up the stairs, Mary Sharon gave a little sigh, "This is truly the place to come if one wants to make contacts, isn't it?"

I looked at her over the chicken wing I was maneuvering into my mouth. "I get the feeling you're not exactly talking about business contacts. Thinking of finding yourself a good woman, are you?" When Mary Sharon moved out here a year ago to start law school, she'd also been extricating herself from a ten-year-long relationship.

Now she shrugged, carefully studying her vegetables. "I think about it from time to time. I'm in no hurry but...I liked being in that long, stable relationship with Clare. I'm basically a down-home kind of girl. You know." I knew, all right, but I doubted many others did. Not many women had ever seen Mary Sharon making omelettes in her pink robe and bunny slippers. "But then, it's probably easier not being with anyone now while I'm in school. Everyone I know who's in law school and in a relationship is cracking up—either individually or the couple. It's tough. Hey, look who's coming in the door." She nodded down the stairs.

It was Angela Dahl, a local comedian just starting to make the national circuit. She was immediately mobbed. Her darkness was beautifully enhanced by a glowing peach-colored mini-dress that could have passed for a long shirt. "Angela's a pretty hot woman, Mary Sharon. Want to meet her?"

Mary Sharon looked scandalized and said, "You expect me to bring a black woman home to Lake Wobegon, Minnesota? My mother would have to cook a meal for the entire membership of the Church of Our Lady of Fallen Grace in order to handle that."

I laughed. "Oh, your mother wouldn't have that much trouble with it. She'd love Angela. Imagine what fun she'd have trying to fatten her up. It's your brother who'd really flip out." We laughed together, thinking of Mary Sharon's narrow-minded, conventional brother, who couldn't bring himself to say the word "lesbian."

Mary Sharon leaned over and kissed my cheek, saying, "Too bad you're such a drunk. We'd sure make a fine couple."

We grinned appreciatively at each other; there was no need for further words. We'd settled this issue a long time ago, back when we were still in college. After a singularly awkward night, we'd both decided that the passion of our friendship was far too precious to jeopardize for a little fleshly passion.

"Do you know Angela?" Mary Sharon sucked on an artichoke, a habit that made me shiver with distaste.

I nodded. "A little. She's a friend of a friend of a friend. Want to meet her? I hear she's between lovers."

She waved a clump of broccoli. "Maybe later."

We had arrived fairly early, when the crowd was still thin. Now the fashionable latecomers were beginning to arrive. While some were still making a fuss over Angela Dahl, Jeanine Anderson caught sight of us on the stairs and waved. She, too, was immediately surrounded by a group of women eager to meet her or prove they knew her or to curry her favor. She was wearing a pair of dark slacks with a simple but elegant white blouse. I nodded my approval.

I turned to Mary Sharon, a half-eaten cocktail wiener in my fingers. "Do you ever think about politics?" Her mouth was full of crunchy green things, and she just looked at me quizzically. "I know you *think* of political things. I mean do you think of going *into* politics? Lawyers do that, don't they?"

She swallowed, shaking her head simultaneously. "Uh-uh. Mainstream politics is too much about compromise. That doesn't exactly interest me."

I nodded, thinking about the juggling Jeanine probably had to do even to get elected to the Board of Supervisors, let alone survive it. About that time, Betsy Zaylor arrived, and all the other "stars" were abandoned for her. She was among the current crop of "lipstick dykes," women who had "reclaimed" their femme selves. She wore lots of make-up, a fifties kind of bleached "do," and a flowing dress of something silky in flowering pastels. She reminded me of my nursery school teacher, wholesome and fluffy. Mary Sharon and I ate and observed in silence for a few minutes, until the Zaylor contingent began to move off into the house.

"Remember when our heroes were writers, thinkers, musicians, activists?" I didn't wait for Mary Sharon to respond. "Now it's 1950s retreads and therapists. What does that say about our community?"

Mary Sharon said, "Betsy is a writer, Tyler." When I cut narrowed eyes at her, she added, "She wrote a book, remember?"

"That doesn't make her a writer."

She grinned. "Some people believe she's the greatest thinker of our decade."

My lip curled. "My point exactly."

"Her book probably reaches more people than anything Mary Daly ever wrote."

I looked at her suspiciously. "Are you playing devil's advocate here?"

She shrugged. "Maybe. But really, Ty, don't you think you're being a little elitist? I mean, don't you just dismiss *anything* that's too popular?"

I popped a moist meatball in my mouth, thinking about what Mary Sharon had just said. "Possibly," I conceded. "But don't you think it's scary that we make heroes out of therapists and transform pop psychology into philosophy? Zaylor and her ilk skim the surface, preach 'love and tolerance,' and seem to have forgotten what feminism is all about. They talk twaddle about 'post-feminism'—whatever the hell *that* is!— and seem to have forgotten that the women's movement was initially the women's *liberation* movement. First we rendered the word 'liberation' ineffective by allowing it to be diminished to 'lib,' now we've allowed it to be excised altogether! Now 'feminism' is in danger of being replaced by—what? Humanism? Queer politics? Progressive politics? None of which, of course, actually addresses women's issues."

Mary Sharon nodded. "We're on the same side, remember? Look over there."

Leslie Briggs, an internationally known feminist poet and lecturer, was being personally welcomed by Jude. A group of women immediately surrounded them. Leslie's diminutive size was lost in the crowd, but I could still see the grizzled head with cropped hair, held at just that angle that shouted "pride." Her erect stature, the women swarming around her— I felt better immediately.

The lesbians, and even the feminists who weren't lesbians, continued to arrive at a steady pace—locksmiths and judges, entertainers and waitresses, plumbers and computer experts. There were women who were well known at least to the lesbian community (and, in some cases, well beyond that), as well as women known only to their friends. Regardless of their differences, they were all women who gave their time and energy and money to women, who made women their first priority.

Mary Sharon and I remained on the stairs, and were joined by others, for the presentation of the Becker Awards which was always done in the spacious vestibule. Women were honored for such activities as "Journalism," "Best Collaborative Effort," "Most Innovative Program Dealing with… (several different issues)," "Most Effective Fund Raising Campaign," "Creative Problem Solving," "Publishing," "Multicultural Efforts," and many others. It was our "Oscars," a truly wonderful event that bridged our differences long enough for us to remember we were all on the same side and to celebrate each other and the work we all did.

After a second run at the food, Mary Sharon suggested, "Well? Should we give up our holier-than-thou stance and go mingle with the common folk?"

I laughed. "I guess so. See you later, pal."

Just as I reached the dining room, in search of a diet soda, Annie appeared at my elbow. "Hi," she said, a little shyly.

"Hi," I responded, perhaps a tad too heartily. "Did you get your ad in the personals?" She nodded, saying no more. "Well, I wish you luck."

She shrugged. "I think it could be fun. We'll see." I smiled agreement. "Where'd you get a name like Tyler?"

I was startled by the abrupt change in subject. "What?" I asked with my usual suavity.

"Tyler," she repeated. "Is it a chosen name or your mother's maiden name or what?"

"Oh," I said, comprehension finally dawning upon me. "Given. My mother thought Jones was so prosaic that she had to give us interesting first names. My sister is Magdalene after the prostitute—reformed prostitute I guess—in the Bible. She's spent most of her life proving that she is more like Mary-the-mother-of-god than Mary Magdalene." Why am I rambling on like this? "Then I came along and my mother was just sort of beginning to understand that there was something wrong with 'paradise,' the prefeminist stirrings of the 1950s I guess, and she named me after her best friend."

"That's fascinating!" Annie said, with what seemed to be way too much enthusiasm.

An uncomfortable silence followed that we both tried to fill with inane remarks about the party. Just as I was preparing a sentence to help me move away from her, she said, "Well, nice chatting with you. I see some friends over there," she waved vaguely, "so I'll see you later. Okay?"

I breathed a sigh of relief as she moved away. For the next couple of hours, I wandered about, picking up a little food here and there, visiting briefly but pleasantly with many people I knew—many of whom I even liked—intersecting occasionally with Mary Sharon, getting caught up on everyone's current activities and/or passion.

Suddenly a pair of hands reached from behind to cover my eyes as a voice whispered, "I bet you don't know who this is." My body stiffened.

"Hey!" The hands were removed immediately. "I didn't mean to scare you. I was just teasing!"

Recognizing the voice, I turned to fall into a vigorous embrace. "Pepsi!" I gasped, as soon as I was allowed enough air to breathe. "When did you get back?"

"Last night," she answered, stretching her arms out and arching her rounded body. "I'm still wiped. Would've called you, but I knew you'd be here tonight, so I decided to surprise you. What's going on? How come you're so easily spooked?"

"A long story. What are *you* doing here?"

She smiled, the most gorgeous smile I've ever known to cover any woman's face. "Another long story, my love. Let's go talk."

We soon found ourselves out in Jude's backyard in an old-fashioned swing under the rhododendrons, talking heart-to-heart. Pepsi Armstrong was the first woman I'd ever loved—not the first woman I'd ever slept with, but loved. Our relationship, now ancient history, had settled into loving friendship. About four months ago, she had followed her then-current heartbeat to Australia, convinced this was a permanent commitment. She relived the unraveling of her dream for me.

"Oh, Pepsi," I said, when she'd given me most of the salient details, "you must be devastated." I gave her a big hug.

She shrugged, her dark eyes moody and withdrawn. "Yeah. I guess so. I'm so tired, Tyler, of feeling anything. I think I've just shut down for a while. So distract me. What's going on with you?"

After I filled her in on the details of "my" murder, she asked, "So what about this Peter kid? Did the cops arrest him? Talk to him? What?"

I shook my head. "Pepsi, I just told the cops a few hours ago. I'm sure they have to confirm my information before they'll act on it. And, especially now, they're not likely to be telling me what they've done or not done. Jeff Adams, at the paper, has all the police sources. When he knows something, he'll tell me."

"What do you think?" she pressed. "Was it Peter?"

I shook my head again. "I don't know. I really don't know. I don't like him much, but that doesn't make him a murderer."

What about the mother and sister?"

"I'll tell you something, Pepsi, I have this feeling about Margarita. That woman is in pain, enormous pain. I'm not saying she killed her father, but I bet she knows who did it. Which makes me more suspicious of Consuelo than I would be otherwise. Consuelo might have killed Jason if she found out something about him and Margarita. Margarita would be tormented if she knew her mother killed her father, especially on her account." I shrugged elaborately. "Of course, I'm just making this all up. I have no concrete facts at all, just a feeling about Margarita. Well, it's more than just a feeling. You should have seen the pain on her face. It was burning in her eyes like a forest fire."

"What's the last name again?"

"Judd," I answered. "Why?"

Pepsi ignored my question. "Margarita Judd." She said the name slowly, as if she were trying to remember something. "Margarita," she repeated, a slight frown crossing her brow. I didn't say anything, just waited. "Margarita Judd. No, that's not it. Marga? Margie? Marge?" Again a little silence. Then her brow smoothed as she said, "Rita. Rita Judd. That's it."

"What?" I asked, feeling a little jump of excitement.

Pepsi now looked a little thoughtful, quiet for another minute. "This is not the kind of thing I can tell you lightly, Ty. Only the gravity of this situation compels me to share this with you, but I must ask you to use this information with the utmost respect."

"Pepsi," I said with frustration, "what are you talking about?"

"Remember that incest group I was in before I left for Australia?" My stomach clenched as I nodded. "There was a Rita Judd in that group. Actually, we only went by first names, but she once referred to herself as 'Rita Judd.' I remember because I thought Judd was an odd last name for someone so obviously Latina. She had exceptionally dark eyes, very fair complexion and short, dark hair. Thin, medium height, probably in her early or middle twenties."

"Sounds like her," I nodded. "Well."

"Yes," Pepsi agreed. "Well."

For a couple of minutes, neither of us said anything, just rocked back and forth in the swing, thinking of the import of this information. Finally Pepsi said, "It seems as if you'd better concentrate on her."

I nodded again. "You're probably right."

Mary Sharon joined us about then, making the expected fuss about Pepsi's presence. Pepsi gave her an abbreviated version of the ill-fated Australian romance.

After making appropriately soothing and affirming noises, Mary Sharon turned to me. "I picked up an odd piece of info tonight, Tyler. For what it's worth."

"Well," I demanded, "what *is* it worth?"

She shrugged. "I was talking to Maura..."

"Ah, yes," I interrupted. "Maura. That name sounds vaguely familiar. Now where have I heard that?"

Mary Sharon glared at me, and Pepsi looked from one of us to the other. "Am I just supposed to guess what's going on here or what?"

Mary Sharon ran her hand through her already wild hair and said, "Oh, she just thinks she's being cute."

"Cute? I never had that intention for a minute." Then I turned to Pepsi and said, "Maura is a woman that I never *really* get to hear any details about, but, for some reason, her name keeps popping up in conversation with this-here gal." I gestured toward Mary Sharon, who was looking, I realized, genuinely upset. I dropped my western drawl and asked, "What is it, Mary Sharon?"

Very quietly, she said, "Tyler, if you must know, Maura is entirely involved with someone else."

There was a little silence for a minute while my mouth formed a perfect O. Then I said, "Mary Sharon, I'm sorry. I didn't know that. Why didn't you tell me? I wouldn't have been such a snot."

She wriggled her shoulders and looked away, some of the anger leaving her eyes. "I don't know. I guess because I was trying not to be attracted to her and then you kept throwing it in my face."

I repeated, "I'm sorry, hon. Really. That's tough."

She frowned. "Yeah. Well. Do you want to hear what I

heard or not?" I nodded. "I was telling Maura about the murder and stuff...She thinks she's heard of F.U.C.K."

"Oh, she *is* up on things, isn't she?" Pepsi said rather drily. Mary Sharon and I missed a beat as we stared at Pepsi, uncomprehendingly. Suddenly we started laughing and Pepsi demanded, "*What* is going on?"

I gave her a quick rundown on F.U.C.K. and Jeff's hunch about it. Then I turned back to Mary Sharon. "What has she heard?"

"It's not much. Just someone talking about this secret society, and she thinks she heard the word F.U.C.K."

"Who's the 'someone'? A woman?"

"Yes, a woman." Before I could bombard her with more questions, Mary Sharon raised her hand. "That's it, Tyler. Maura thought she heard something, and no one she's talked to confirms it. No more."

"Mmm," I responded, turning this bit over in my head. "Curiouser and curiouser."

We looked at one another. Finally I broke the silence. "What do you think? Is this the legendary feminist hit-squad?"

Mary Sharon agreed quickly. "At last. Finally." Her voice indicated she could now sleep at night. I grinned at her.

Pepsi's eyes widened. "You guys are kidding, right?" We shrugged simultaneously. "Come on. I mean—really."

I said, "Okay. We're kidding. I guess. But who knows?"

"Yeah," Mary Sharon agreed again, almost wistfully. "It could happen, you know?"

The three of us kicked around some ideas regarding Jason's murder, and we talked about who we would want "eliminated" if there really were such a thing as a feminist hit-squad. Mary Sharon's first vote went to the man who raped a fourteen-year-old with a hot curling iron. I'd just dealt with an eighty-year-old woman who'd been beaten and raped by neighborhood teenagers; my vote went to them. Pepsi wanted to know if she could suggest ex-lovers. We remonstrated, insisting the victims had to be men. Not that we condoned such an idea, exactly.

Pepsi and I hugged each other good-bye, promising to get together soon and do some proper catching up. At home, Mary Sharon and I lingered on the deck, dissecting the party and talking about Mary Sharon's ill-fated, not-to-be-acted-upon attraction to the already-committed Maura, while Aggie checked out the backyard and then was content to lean against my leg.

23

I thought how glad I was that she was no longer mad at me as she took each of my toes into her mouth as carefully as if they were paper flowers. Her tongue darted between my toes, bathing the delicate, virginal tissues there. Then she slowly swirled that soft wet mass around each toe, her mouth like that of a small guppy—sucking, sucking until—thwpp—she released it before moving onto the next one. She transformed each of my toes into a projectile, shooting liquid fire up my legs toward my crotch.

Next, that traveling tongue began a leisurely stroll—up, up, up my legs, her fingers doing a kind of advance dance, a reconnaissance trip, as it were. Long before that merry troupe reached the top of my thighs, I was dripping wet and straining toward her with anticipation and anxiety. But she ignored all that, her fingers merely flitting over my brush, her tongue barely flicking across the upper edge of my need, sending a shudder through me that she also ignored as she moved that tongue into the vicinity of my navel. Now the licks of fire were moving downward, but disappointment had blunted their burn capacity.

Before I was allowed, however, to get too complacent, her mouth had closed over a large nipple. From a guppie, she had changed into a lamprey eel, sucking with such intensity—her tongue whipping back and forth across the very tip—that the liquid fire now doubled, tripled. Shock waves rippled from my breasts to my crotch as my body again began to strain, trying to release itself beyond its mere physical boundaries. This exquisite yearning and reaching continued as she moved her mouth to my other breast and her hands ran up and down my sides, across the valleys and humps of my body, never stopping, just moving, searching for a resting place. Suddenly her mouth was on mine as her hands at last found their home between my legs, but her fingers, still restless, moved ceaselessly—caressing, tickling, poking, exploring those folds of soft flesh. Her mouth left my mouth, trailed down my neck, returned briefly and then headed south.

That mouth moved down my Mississippi River toward New Orleans, where her fingers were already diving into my Gulf of Mexico. Momentarily, I wondered at my passivity, then lost that thought immediately in the concentration of my entire being toward releasing the energy now amassing between my legs. My hips rose and rose to meet her. Just as I knew her tongue was going to swim in my waters, I heard the clank of metal.

"Oh no," I thought, "she's getting out her handcuffs!" I stiffened, hearing the metal clank again.

I was sitting straight up in my bed, no Carla George beside me. Or was that Pepsi? Did she stay over last night? I shook my cottony head, trying to clear it. Aggie was sitting next to the bed, her leash in her mouth. When she shook her head, the metal of the leash jingled a little and I half-moaned and half-laughed. Damn! "Not yet, sweetie," I told a puzzled Aggie as I lay back down in my bed, putting my hands between my legs where a distinct throb still pulsed.

By ten a.m., I was dressed in my "respectable" journalist clothes—grey flannel slacks, crisp white blouse, navy blazer, and navy flats. I did draw the line at wearing one of those blouses with floppy bows. The funeral was at eleven.

Unlike Harold and Maude, I didn't really enjoy funerals. In fact, I'd spent most of my adult life avoiding them. Why would anyone want to gaze at a dead body? At least the casket would be closed. Even the wonders of forensic make-up wouldn't be able to cover up a bullet hole between the eyes.

The fashionable church on Nob Hill seemed to be the kind of church where it was likely that people went to be seen rather than saved. Certainly the people entering that morning were something to gaze upon. The animal rights folks would have had a heyday with the herd of furred ladies present. Funerals had changed over the years. Although the men were in dark clothing—the same dark clothing, I suspected, they wore most days of their lives—the women wore anything from raspberry red to lemon yellow to watermelon green. (Raspberry? Lemon? Watermelon? Maybe I should have eaten breakfast.)

I slipped into a pew at the back of the church. Expensive clothing and jewelry, perfectly coiffed hair, smooth emotionless faces, and cool demeanors all seemed to indicate the presence of money. There was a handful of younger people, somewhat scruffier and more casual than their elders, presumably friends of Peter and Margarita. Nearer the back was a group of people whose clothing and haircuts and a certain toughness in their faces indicated working class. They were mostly Hispanic—perhaps workers who had been employed by Consuelo at one time or another or maybe relatives. I wondered if any were members of AMIGAS.

I was not the only watcher. Inspectors Dwyer and George were also sitting apart near the rear, carefully eyeing the mourners. Dwyer caught my eye at one point and gave me a quick grin. George, however, looked right through me. I guess she was really pissed.

I don't know what I expected to see or find. Maybe

nothing. My eyes scanned the back rows, looking particularly at the women. Wasn't that where a mistress would sit? What was her name? Laurel something.

Just before the service began, the family entered. Consuelo, elegant in black, her eyes hard and dry, leaned lightly on Peter's arm. Peter, in his dark, conservative suit, moved very stiffly. Margarita, also in black, appeared more rumpled than elegant. Her eyes were red and puffy and still tortured, and she leaned heavily on Sam. Following more slowly were Victoria and Jorge Alvarado. Victoria looked down, stumbling a little, while Jorge pulled at his collar and looked like a rabbit about to bolt. They sat in the front pew with the family. That was unusual enough for me to think about the apparently close bonds they had with Consuelo. Might they have killed Jason to protect her?

Throughout the long, tedious service, the backs of the family revealed little. I looked about, discerning nothing of any particular import. I curbed my fidgeting by wondering if the cops had followed through on the information I'd supplied them about Peter. Had they already talked to Peter and released him? Or were they still waiting for corroboration of my story from their colleagues in L.A.?

At last I followed the mourners to the cemetery. George and Dwyer were there, too, keeping a discreet distance. Consuelo nodded somberly at me. After the ritual, the priest announced that the family welcomed "friends and loved ones" to their home for a light repast. I hoped it wouldn't be too light; by then I was famished.

Stifling the urge to swing by a McDonald's, I dawdled on the way back to the house. I had no intention of attending this little gathering if it was, indeed, little. I wanted to be fairly inconspicuous and certainly wouldn't be if there were only ten or so people present. I very obligingly got lost again in St. Francis Woods and arrived late enough to have to park a couple of blocks away. I was pleased at the number of cars.

Entering the front door, I found myself at the end of a line that moved slowly toward the family in the living room. I ducked into the dining room and watched for a moment. Peter seemed distracted, his eyes sliding around the room aimlessly. Near the fireplace, Margarita had collapsed into a chair and was making no attempt to talk to anyone. Sam bent over her, his hand resting on her shoulder. Consuelo's hands reached out continuously as she welcomed her guests.

I wondered briefly at what I was doing. If one of these people killed Jason, did I really want to uncover that fact, expose it? Didn't I believe in justifiable homicide? I felt like a voyeur and I realized again that I didn't know what I intended to do with the truth.

I turned toward the dining room table, heavily laden with miniature quiches, petite sandwiches, fruit, and tarts. I was glad I hadn't stopped at McDonald's. Victoria, with an apron over her funereal clothes, nodded at me as she brought more food in. Jorge was presiding over a shank of lamb; if he recognized me, he didn't indicate so. Carrying a full plate, I casually wandered toward the back of the house. I was pleased to discover that some people were gathering in the sunroom as well as in the courtyard out back. It was important that I not be the only one absent from the living room.

I stood in the hallway overlooking the back garden and looked all around me. When I was quite certain no one was paying any attention to me, I slipped into Jason's study. Still hungry, I set my plate on the corner of the desk, knowing I must look through this room quickly while the family was still preoccupied.

Jason's desk chair, ample and comfortable, swiveled smoothly. I moved my food right in front of me so I could appear to be eating if anyone should come in. I popped a quiche into my mouth before I got up and went back to the door to see if I could lock it. A simple push button. I hesitated. Would it be worse if I locked it or if someone walked in on me rifling the desk? I pushed the button in.

I began opening drawers, finding the usual desk contents: pens, stamps, paper clips, rubber bands, unpaid bills, unbalanced bank statements, unopened sweepstake notices, cancelled and unused checks, personal correspondence. I looked at this a little more carefully. A colleague in New York had sent information about an upcoming conference. There were several requests for Dr. Judd to lecture. Nothing else caught my eye.

I froze momentarily at the sound of voices just outside the door. Rising slowly from the desk chair, I closed the drawer I'd been going through, my eyes glued to the door handle. After a minute or two, the voices drifted away down the hall. I slumped in the chair, exhaling my withheld breath as my heart began to hammer.

The bottom two drawers on either side turned out to be file cabinet drawers. I scanned the folders: credit card receipts, utilities, tax returns, medical receipts, bank statements, stockbroker statements, and other financial matters. I pulled out most of the files and glanced inside, just to make certain they were what they purported to be.

The other file drawer had various other headings: lectures, social security numbers, sprinkling system, security system, warranties. With a start, I found myself reading my own name. Jason had filed every column or article of mine that had been published since his assault on me last spring. The papers filing suit against him were in there also.

I was tense, listening for any sound in the hall. I searched through the clippings—for notes in the margins, any reactions to my words. There was nothing. I ate some sandwiches and fruit while I thought about this file. Why hadn't the cops confiscated this? Did they just copy everything these days? I forced myself to go through the file again but found no further clues. I put it back in the drawer.

I glanced at my watch. I'd been in there for forty minutes and figured I'd better get out before the party started to break up. With something niggling at the back of my mind, I pulled a couple of volumes out of the bookcase and paged through them. There was nothing hidden inside, no sinister messages written on the flyleafs.

The closet door was locked. Locked. What was I trying to remember? A safe. Jeff told me Jason kept a gun in a safe. Plus the missing money. Where was that safe? In this closet? The lock was the kind that could be easily picked with an unbent paper clip. I opened the door and caught sight of the safe, then stepped back in dismay. Surrounding it, stacked on built-in shelves from the floor to the ceiling, were pornographic magazines. Hundreds, maybe thousands of them. I couldn't bring myself to touch them, but the covers were brilliantly colored and graphically violent. Not the soft slicks like *Playboy*, but the truly disgusting hard-core stuff: wild animals crawling across women's naked bodies, other women being "snuffed" or, more accurately, murdered while being fucked, and random body parts. And all of this just on the covers. Sickened, I closed the closet door.

Just then I heard a metallic click. Someone was trying the hallway door. Adrenaline shot through me, making me feel almost faint, and I struggled to breathe evenly. There was a knock and someone pushed slightly against the door. I quickly looked around the room, making certain all the desk drawers were closed. Then I reached over and swung the door open, finding myself face to face with a glowering Peter.

$$24$$

Peter's eyes crawled suspiciously around the room. "What are you doing in here?" he snarled at me.

I swallowed and sent a message to my heart to calm down. "I just came in here to eat my food alone." I gestured toward the almost-empty plate on the desk.

He sneered at me. "With a locked door?"

"You know," I said, furrowing my brow in feigned puzzlement, "I don't know how that door got locked." I scrutinized the doorknob a moment. "I must've pushed that button in unwittingly when I came in here."

"Right," he snorted. "How dumb do you think I am, lady?" I didn't answer, instead tried to think about getting around his body and getting out of there. "You have no right to be in this room. No right even to be in this house."

I nodded agreement. "Fine. I'll just leave then." I tried to brush by him, but he put out a restraining arm.

He leaned toward me and whispered, "I know you killed him. No one else knows, but I do. I know you did it." His eyes were blurry with rage and invective.

I felt a stab of fear at the base of my neck that began to tingle down my spine and out my limbs. I shook my head, "I didn't. Really. I don't know..."

Suddenly Sam was there, behind Peter, saying, "Hey, Tyler. I've been looking for you." He reached past Peter and pulled me out the door. "Come on. Consuelo told me to be sure to show you the garden."

I blinked in confusion, doubting such a message from Consuelo, but followed Sam with alacrity—glad to get out of that room. No one was in the garden. I felt my chest tighten as I compared this light, airy loveliness with the insidious ugliness in Jason's closet. I shuddered, thinking about a doctor to whom you entrusted your body—a doctor who had so little respect for women's bodies that he found it pleasurable to gaze at them being tortured, abused, degraded. The nausea returned, and a bark of a sob escaped my mouth before I could control it. I stuffed my fist in my mouth, squelching further outbursts.

"What is it?" I had forgotten about Sam. I shook my head, and he put his hand on my arm. "Tyler? What did Peter say?"

I shook my head again, managing to say, "It wasn't anything Peter said." Sam steered me toward a stone bench, and I put my head down between my knees. Gradually my breathing changed from ragged gulps to deep inhale, slow exhale. Finally I said, "He was a monster, Sam."

"Peter?"

"No. Jason."

"Oh. Yeah," he agreed, without asking more questions. Maybe he knew about the closet.

"Peter thinks I killed him."

"Did you?"

"No. Did you?" I shot back.

"No," he answered, "but I guess neither of us cares too much about his death."

"How's Margarita?"

He shrugged. "She's having a hard time. She went to lie down for awhile. The doctor gave her a sedative. What do you know about this case, Tyler? The S.F. cops aren't exactly confiding in me."

"Because of your personal involvement?"

"Presumably."

I smiled slowly at Sam. "I do know that you're a suspect, Sam. But then—so am I."

"And everyone in the family?" he asked and I nodded, watching him closely. "It's not that she cared about him at all." I knew he was talking about Margarita. Was he worried that she'd done it herself? Did he know? "He was a bastard, you know, a real bastard. He made guys like me look like amateur night. Not to dismiss what I did to my wife and kids, but *this* guy...you know?" He looked at me beseechingly, obviously wanting some confirmation. I nodded again, wondering about all these you-know's. "It wasn't enough for him just to push his wife and kids around." I thought about an entire closet filled with pornography, and I looked at Sam's clenched fists. My bet was that he knew about the incest.

I put my hand on his forearm and patted it, saying nothing. What was there to say? If Sam or Consuelo or Peter or Margarita had killed Jason, what would I do? Jason Judd deserved to die. If the cops found out who murdered this brute, then fine, it was out of my hands. But if I found out, I would have to make a decision. A decision I wasn't sure I *wanted* to make.

"So, Tyler," Sam interrupted my reverie. "Are you going to tell me what you found in Jason's study?"

I looked at Sam for a few seconds, at the blond hair that had worked its way free of whatever taming agents he used and now flopped boyishly across his forehead, at his soft, sad brown eyes, at the notch in his chin. It was hard to imagine him a murderer. But then, it was hard to imagine him a wife-beater, too, and I knew he'd been that.

"He had a file on me, Sam. With my name on it and stuff about me in it," I said.

Sam nodded. "I gather he didn't like you very well."

"No, I guess not. But a file..." I let the sentence drift off as I thought about this ominous file, about Jason hiding in the bushes at my park, about his seeming obsession with me. "I think he intended some sort of revenge against me."

"That would seem in character. Anything else?" Sam prodded me and when I looked puzzled, he added, "Anything else in there?"

"Did you intend to check the room out yourself, Sam, when you rescued me from Peter?"

He shrugged. "Maybe."

We smiled at one another, and I said, "Pornography. A whole closet full, Sam. Bad stuff. Not just the usual icky stuff but *really* bad stuff."

He nodded, his fists clenched again. "He wasn't a nice man."

We exchanged other bits of information. Sam wondered if Peter was "milking" his dad, using his knowledge of his father's private life, perhaps, to extract big bucks from him.

"Why would you think that?" I asked.

"I have no proof," he responded. "It's just a feeling I have. Peter lets little hints fall, maybe to humiliate or discredit his father. But they've always been so oblique. Anyway, I just think it's unlikely he'd murder his golden goose."

"But if the goose decided to quit laying golden eggs?"

Sam shrugged, then nodded. "Yeah, maybe. I just don't know."

"Does Margarita know who killed him?" I asked him quickly, feeling myself on shaky ground.

He didn't anwer right away, just gazed out toward the fogged-in ocean. Just when I thought he wasn't going to answer, he said, "I don't know. I guess I think she knows... something."

I nodded. "That's my gut reaction, too." I changed direction. "Ever hear of an organization called F.U.C.K.?" I spelled it out.

He frowned, shaking his head. "F.U.C.K.? Never heard of it. Who are they?"

"I don't know. Just a line I've gotten and can't seem to reel in."

"F.U.C.K.," he said slowly, looking away again. "Can't help you. Can't say I've ever heard of them. Them? It? Whatever it is."

I looked at my watch. "I've got to go. I didn't realize how late it's gotten." I stood up and offered my hand to him. "I wish you well, Sam, and hope everything'll work out with Margarita."

He nodded, also getting to his feet. He took my hand and shook it warmly. "Come on," he said. "I'll walk you out."

The house looked quite deserted as we passed through it. I heard low murmurs in the kitchen—probably Victoria and her husband. Maybe Consuelo was out there. We encountered no one else. Sam walked me to the front door and made as if to go to my car, but I informed him it was up the street.

He stretched his hand out again and said, "Let's keep in touch, Tyler, okay?"

I agreed and walked uphill toward my disreputable but always reliable bug. A car cruised by me and turned into Consuelo's drive. I recognized Carla George's salt-and-pepper hair and the bearlike head of Allan Dwyer next to her. I smiled to myself, thinking, Time for some answers, Peter.

$$\widehat{25}$$

Instead of going home, I drove directly to the address on Telegraph Hill that Jeff had given me. "Laurel Scott," read the note I'd left in my car. Thirty-three years old. Not that much older than Margarita. Ms. Scott lived in one of those places on Telegraph Hill that could only be reached by walking up steps. Saturday afternoon meant that there was nowhere to park in the neighborhood, what with residents being home and tourists on the prowl. I counted myself lucky to have found a parking place that was only one zip code away. Of course, it was straight uphill to the foot of the stairways that ascended even higher to Scott's address. I had to start exercising more or move out of this city, I thought, as I puffed my way up. I consoled myself with the thought of the descent.

When I reached a post that indicated the correct address, I was thoroughly winded. After giving myself a couple of minutes to catch my breath, I proceeded on an overgrown path, conveniently private, to Laurel Scott's front door. Her house was actually a cottage, directly above and below other houses on this steep incline, promising a spectacular view of the bay and Marin County. I knocked on the door. Very pricey, this location and view.

The door was opened almost immediately by a slender woman in jeans and paint-splattered sweatshirt. She wasn't conventionally beautiful, but her high cheekbones and bright green eyes made her noticeable. Her dark blond hair was pulled back in a loose ponytail, and she looked younger than I expected, less brittle. Her eyes were puffy and red. I wondered if Jason had treated her better than the other people in his life.

"Yes?" she asked, when I said nothing.

"I'm looking for Laurel Scott," I said.

"You've found her," she responded. "What can I do for you?"

I hesitated, then blundered on. "I'm Tyler Jones. I want to talk to you about Jason Judd."

Her eyes widened slightly before she asked, "Are you a reporter? Police?"

I shook my head. "Neither of those. I do work for the *Chronicle*, but this is on my own. I'm a friend of Consuelo's and"—what to say next?—"I'm involved in Jason's murder because I found his body."

She just looked at me for a few seconds, then opened her door wider. "Come on in." She preceded me into a small but beautifully furnished living room. "You want some coffee?"

"That'd be great," I answered. The view was, as I'd expected, fantastic. There was no masculine presence that I could detect in this room. The colors were pale yellow and white with a touch of royal blue in a couple of accessories. The bric-a-brac was all delicate and reflected the owner's appreciation of fine art—a couple of unusual vases, a beautifully worked bowl, an antique doll. In a place of prominence above the tiny mantel was an arresting painting, abstract, with the feeling of something concrete trying to materialize. Here was concentrated all the color that was absent in the rest of the room: emerald green, vivid orange, splashes of scarlet, deep blue-purple. I was just making out the artist's name when Laurel returned with a tray.

"Do you like it?" she asked me.

"It's stunning," I answered, turning to her. "You painted it?"

"Yes. My agent is trying to get me to put it up in a gallery, but..." She shrugged. "I'm not sure I can part with this. Sit down," she added, as she handed me a cup of coffee. "Milk or sugar?"

"Milk," I said, staring at her in confusion.

"I'm not what you expected, am I?"

I suppressed a smile of embarrassment and said, "I guess not." My eyes strayed again to her painting as I sipped the excellent coffee. "I guess...I don't know how to say this, so I'll just be rude and blurt it out. You don't seem to be the kind of woman who would choose to be a 'kept' woman. I guess I expected someone less independent and..."

"And less talented? Capable?" I nodded my agreement. "Have you ever tried to make a living painting—what did you say your name was?"

"Jones. Tyler Jones."

"Ms. Jones? Have you?" I shook my head. "Well, I have. I'm good, I think you can see that, but it makes little difference in the art world if you're good or not. Especially if you're a woman. What matters the most is who you know. And your ability to hang on—financially and emotionally—until your paintings start to sell or even to be noticed. Even then, you might never make enough money to live off of your work. At least not while you're alive."

I listened without interrupting. She got up and moved about the room—adjusting a vase, an ancient music box, straightening a painting that didn't need straightening. "I was twenty-eight when I met Jason at an art opening. I'd been waiting tables, scrubbing floors, typing letters endlessly for ten years—whatever I could do to support myself. There's nothing wrong with what I was doing, mind you. It's just that it leeched most of my energy, leaving very little for painting. I'd been in one group show and sold a couple of things. I just didn't have much done, or time or energy to do more."

She was standing at the window now, staring at the sailboats in the bay. "Jason offered me ease, time, possibility. He also knew a lot of the right people in the art world. I'm not sure I even hesitated. It seemed such a worthwhile exchange. I knew plenty of women artists who had married, mostly for support. I was being offered an opportunity for the same support with no marital ties. He bought me this little house, paid my bills so I didn't have to work, and rented a fabulous studio within walking distance from here."

She came back to the coffee and poured herself another cup. "More?" she asked, and I held my cup out again. "He asked very little in return. He came here once or twice a month, sometimes less often. I guess I was a prostitute. I didn't think much about that. In five years, I've been in three shows. One of them was my own. I have an agent now. I've sold lots of stuff and hang regularly at a couple of sale galleries in town." She wound down and said no more.

After a couple of minutes, I said, "Was he violent with you? Did he want you to do"—I was thinking of his pornography collection—"odd things for him, with him?"

She pulled the sleeve of her sweatshirt up. There were fading but obvious bruises on her upper arm. "The answer to both of your questions is 'yes,' and I don't want to talk about it."

Again we were silent for a couple of minutes. "Were you at the funeral this morning?"

She shot me an amused look and shook her head. "You don't understand. I'm not sorry he's dead. I'm not mourning him. I wouldn't think of going to his funeral. I'm mourning... the loss of my security, I guess. Maybe I can do this better on my own now. My time with Jason..." she shrugged. "I got what I needed." She suddenly got up and went to a teacart masquerading as a bar. "Would you like something to drink?" she asked, as she poured a very stiff tumbler of whiskey, straight up, and downed it with one gulp.

Yes! I almost shouted; instead, I politely said, "No thank

you." She poured another tumbler and brought it back to her chair, sipping it more carefully. "The price was probably too high," she went on, "but now I don't have to make a decision about giving this all up. I just have to do it. What I don't have to give up is the confidence and contacts and talent I've developed while he supported me. I'm not exactly grateful to him—it was an exchange, after all—but I am glad to have gotten the things I have gotten."

I put my cup down. "Ms. Scott..."

"Laurel," she interrupted me. "Please call me Laurel. Right now you know a lot more about me than most people do."

I smiled. "And I'm Tyler. Laurel, do you have any idea who might have killed Judd?"

She shook her head. "No. Except anyone who knew him well or intimately. He was not a nice man, Tyler." That sounded familiar. "Not nice at all. He told me some things about his family..." She hesitated, then continued, "I'm not sure why they didn't murder him long ago. And I can't begin to think why his wife would stay with him. But then...I'm a fine one to talk. People in glass houses and all that."

"What kind of things did he tell you about his family?"

She just looked at me. "Why all these questions, Tyler? What's your interest?"

I sighed. "I'm a prime suspect, so partly I want to clear myself. But also..." I told her an abbreviated version of the story about the Judds and me.

She nodded thoughtfully. "Do the police know about me?"

I told her I didn't know. "If I could find you, Laurel, they can. It might be better for you to go to them than wait and hope they don't find you."

"You think?" she asked earnestly. I nodded.

"Laurel? What did he tell you about his family, about anything?"

She shook her head slightly. "He drank a lot, and he lied a lot, both drunk and sober. He told me he beat his wife and 'took' her if she, in his words, 'held back.' Then he told me his daughter had seduced him when she was only eleven." I shuddered and Laurel nodded. "I know. Seduced. That's the word he used. As if an eleven-year-old is capable of seducing anyone! Supposedly he fucked all his nurses on examining tables, sometimes on operating tables. That story I didn't believe. I know one of his nurses, and I asked her about it. She was astounded. I don't think she really believed that Jason had actually told me that. Apparently he was quiet and polite and well-mannered at work. He even told me that he'd fucked one of his patients after he lost her. You know, she was dead..."

We were both silent as she began pacing the room again. "After a while, it didn't matter whether it was true or not. It was horrid, one way or the other. I never knew how much of it he made up or...He really wasn't bad with me, except some of the things he wanted to do were"—she shook her head a little—"at best, odd, at worst, downright creepy. But he didn't hit me or anything. These bruises came from him just grabbing me too hard and pulling me around. I'm not trying to say he was a sweet guy or anything. He wasn't. It just wasn't as awful as it seems." She went over to the bar and poured herself another drink.

I didn't say anything. Some of the nausea from earlier had returned, and I was thinking it was probably time for me to leave when she said, "I guess I want to make it seem not so bad, because I want to justify my putting up with it. It's simple, though, isn't it? I put up with it for this." Laurel moved her arms around in a circle. "I'll have to move. I can't afford this. But at least I won't have to give up the toehold I have in the art world now."

"So this place is in his name?" I was thinking how soon

the cops were likely to find her. And also how the family was going to find out about this part of dear old dad's life.

She shook her head. "No, it's not in his name. It was initially, but two years ago he had it transferred to me. Unusually kind of him—for both me and his family. It doesn't matter though, because I can't afford the taxes. At least when I sell it, I'll have something to live on for awhile."

I nodded, getting up. "I wish you well, Laurel," I ventured, not knowing what else to say. I looked at the painting above the mantel again, suddenly recognizing what was trying to materialize: her talent, maybe even her self. On the other hand, the vivid colors—colors of bruises and bumps and blood—made me think of the price of that self-discovery. "You have tremendous ability. I expect you'll do fine." She gazed at the piece, too, smiling. I turned toward her. "I'm curious. How come you invited me in? Talked so openly to me?"

She shrugged. "I've been waiting, ever since he died, for someone to come talk to me. And...I don't know. I guess I needed to talk about it." She walked me to the door. "Thank you," she said. "For your kind words, but even more for the chance to talk."

We shook hands, and I left.

I thought about Laurel Scott. She didn't seem like the kind of person who would kill someone. She was too nice. I smiled at myself. Too nice. As if that eliminates the possibility of murder. Still, it didn't seem to be in her best interest. Talk about killing the golden goose. On the other hand, if she didn't really need him anymore or if he grabbed her or pushed her around one too many times...I guessed she was as much a possibility as anyone else. And I still thought she was genuinely too nice. The walk back to my car wasn't nearly as pleasurable as I'd expected. I always forget that my calves scream louder on downhill grades than uphill.

26

Mary Sharon was slipping into one of her rambling, back-home stories. "Now this is very pertinent," she insisted.

"Sure," I murmured.

As always, she ignored my lack of exuberance and proceeded. "One spring, Johnny Callahan's body was found near the creek running through the Tidwell's farm."

"Callahan?" I repeated. "Are those the Callahans who ran the hardware store?" I'd heard of almost every family in Mary Sharon's home town of Rocky Ridge, Minnesota.

"That's right!" she responded, obviously delighted I'd remembered.

"But the Tidwells..." I couldn't place this name.

"You remember the Tidwells," she encouraged me. "The ones who named all their kids after the saints: Teresa, Bernadette, Mary Maria, Frank, Agnes, George, and Patrick."

"Frank? There's a St. Frank?"

Mary Sharon pursed her lips. "I hate it when you think you're cute. St. Francis, of course."

I nodded. "Oh yeah. I remember that family. But you never told me that Johnny Callahan got murdered."

"I didn't say murdered, did I? See how quickly we jump to conclusions? Although, at first, that's what everyone thought. There he was, stretched out on the bank of Blueberry Creek, a gunshot hole in his head and no gun around. What else could it be but murder?"

I nodded my head sagely. "Sure looks like it."

"And that's the whole point. Things aren't what they look like sometimes. Now listen," she said. "There were powder burns on his face, which means the gun was held close to his head. We all figured someone he knew had come right up to him and put that gun to his head and pulled the trigger. And everyone in town knew he and George Tidwell had been fighting for months over Evelyn Ronning and now...the field was clear for George, wasn't it? Only not so clear after all, because they arrested him for the murder of Johnny. He insisted he'd never done any such thing and no gal was worth murder and so forth and so on. But everyone figured he'd done it. Who else could it have been?"

Mary Sharon got up and poured more coffee for us. It was Sunday morning. Light splashed across my kitchen table, cluttered with breakfast dishes and the Sunday papers. In spite of my reluctance, I had to admit I was hooked on her story. "So. What happened?"

"Sometimes I wonder," she said musingly, "if George would've been convicted. Of course, it was all circumstantial. At that point, they hadn't found a gun or any other evidence indicating George had actually done it. But someone had to have done it and George seemed the likeliest. He kept insisting that he 'wouldn't of been so stupid to do it' on his pa's land and leave the body there to incriminate himself, but, frankly, everyone in town thought he probably *was* stupid enough to do that. But, then, no one really thought he was smart enough to hide that gun so well. So where was that gun?" She stopped to sip her coffee and gaze out at the incoming fog.

I stirred restlessly. This was part of Mary Sharon's story-telling technique. Lots of lengthy pauses with the expectation that I push her. "But he wasn't convicted?"

She turned back to me. "No. Just as the trial began, a hobo was picked up for vagrancy over at Granite Falls, some little way from Rocky Ridge. He had a gun on him, and the sheriff's office knew about our murder case, of course, so the two sheriffs got together and, lo and behold, the shell found by Johnny's body matched that gun. *Voilà!* They had the murder weapon. They questioned the hobo some more, and he said he'd found it by the town dump. All the pieces, you see, were coming together. Everyone figured George had shot Johnny and then threw the gun into the dump, and the hobo had found it and made off with it."

She paused again, and I realized I was getting confused. I asked her, "So why wasn't he convicted?"

"Well, the funniest thing. A pawnbroker down in the Twin Cities had been following the case and called the sheriff's office to say he'd sold a gun of that sort just the week before the murder. The registration numbers checked and guess who he'd sold the gun to?"

"St. Francis?"

"No," Mary Sharon decided to ignore my wit. "Johnny Callahan had bought the gun himself!" I frowned. "It had been suicide all along. No one had ever thought to check Johnny's hands for powder burns, and by then it was too late. The only thing to do was push that hobo a little more, and so they did. He finally admitted that he'd come across Johnny's body with the gun lying on the ground right next to his hand. He didn't want to get in trouble for not reporting the body or for taking the gun, so he'd made up the story about finding it by the dump. That was it, then. The charges against George were dropped, and he and Evelyn got married the following fall."

I waited a minute to make sure she was done before saying, "Are you now telling me that the town has always wondered if Johnny really killed himself or not? After George and Evelyn got married?"

"No, no," Mary Sharon exclaimed. "Everyone accepted Johnny had killed himself. His ma admitted, after all was said and done, that he'd had long bouts of depression. No, the wedding was just an addendum."

After another short silence, I said, "Well, Mary Sharon, I hardly think that Jason knocked himself out with a rock, then shot himself, and a hobo made off with the gun. Do they actually say 'hobo' in Minnesota?"

She shot me a disgusted look. "Back in the fifties, when this happened, they did. You've missed the whole point, Tyler. It's not about who did it or whether or not it was suicide. It's about things not appearing to be what they are."

It was a good point, actually, and I silently digested this message. The problem was that nothing about Jason's murder made much sense. I couldn't figure out what things *appeared* to be, let alone what they *didn't* appear to be.

27

On Monday morning, I was eager to talk with Jeff, but just as I picked up the phone, George and Dwyer arrived at my door with a search warrant and a couple of blue boys. I was dumbfounded. I followed them around, asking them what they were looking for and why they were looking for anything at all at my house. They wouldn't tell me anything except that they wanted me to come downtown, when they were finished, for an official chat.

This was certainly not what I expected to happen when I blew the whistle on Peter. Mary Sharon came up to see what was going on but was politely asked to leave. I didn't hesitate this time or wait for Mary Sharon to tell me to call an attorney. Corinne agreed to meet me at police headquarters.

The questions were not new. Over and over, they asked about the morning I'd found Jason's body, about my previous connection with Jason, about my activities the night before he was killed—every detail, every memory, every single thing we'd already discussed. George was clearly hostile and Dwyer seemed almost apologetic. Good cop, bad cop routine, I thought. They actually do this in real life. Corinne's presence was comforting but hardly necessary. It's not as if I could say anything that was truly incriminating. They were just whistling Dixie, and I suspected they knew it.

Finally, after a couple of hours, Corinne said, "That's it. This interview is over. Either you arrest and charge Ms. Jones or we're out of here." I felt a shiver of apprehension. Was this a calculated risk?

Dwyer and George left the room, and I turned to Corinne. "Are they going to arrest me?"

She shook her head. "No. They would've done that already if they had anything concrete. Apparently they expected to find the gun or something else incriminating at your house. But they didn't find anything or they'd be doing more than questioning you."

I shook my head. "I don't get it. Why wait all this time, and then they suddenly jump on me?"

"Someone probably put them up to it. They're convinced you're involved, or they wouldn't waste all this time. But they can't prove it. They're hoping to trip you up somehow."

"That's kind of hard to do when I'm not hiding anything."

She nodded and opened her mouth, but Dwyer reentered the room at that moment. "You're free to go, Ms. Jones. I want to remind you that this is a homicide investigation. We not only expect your full cooperation but also your discretion. And Ms. Jones? We'd appreciate it if you'd stay in the vicinity for the time being."

After Corinne dropped me at home, I called Jeff at the *Chronicle*. He laughed when he heard my voice. "Spend some time in the slammer this morning, girl?"

"You do have quick sources, don't you?" He chuckled. "Jeff, what's going on? How come I got hauled in there this morning? And how come they had a search warrant for my house?"

"Hot tip, Tyler babe. Hot tip."

"That's it? What's going on with Peter? You must've heard something."

He laughed again. "I don't know, Tyler, I might get in trouble passin' info to a criminal type such as yourself."

"Very amusing, Jeff. Give me what you've got."

"Okay, okay, keep your shirt on. I'm just funnin' ya."

"Jeff." I mustered all the threat I could into that one word.

"Let's see what I got here," I could hear papers shuffling.

"How much you want to know, Tyler?"

"Everything, Jeff." He sighed audibly.

"Everything" turned out to be quite a lot. The police picked Peter up after the funeral. He denied everything until he found out that his roomie had broken down. Then he insisted that he'd gotten homesick. Arriving late on Tuesday night, he found his father in the study, got into a fight with him, and drove down to the family place on the ocean near Half Moon Bay to spend the rest of the night. When he found out Jason had been killed, he knew his activities would look suspicious, so he called his roomie and bribed him before heading back to S.F.

The cops nattered away at him for awhile, then let him go. On Sunday morning, they got some new info. Turned out that Peter had been the campus dealer. His operation was large; he dealt with local suppliers but didn't seem to be "controlled" by any of them. It looked as if he had his own bankroll. This part fit in with what Sam had told me.

Peter was hauled back in, this time with a very pricey criminal lawyer. He kept to his "homesick" story at first, but, as more and more information about his college activities came out and the cops leaned harder on him, he apparently got scared. This time he told a different story.

He started talking about his drug business. It had started in high school in a small way. When he got to Cal Tech, he realized he'd struck gold. These mostly rich, compulsive kids were like sitting ducks: they wanted pick-me-ups and downers and the high-fly of cocaine. Peter didn't want the mob or anyone else pulling his strings. He went to his father and told him he'd go public about the abuse and pornography if he didn't give him whatever bucks he needed to start his own business. Peter had pegged his father just right: Jason was not willing to tarnish his respectable image. When Jason tried to

beat him, Peter fought back—no longer the quiescent son, afraid of his old man. In the end, good old Jason had given in and bankrolled his son's drug business.

"Whew!" I said. "This is quite a story, Jeff."

"It's something, inn't it?" he agreed. "This is life in the fast lane, I guess."

"So what does this all have to do with Jason's murder?"

"Patience, girl, I'm gettin' there," Jeff promised.

Peter hadn't needed constant funds from his father. After that initial bankroll, the business mostly financed itself. On occasion, however, he'd overextend himself in personal spending or credit, and he'd need a little cash to keep his suppliers happy. Then he'd return to Jason to augment his funds. Apparently, he never paid his father back. After all, what was Jason going to do? Turn in his son for unpaid debts?

On Tuesday, Peter had called his father at the hospital to request that some money be sent to him, just to tide him over. Jason, according to Peter, had refused. Peter made his usual threats and Jason, in turn, threatened to blow the whistle on his son's activities at Cal Tech.

But Peter was quite anxious about his affairs and decided that evening to drive home and be more persuasive or threatening, as the case might be, to get what he needed. He left L.A. about 7:00 p.m., drove hard, and arrived home about 1:30 a.m. He found his father, drunk and bellicose, at his desk. They had a terrific row and no progress was made. Peter was about to go to bed, thinking he'd just sneak down later and steal the money from his father's safe and wallet, when Jason—as drunks are known to do sometimes—changed the subject and asked Peter if he wanted to know a secret. Curious about his father's conspiratorial tone, Peter agreed.

They drove to the park together in Jason's car. On the way up, Jason talked about this "bitch" he was going to get even with. That was me, of course. At this, I felt some pleasure that I'd figured right about his presence at my park. Jason told

Peter I always went to the park at the exact same time every day—he'd been watching me for weeks. Uh-oh. The cops were right on that one. He showed Peter how he was going to crouch in the shrubbery and wait for me to come by and then scare the bejesus out of me. Maybe even rough me up a little. He was just waiting for the right time, he informed his son. While he was crouched there, Peter picked up a rock and conked him on the head. When he found out his father had already emptied his pockets, Peter took his keys and drove back to the house, stole the money from his wallet and out of the safe, and then took off.

He figured his father was going to be plenty pissed off when he came around, but, as always, what would he—what could he—actually do? Peter went to the ocean home to sleep a little before proceeding to L.A. He got up around 10:00 a.m. to get back on the road and had just left when he heard the report of his father's death on the radio. Of course, there was no name mentioned yet, but Peter was quite certain from the description of the body found in a small park in the Sunset that it was his father.

He knew he was in big trouble. He returned to the ocean home and called his roomie. As both were wont to do, the roommate had already covered for him when Peter's mother had called. So Peter offered him the money to lie about the night before. Then he called Consuelo, pretending he was at school, and promised to come home. He got some more sleep before driving back to San Francisco, arriving when he would be expected to arrive after the longer drive from L.A.

"He's convinced," Jeff assured me, "that you did it, Tyler. He thinks you found his father lying there in the bushes and plugged him."

"So that's why the cops got the warrant to search my place. They really are looking for the gun, aren't they?"

"Yup. Did they find it?"

"Ha, ha. And they're not convinced I didn't do it, are they?"

"What? Sometimes you don't make any sense, babe. Yes, they're convinced that you maybe did do it—if I'm correct in figurin' that's what you were tryin' to say. Oh yeah"—more shuffling of paper—"you might be interested to know that it was Peter who called you and whispered sweet nothings that morning."

"What! Why did he do that?"

"He said he wanted to let you know that someone out there knew you'd done it."

"But I didn't!"

"That's not how he sees it."

"Why would he admit to that call, do you suppose?"

"I dunno. Probably because he was afraid that they'd be able to check phone records and see that it had come from his mother's house. You understand, he was spilling the beans at this point. After lying twice already, he wanted to convince the coppers that he was tellin' the truth this time. One way of doing that is to come clean about every possible detail."

One step forward, two backward. Every new piece of information I got seemed to clarify a little bit and muddy a whole lot more. I wrote down everything I knew, had heard, and had guessed on index cards and tried to fit them together, to make some kind of sense out of them—as if I were putting together a jigsaw puzzle. Nothing fit.

(28)

I had been thinking about quitting my investigation of this murder. It was becoming clearer and clearer that it had been committed by someone in the family. Or someone close to the family. Peter or Margarita or Consuelo. Sam or Victoria or Jorge. Or some combination of any of these people. There was always Laurel. Did I want to expose any of them? On the other hand, did I want to go on being dragged in for questioning? The only person I knew for sure hadn't done it was me. Unfortunately, the cops didn't share my conviction.

I wouldn't mind exposing Peter, but even I had to admit his story had the ring of authenticity. Then I thought of Mary Sharon's parable: nothing is necessarily what it seems to be. Peter might seem to be telling the truth now, but that, too, might be a technique. Tell them *some* truth, then they'll think that's the *whole* truth. No, I couldn't entirely dismiss Peter.

Anyway, I knew I wasn't ready to quit searching. Tuesday morning found me slouched down in my bug outside Margarita's apartment house in Berkeley. I hate doing surveillance. It is without a doubt the most boring of jobs. I didn't know exactly what I was looking for. I just didn't know what else to do at this point. Maybe I'd spend a week following each of them. Maybe not. Alone, I could miss whatever it was I needed to know, because I clearly wouldn't be able to do this twenty-four hours a day. But this was all I could think to do.

It's not easy to look inconspicuous when you're on a stake-out. Of course, it's much easier if you're an undercover cop, and you get to set up a van with sophisticated surveillance equipment across the street from the victim's abode. Not having those options, I had to do it the old-fashioned way. It helped a lot that Margarita lived in Berkeley. There is almost no "normal" in Berkeley, so sitting in a car all day was a little less strange. Also, my slightly disheveled VW—once a rich green, now a dull, faded green speckled with rust, picked up mostly during my Minnesota college years—blended well into Berkeley's generally down-scale look. It would blend even better if it were a little more beat up and had some Deadhead decals on it as well as some save-the-whales or anti-nuke or out-of-Central-America bumper stickers.

Having had to do this occasionally for journalistic investigations, I had developed one habit that made surveillance more bearable. I brought my Walkman (was mine a Walkwoman?) and some of my favorite cassettes: Billie Holliday, Charlie Mingus, some Mozart concertos.

Margarita's apartment was across the street and a little down from where I was situated. I arrived between 7:30 and 8:00 a.m., hoping to get a parking place that'd been vacated by someone leaving for a regular nine-to-five job, figuring anyone who worked in S.F. would have to leave an hour or two early to get across the Bay Bridge. It had worked.

Before settling in to watch, I walked around Margarita's building. It was an old house that apparently had been cut up into flats and seemed to have only two entrances. I worried about the back entrance until I realized that the small parking lot in back was enclosed by a fence. Margarita's silver Toyota Camry was parked in back. I had had a friend at the DMV run a check for me, so I had Margarita's license number.

Of course, I didn't know if she was in there. The fact that

her car was in back boded well, but didn't guarantee any-thing. When Sam strolled out the front door at about ten to eight, I felt reasonably certain that Margarita was, indeed, inside. I ducked down when I caught sight of Sam. His car, a slightly rumpled and not very new canary-yellow Nova, was parked in the other direction from mine. Good, I thought, now I'll know to look for that in the morning when I come. I ducked down again as he drove by me, I assumed on his way to work.

Close to an hour later, Margarita's car appeared from behind the house. I followed her discreetly to Mills College in Oakland, about fifteen minutes away from her flat. At the front gate, I kept her car in sight, telling the gate guard I was visiting my "niece," Carla Fogleby. Mentioning Ethel Moore, an on-campus dorm, convinced him I knew my way around, and he passed me on.

Margarita spent the next four hours on campus, so I did, too. It was not as easy to look inconspicuous here, although the sheer number of women helped. I was afraid to lose sight of Margarita's car and equally concerned that someone would report me. So I sat in Lady Bug for awhile, went for a leisurely stroll, sat under a tree, then started the process all over again. About the third time through, I gave up and walked over to the tea shop to use the rest room and get myself something to eat. Luckily, when I returned, Margarita's car was still there.

In the afternoon, I followed her back toward Berkeley. She stopped at a Safeway on College. After stowing the gro-ceries in the car, she walked down the street, stopping at a bakery and a drugstore, and made herself comfortable at a table in a wood-and-fern restaurant on the corner. The other customers, mostly students, were talking earnestly with one another or perusing books. I found a table some distance away from Margarita. Seeing only coffee in front of her, I ordered the same and pulled a book from my bag—it was a Barbara Wilson mystery—and allowed myself to read a little, still keeping an eye on Margarita. When a friend joined her, I ordered a lemon tart, paying immediately. Chewing slowly, I watched the two through lowered lashes. Margarita's friend was an African-American woman about the same age as Margarita. She was short and stout, with a tough look to her body movements and her facial expressions. I was not close enough to hear any of what they said, but the talk seemed intense. They leaned toward one another, almost conspiratorily. Mostly the other woman talked and Margarita listened intently. Neither one smiled or laughed.

About half an hour later, the friend touched Margarita's arm lightly, definitely in a gesture of consolation. She looked around in a cursory manner and left the restaurant. A few minutes later, Margarita paid the bill and walked out. It was just after 4:30 when she pulled her car behind her building. I settled down to listen to a Cassandra Wilson tape and tried not to get sleepy. About an hour later, Sam walked right by my car and then cut across the street to Margarita's building. Ah, domestic bliss, I thought wryly. He was either living with Margarita or spending most of his time there.

I decided to call it quits at that point. An agreeable little surprise on the Bay Bridge made the long day worthwhile. Stuck in a long line of cars, one of several such lines moving slowly toward the the toll booths, I amused myself by gazing almost unseeingly at other drivers. My attention focused more clearly when a sports car pulled up alongside me, driven by a woman who radiated dyke energy. She flashed a smile, hands motioning a request to cut ahead. Momentarily charmed, I let her in, then returned to my absent-minded musings. When I reached the toll booth, a smiling attendant informed me that my toll had just been paid. The woman in the sports car! I sped up, searching for her in vain among the influx of cars all emerging simultaneously from toll booths. Too bad I hadn't thought to check her license plate. I drove the rest of the way home with a pleased smile on my lips.

$\boxed{29}$

The next week varied only in the places to which I followed Margarita. I found a parking spot across the street from Mills, which naturally was a regular destination. There didn't seem to be much point to my being on campus—I couldn't really follow Margarita into her classrooms anyway—and I was afraid of arousing suspicion by hanging around. She had to leave, when the time came, by this one access gate.

Most of Margarita's forays were pretty routine. She went shopping, visited her mother frequently, got her hair cut, attended a dance class, met a friend for lunch, went to the movies with Sam and his kids one night, went to dinner a couple of times (also with Sam), attended a meeting that appeared to be some kind of La Raza gathering (this I surmised because everyone who entered the building into which Margarita had disappeared seemed to be Latina or Latino), and several trips to the library. When she entered an unfamiliar building in Oakland, I scanned the names on the placard inside the foyer. The only one she was likely to visit was a woman therapist, Becca Bond. I did a little checking on this Bond woman—put the word out to my friends in the business—and discovered that she specialized in working with women who had survived incest.

The fact that Margarita was going to some kind of Latina/o gathering made me wonder if she was involved with AMIGAS, so I tried to find out more about it. I didn't have much luck. I pushed Jeff–had the cops found out more about this organiza-tion than I had? Apparently the police were running into the same road blocks I was.

Aggie was not happy about these new activities. I thought about bringing her with me but decided that just wasn't practical. She might bark if someone walked by the car, plus I would have to get out to walk her or let her relieve herself. She was very dejected, day by day, watching me get ready to leave. I'd keep a steady chatter going with her.

"Now, Aggie, don't look that way. I'll be home tonight, and we can spend some time together then. Won't that be nice?" She didn't look convinced.

This is what single mothers must feel, I thought guiltily. If I have trouble leaving Aggie every day, what must it be like for mothers leaving their children? Especially with the constant childcare crisis. It wasn't as if most mothers had access to decent or affordable childcare, or even the comfort of knowing their children were in good hands.

One day I abandoned Margarita on her campus to have lunch with Mom. She lived in a shabby yet still elegant three-storied Victorian, not far from the Berkeley campus. By renting her overflow bedrooms to women students, Mom always managed to have someone in the house when she took her yearly trips to the countries south of us.

I was maneuvering around the large boxes stacked on the front porch when my mother burst through the front door. "Tyler!" She hugged me warmly. "I'm so glad you suggested this. I'll be leaving soon now, so we should try to spend some time together before I'm unreachable." I felt a twinge of guilt, knowing that I was here to pick her brain about AMIGAS, rather than feeling any loss about her impending trip.

My mother's kitchen overlooked her minute backyard, which was a riotous disarray of radiant flowers, barely surviv-ing vegetables, and unrestrained weeds. Mom served gazpacho and tore hunks off a fresh loaf of sourdough bread.

Sitting at her bright yellow-and-red table, I cheered at the oblivious casualness of her life. She asked me what I was grinning at.

I could only answer, "Oh, you. And life, I guess." She smiled back. As I sipped the delicious soup, I said, "This is wonderful! Did you make it?"

She laughed. "Don't sound so surprised. Of course I didn't make it. There's a great Mexican deli over on University." Like mother, like daughter—I thought. Delis feed me oftener than my own culinary efforts, too.

The phone rang almost continuously, but there must've been someone answering it—or a machine, I guess—because Mom didn't get it. I tried to get some more information about AMIGAS, but it was hard with all the interruptions.

"Adios, Weezie," someone called from the front of the house. "Later."

"Wait," my mother called, waving apologetically at me as she bustled out to the front door. I heard snatches of a half-Spanish, half-English conversation.

"I'm sorry," Mom apologized when she returned. "Now where was I?"

Then someone might call from upstairs, "Weez? I think you better take this call!" Then she'd get on the phone and Spanish would flow fast and furious from her mouth. Again she would apologize.

"Weezie?" Someone entered the kitchen, adding, "Oh, sorry," upon seeing me. "Did the mailman come already?"

"One of my boarders," Mom informed me after she'd dispensed with that interloper.

When I was a little girl, it wasn't students or SALSA or political activism. It was the cancer drive, the Red Cross drive, UNICEF, March of Dimes. It made me tired—not because Mom was so busy, but because I wanted to sleep more than I wanted to confront my anger at her unavailability. I'd always felt there were no pieces left over for me. I knew this was selfish and childish, but I also knew this is what I felt. I didn't stay long.

By the end of the week, my music knowledge and appreciation had been pretty well expanded to the point of satiation. And I was convinced that I was just not going to get anywhere on this tack. One more weekend, I thought, and that's it. I ought to be getting credit for this at Mills!

On Saturday morning, when I was deeply engrossed in the various nuances of Nadja Salerno-Sonnenberg's interpretation of Brahms' Concerto in D, Margarita's silver Camry pulled out from behind her building. I put Nadja aside for the time being and slid my car onto the road, following at a discreet distance. It occurred to me that I hadn't seen Sam's car earlier. He'd been there every other night that week. I was getting kind of used to the guy. Well, he did have kids; maybe he spent his weekends with them.

Margarita worked her way east, toward the hills, finally getting on the expressway. She headed south on 13 for two or three exits, before pulling off and turning east again into the Oakland hills. The streets grew increasingly narrow as they wound upward. I was afraid of losing Margarita around a corner but didn't dare to pull up closer in the light traffic. My gearshift was getting a workout on these hills. On any other day, I would have enjoyed the view.

Rounding a corner a little too fast, I caught sight of Margarita's car in a driveway. A little further up the hill, I turned my car around, then parked just out of sight. What to do next? I couldn't pull in view of the house. With the curves, I'd end up directly in front of it. How was I going to know when Margarita left? I could try to park just downhill from the house, hoping to see her as she left. But what if she headed further uphill? There might be another route back.

It made sense to try to get the address. I slipped out of my car, softly closing the door and slipping the keys in my pocket. The neighborhood was very quiet on this sleepy

Saturday morning, no people around at all. In the distance, a lawn mower hummed. Somewhere nearby, a dog was barking.

Margarita's car was parked at number 4775. Damn. Where were the street signs? I'd lost track—way back in these hills—of what street I was on. I strolled past the house across the street, pretending I belonged in the neighborhood, then crossed the street and moved alongside a hedge next to the Camry.

From this vantage point, the house looked abandoned. It was an ordinary California ranch with attached carport. The yard was neat but nonetheless neglected. There was a hollowness about the windows, and no furniture or drapes were visible.

I moved cautiously along the side of the carport, peering through the latticework of the outside wall into the parking space. It was empty. Lawn mowers, paint cans, garbage cans, hoses, rakes—all were absent. The backyard butted up against a hill that rose to the twist of road above it. I craned my head backward to see if anyone up there could be looking down. There was no sign of a house up there, just lots of trees and shrubbery.

The yard was small, a shabby little patch of poorly maintained grass—mostly weeds—and rocks and scruffy shrubs. I stood very still but heard only distant neighborhood sounds; their very ordinariness made me feel creepy. On this sunny, pleasant morning, not hot but warm enough to have a window open, no voices floated out of this house.

I had to try peeking into a window. I carefully placed a foot, hesitated, positioned the other foot, and kept moving across the back of the carport. Some little noise—a tiny breath, a shoe against a pebble?—alerted me and I began to turn around when something hard was pressed into the small of my back and a low voice said, "Don't turn around. Don't move." I froze. The voice, a woman's voice, continued, "Just do exactly what you're told to do and nothing will happen to

229

you. Do you understand?" I nodded. "Put your hands behind your back." I hesitated and the something hard pressed into my back more insistently.

I put my hands behind my head. "At your waist," she said, and I moved my hands down. A soft scarf was used to tie them together, not too tightly but snug enough, I discovered, when I tested the knot. Another scarf or some sort of soft material was placed over my eyes. My body stiffened. I hated feeling this vulnerable.

"Okay," the voice said. I felt a hand on my shoulder. "This way." The hand turned me to the left and guided me into what I thought must be the carport. A turn to the right. "There's a single step here," she warned me as I was escorted through what must be the door from the carport into what was probably a kitchen. I could discern a bare floor, then carpeting. Suddenly I was aware of the presence of people, many people. I heard the shifting in chairs, the whisper of breath, some low murmuring. I smelled body odor, soap, shampoo, perfume—sweet odors, artificial odors, not-so-sweet odors.

I was nudged slightly. "Move," said the voice. I was led a few more steps, then the hand resting on my shoulder pressed slightly downward. "Sit," she ordered and I did. The chair was hard and metal, a folding chair, I presumed.

I swallowed and said, just as if I wasn't terrified, "What's going on here? I demand to know!" A wave of mutters spread through the room, and the fingers of a hand wrapped around my upper arm and dug into my flesh.

"You are here to listen, not talk. I suggest you do that, starting now." This was a different voice than the first. Clothes rustled and chairs squeaked as people seemed to settle in. "All right," the second voice said, in a tone suggesting that something was about to begin.

30

A spectacular sunset was out there somewhere, I knew, beyond the fog that had inexorably rolled toward shore for the past hour. Perched here on my deck, I could still see the line of breakers at ocean's edge, but just beyond that the fog rose like a wall of bleached cotton candy. An unopened bottle of Cutty Sark stood watchfully on the table at my side, and I felt as drained as a newly unclogged sink. The lights were coming on in houses down below, one by one, as darkness spread like an ominous oil spill.

Aggie bounded down the stairs and barked sharply in greeting when we both heard Mary Sharon arriving home. I barely noticed. My hand reached toward the bottle, and I lightly ran a finger down its curve.

Mary Sharon called from below, "Tyler? You up there?" When I didn't answer, she said to Aggie, "Where's your mommy? How come the lights aren't on?" and repeated, "Tyler?"

"I'm here."

There was a moment's quiet. Then she said, "Okay if I come up? Or do you want to be alone?"

My eyes flickered toward the bottle. "You can come up."

She and Aggie clambered up the stairs, showering affection on one another. "How come you're sitting here in the dark? I thought you weren't home," Mary Sharon said, dropping into the chair beside me. I didn't answer, but in the silence all sorts of words were being shouted. I knew that she was staring at the Cutty.

Finally I said, "You want to get rid of this before I drink it in one gulp?"

She shot out of her chair and snatched up the bottle. No! I thought, but forced myself to keep silent. In a moment, liquid was gurgling down the drain, and my body strained toward the sound like a horse toward the barn at the end of the day. Mary Sharon said, "You want a cup of tea?"

Tea seemed too weak, too ordinary. But then, everything seemed too weak. Except for booze. Damn. Damn-damn-damn. I nodded, then realized she wasn't going to see that and said, "That'd be fine. Thanks."

She busied herself in my kitchen. The last of the light faded from the sky while the light from the kitchen splashed across the deck, melting away into the dark all around me. Mary Sharon was murmuring to Aggie. "Are you starving to death? I know, your mommy never feeds you, does she? Just leaves you to fend for yourself, poor darling. A little cheese, maybe? Just to lessen the pangs of starvation, mind you. Not a real meal, of course." She raised her voice, sending it out toward me. "English breakfast? A little milk?"

"Cream," I corrected her. She was always trying to con-vert me to something or other. "Thanks," I added, reminding myself not to blame Mary Sharon.

She came out in a minute, carrying a tray of tea and crack-ers and cheese, even peanut butter for spreading. One of my favorite snacks. I smiled in spite of myself and said, "Your mother stop by in the last minute or two?"

Mary Sharon just smiled back, lighting a candle she'd also brought out, then settling herself in the chair next to me. We both sipped tea and munched crackers. I felt as if I were coming out of a cave. The food and the tea made me feel more human, but I would've preferred something stronger.

After a bit, Mary Sharon said, "So. You want to talk?"

She waited patiently as I continued eating for some minutes. I poured myself another cup of tea, stirred a little cream in. Then I told her. I told her about following Margarita that morning up into the Oakland hills. It hardly seemed possible that it could have been just that morning. It seemed like days ago, weeks ago. I told her about the object pressed into my back, the blindfold, and the room full of murmurings and shiftings and breathing. I told her about the stories. All the stories she and I had both heard, over and over again, in the years we'd worked for the eradication of violence against women, all the stories we *never* got used to: stories of rapes and beatings, incest and abuse, overt and subtle violence, stories of being dragged into alleys, cars, parks, stories of being invaded in one's own home, stories of being publicly beaten, privately beaten, stories of disgusted or indifferent cops, doctors who looked the other way, families and friends who blamed you or just felt helpless, terrified children, scarred children, dead children.

When I stopped talking, she remained quiet, waiting. After a minute, she got up and went into the house, returning with a Kleenex box. Tears were streaming down my cheeks. I remembered that someone had wiped away my tears, the tears that kept leaking out from under my blindfold.

I continued telling Mary Sharon more stories, everything I could remember from the women this afternoon, every detail—as if I could exorcise the reality of these stories in the telling of them, the breaking of silence. I told of threats, slaps, pushes, kicks. Of being pushed down stairs, against walls, over chairs. I told of weapons—broken bottles, guns, knives, ropes, lamps, hands, whips. And of broken bones, bloody faces, black eyes. Broken spirits. I told of being stalked—hiding under covers, under beds, in closets, under steps. I told of things that little girls gazed at while flat on their backs—their bodies being invaded, violated, assaulted, mutilated: a network of cracks on the ceiling that resembled

Africa; a lamp that looked like an inverted bowl; the glittery stars a mother had lovingly glued to the ceiling; the flutter of gingham curtains; a water stain that grew each year; a spider spinning a web in the corner; car lights tumbling across a dark wall. Things, shapes, glimpses that still infuse a bubble of terror and nausea in these same women, years later. I told of bodies that still cringe, of minds that still scream or shut down—years and years after the abuse has stopped.

The tears kept streaming down my face. Mary Sharon was helping herself to Kleenex. When I finally stopped, exhausted and wrung out, we sat quietly together for some time.

After a while, Mary Sharon said, "How long were you there?"

"I don't know exactly. Margarita—or whoever it was—left her house shortly before ten this morning. It was almost four when I could next look at a clock."

"Where were you then?" Mary Sharon interrupted me.

I took a deep breath, noisily blowing it back out. "Let me do this in some sort of chronology. After they told their stories, I was ordered to get up. I had several dozen questions I wanted to ask and yet...there didn't seem to be any point. I knew they weren't going to answer me. They'd given me all they intended to give me. Anyway. I was taken to my car, still blindfolded. Earlier they had gotten my keys out of my pocket. At that point, I was afraid they were going to kill me. Why would they need my keys? Instead, they used the keys to move my bug into the carport. I was told to lie down in the back seat, not much room for that, but I did the best I could. Then someone drove for awhile.

"When she stopped, I could hear lots of traffic, people. She leaned back and pushed this gun or whatever it was in my ribs and said, 'Count to 100. Then you can get out.' She loosened the bonds on my hands and opened the car door. 'Wait!' I said. 'What does F.U.C.K. stand for?' I knew she was still there. 'You are F.U.C.K., aren't you?' Without answering yes or no, she whispered, 'Feminists United against Cold-blooded Killers.' I heard the car door close as she left.

"I counted to 100. I suppose I didn't have to, but I did. I was being a very 'good girl.'" I snorted, and I could see Mary Sharon nodding in the candlelight. "While I was counting, I grappled with the scarf tying my hands and got free of that. When I reached 100, I took the blindfold off my eyes. I felt a little dizzy at the brightness and I was stiff, both from having my arms in that position for so long, and from being cramped in the back seat."

"Where were you?" Mary Sharon asked.

"On Channing, just off of Telegraph in Berkeley. Lots of people around, no one paying the least bit of attention to me. I got out of the car and stretched and rubbed my hands and arms, squinting all the time. Then I drove right to Margarita's house and pounded on her door. She looked sleepy when she finally opened the door. I asked her where she'd been at ten that morning. I was already feeling pretty certain that tracks were going to be covered in every way, but I needed to play it out.

"She was affronted, said I had no right to ask such questions and who did I think I was and so forth and so on while I shouted back at her and finally she said, as I knew she would because I was so certain she'd have an airtight alibi, 'It's none of your business, and I don't have to tell you anything, but I want you to get out of here and leave me alone. I had a therapy appointment at ten this morning. My therapist's name is Becca Bond.' She started to close the door and I said, 'Did you leave from here?' And she said, very quietly and very firmly, 'That's it. I'm not answering any more questions. I suggest you leave me alone or I'll call the police.' I left her alone. I sat in my car, rubbing my wrists and thinking. The therapy stuff didn't surprise me. I was certain she'd be covered."

Mary Sharon was frowning, "Do you think the therapist is involved?"

I shrugged. "It's hard to say, but it certainly wouldn't be necessary. Margarita makes an appointment, stays overnight at a friend's house, maybe Sam's, and someone else takes her car and leaves Saturday morning, knowing I'll follow. They clearly knew I'd been following Margarita."

Mary Sharon shook her head slightly, pursing her lips, "This was very carefully planned, wasn't it?"

"Yeah, more than you know. After leaving Margarita, I drove up into the Oakland hills. It took me awhile—when you're following someone you're not always paying the best attention to what you're doing—but I found the house. It had a For Sale sign in front that had not been there this morning. I peeked in the windows and walked all around, no sign of any use or occupancy."

"How about the realtor?"

"That's what I did next. Drove right to her office, and she happened to be in. I questioned her about the place, at first as if I might be a prospective buyer. Then I asked her who had keys to it besides her. She was startled—or seemed so—by the question and asked why I wanted to know. I told her there'd been a large group of people in there this morning, and I wanted to know if she'd given them permission to use the house or had they used it clandestinely.

"She seemed to be genuinely puzzled and angry—insisting she knew nothing about anyone using the house, had not given permission or keys to anyone, and finally started questioning me about my involvement—how I knew it had been used and so forth. When I dodged her questions, she became angry and said she'd call the police if I didn't leave her alone. She also told me that my story was absurd because she'd shown the house at eleven that morning."

Mary Sharon whistled. "They didn't forget anything, did they?"

"I don't think so," I agreed.

We sat in silence for a few minutes before Mary Sharon said, "Did the realtor seem to recognize you?"

"Not that I could tell. Was she one of the women in the room with me? If she did know who I was and why I was coming to see her, she was very good at hiding it."

"How about her voice?"

"I thought of that, too, but I can't tell you. I just don't know. A lot of these stories were whispered or almost whispered and even those that weren't—after awhile so many women had talked, I couldn't distinguish one voice from another." Again a few minutes of silence and I said, "I guess, on Monday, I could go to all the chair rental places in the East Bay and try to find one that rented and returned that same day. I think I was sitting on one of those metal folding chairs. But they might each have brought a chair from home. Or one of them might work for or own a rental place. Or someone might've brought chairs from Costa Contra County or even further away. Or all the others—besides me—might have been sitting on the floor, for all I know. I guess I should try and seek it out but..."

I made no attempt to finish that sentence. We listened to the distant moaning of a fog horn, the tinkling of Aggie's tags, our breathing.

At last, Mary Sharon took a deep breath and said, "So. Not much point in going to the cops, is there?"

"I don't think so. What could I prove? They don't take women and certainly not women's organizations seriously anyway; this would just be more of the same crackpot stuff to them. I mean, Mary Sharon—listen to how my story would sound. I was kidnapped, maybe at the point of a gun. I was blindfolded and hands tied behind my back...Sure, lady."

"What about the blindfold and whatever they tied your hands with?"

I shook my head. "Rags. Nothing to identify them." She nodded and I continued. "And what do I tell them next? That I was forced to listen to the truth of women's lives for several hours? That these women are some kind of revenge squad? I followed a woman who was not where I'm saying she was at that point. I was in an empty house with a lot of other women who couldn't, according to the realtor and probably some other witnesses, possibly be in that house at that time or any other time. These women have made absolutely certain that I have nothing but the truth—no facts, no proof, no links, nothing. But the truth, yes. I know it now, and so do you. We can't really do anything with it." After a pause, I said, "I think I'm glad they did that so well."

Mary Sharon said nothing but nodded again. Eventually she said, "Let's walk through it."

For the last time, I imagined myself in the park, early on the morning of Jason's death. "Okay," I said. "Jason and Peter went up to the park. Jason crouched behind the bush to show Peter where he intended to wait for me..."

"And Peter picked up a rock and hit Jason on the head from behind," Mary Sharon finished. "Then he checked his dad's pockets, found them empty, took the car, and went back to their house. Stole money from his dad's wallet and safe and lit out for their beach house. Then what?"

I jumped in, saying, "In the meantime, Jason is still lying there. Isn't it interesting, Mary Sharon, that he was watching me while *they* must have been watching him?"

"You mean F.U.C.K.?"

"Sure." I nodded. "They must've been watching Jason and waiting for the right moment and—"

"Suddenly he was lying on the ground, unconscious, in a deserted park in the wee morning hours, so—"

"Someone leaned over him, put a gun to his forehead, and pulled the trigger. Probably had a silencer. Got in a car nearby and drove away."

We were both silent for a moment until Mary Sharon asked, "Do you think Margarita killed her father?"

"No!" I answered vehemently, then expelled a cough of a laugh. "Now what makes me think I know that? I obviously have no idea at all. I guess...I guess that's simply projection on my part. Or desire. Desire to not have any member of Consuelo's family be the murderer. I have no way of knowing—F.U.C.K. certainly was never direct about anything—but my guess would be that the women who are related to or abused by the victim-to-be have nothing to do with the actual execution." After a couple of seconds, I added, "I guess that's how I'd do it, so I think that's how they'd do it."

Neither of us said anything again for a long time. It was getting chilly on the deck, but I was loath to move, to have to find a way—I thought—of operating as if nothing had changed. Aggie sat at the edge of the deck, her head lifted as she sniffed deeply and expressively. She seemed to embody contentment. How simple life was for her, I thought, not for the first time.

"The legendary feminist hit-squad really does exist," Mary Sharon breathed the words.

"Mmm," I agreed. It was already beginning to seem like a dream. I thought of a good hook for my column. "Most of the eyes at Jason Judd's funeral were dry." Not true, of course, but this was poetic license. "His widow was not crying, because..."

The fog horn moaned distantly, the lights below us had narrowed to a mere strip as the fog moved closer and closer.

Photo by Sher Stoneman

Joan Drury lives in Lutsen and Minneapolis, Minnesota. She shares her life with dear friends and a daughter, two sons, a daughter-by-marriage, and a granddaughter. She dreams, she talks, she edits, she reads, she writes.

Spinsters Ink was founded in 1978 to produce vital books for diverse women's communities. In 1986 we merged with Aunt Lute Books to become Spinsters/Aunt Lute. In 1990, the Aunt Lute Foundation became an independent non-profit publishing program. In 1992, Spinsters moved to Minneapolis.

Spinsters Ink is committed to publishing full-length novels and non-fiction works that deal with significant issues in women's lives from a feminist perspective: books that not only name crucial issues in women's lives, but more importantly encourage change and growth; books that help make the best in our lives more possible. We are particularly interested in creative works by lesbians.